Welcome to Blooms

Joanna Monahan

Praise for Welcome to Blooms

"A beautifully written story about the ties that shape us. *Welcome to Blooms* is equal parts laugh out loud funny and a moving, heartwarming reminder of the joys of home and family."

— Shail Rajan, author of *The Summer Breeze* series and *The Recipient*

"I love this book! Joanna Monahan assembles an assortment of characters, shenanigans, and heartfelt moments into a bouquet of family, home, and what really matters in life."

— Elisa Lorello, author of *Faking It* and *All of You*

"Would you rather be a cactus or a daisy? It seems like an easy choice—until life makes it complicated. Event planner Daisy Greene has spent years staying as far away from her family's floral business as possible. When her brother, Bud, calls her home after their father is hospitalized, Daisy is forced to confront everything she's been avoiding. It's only when she returns to the place she least wants to be that she begins to discover who she truly is and where she belongs. A heartfelt, feel-good story about finding your way back to yourself, *Welcome to Blooms*, Joanna Monahan's sophomore novel blooms with charm, wit, and emotional depth. Its richly drawn characters will inspire you to think about your own life on your own terms. This one is a must-read!"

— Donna Norman-Carbone, author of *Of Lies and Honey* and *All That Is Sacred*

PRAISE FOR WELCOME TO BLOOMS

"*Welcome to Blooms* by Joanna Monahan is a poignant exploration of family dynamics and second chances. Daisy Greene returns to her family's cherished flower shop, confronting the intricacies of mother-daughter conflict alongside her own hesitance to embrace her familial legacy. Through a blend of humor and tenderness, Joanna beautifully illustrates that healing begins when we shift our perspectives, viewing our loved ones not as challenges, but as relationships to nurture. In this richly woven narrative of love and resilience, Daisy learns that amidst life's trials, the most exquisite blossoms often emerge from the fertile soil of our past."

— HOPE GIBBS, AUTHOR OF *WHERE THE GRASS GROWS BLUE*

Welcome to Blooms

Copyright © 2026 by Joanna Monahan

All rights reserved.

No part of this book may be reproduced in any form or by any electronic or mechanical means, including information storage and retrieval systems, without written permission from the author, except for the use of brief quotations in a book review.

Welcome to Blooms is a work of fiction. Any references to historical events or real people and places are used fictitiously. Other names, characters, places, and incidents are either a product of the author's imagination or are used fictitiously.

Cover by Laura Hollingsworth

ISBN: 978-1-948449-26-7

Library of Congress Control Number: 2025951385

Published in the United States by Blue Ink Press, LLC

To Millie and John, my forever reasons why.

Chapter One

Smother calling.

My phone screen lit up in warning a moment before my ringtone blared, bouncing off the austere walls of the Kansas City Art Museum's newly renovated reception hall. Heads swiveled from every direction as I juggled my notebook and pen, fumbling for the *Decline* button.

For a second, all three items hung in the air. I lunged and grabbed the phone while gravity did its job and sent the other items plummeting to the marble floor with an embarrassing crash. I jabbed at the volume button, sighing in relief as the sound bars winked to zero. I deposited the phone unceremoniously into my bag, where it continued buzzing in accusation.

The encounter took less than ten seconds, but I felt as though I'd run a marathon—out of breath, heart pounding through my chest, sweat beading along my hairline.

In other words, a totally normal reaction to a phone call from my mother.

I stooped to recover my things—and my composure—before standing to find myself face-to-face with Reginald Davis, the museum's director and my potential new client. His dark eyes gave away nothing, while his thin lips quirked with... amusement? Displeasure?

Had I already blown the most significant client meeting of my career?

The museum had secured an exhibition of reclusive artist Millie Maxwell's never-before-displayed personal pieces to launch its grand reopening after last year's shutdown. Fiona Gray, owner of Event Artistry, and my boss, had been furious when the contract to manage the opening-night gala went to one of our competitors three months ago.

I pulled back my shoulders and raised my chin in a practiced ice-queen stance. "I apologize, Mr. Davis. I didn't realize my ringer was on. It won't happen again. I assure you, Event Artistry prides itself on professionalism."

By some miracle (I was hazy on the details), I had received a frantic call from Fiona last night telling me to put together my best plan and meet with the museum director first thing this morning. I'd pulled an almost all-nighter, finally falling asleep at my desk. I rubbed self-consciously at my cheek, hoping the keyboard impressions had faded, and held the gaze of the gatekeeper of my entire fate, praying he couldn't sense how nervous I felt. Would this meeting end before it started?

He folded his arms and shook his head. "I'm very disappointed, Ms. Greene."

My heart sank. From the bottom of my bag, my phone resumed its buzzing. My right eye twitched in response.

Not now, Mom.

To my relief, Reginald Davis's posture relaxed, and he laughed. It was an oily sound. "I'm only joking," he said in a tone that made me think he wasn't. He touched my shoulder, and I forced myself not to flinch at the unexpected contact. "You think a phone call is unprofessional? You're here because the event planner I hired decided to quit her job and leave town." His snub nose flared, and his dark eyes blazed, making him look vaguely reptilian. "Can you imagine? Walking away from an opportunity like this?" His grip on my shoulder tightened, then relaxed as he ran his other hand over his jet-black hair, slicking it off his high forehead. "Not that I expect that type of behavior from you." His voice lowered, conspiratorial. "Fiona tells me that you are extremely professional and available to your clients at all hours." He removed his hand, brushing his fingers against the sleeve of my blouse. "I imagine your phone rings quite often. And please"—he winked—"call me Reg."

I pasted on my most professional smile and gestured around the expansive room, tactfully creating space between us. "Shall we walk the main hall?" I asked, cocking my head in a "follow me" gesture. "I want to share our decoration plans. With Event Artistry's help, this exhibit will be the jewel in your museum's crown." From the slight lift of his eyebrows, I could tell he appreciated my allusion to royalty and the reference to "his" museum.

I started down the hallway, heels clicking in the soaring space, with Reginald "Call-Me-Reg" Davis following in my wake.

Thirty minutes later, we were in his office. Outside the door sat a bullpen of cubicles, empty save for the young brunette woman who appeared to be an assistant. She glanced up from her phone as we walked by and hurriedly began typing on her keyboard, the very picture of productivity.

I lowered myself into a hard plastic chair opposite Reg's imposing mahogany desk and smoothed my black pencil skirt. I pinched a rogue piece of lint between two French-tipped nails and dropped it into my purse before producing the event proposal and handing it across the cluttered desktop.

He barely glanced at it. Instead, he folded his hands across his stomach and leaned back, regarding me. I mirrored his posture and waited, my face a politely patient mask despite the cacophony of nerves in the pit of my stomach. My orders were clear: "Get this account or look for new employment." Fiona believed in the literal interpretation of "go big or go home."

Reg broke first. "I'm impressed, Ms. Greene. Your vision for our event is classic yet modern, exactly what I asked for. I can see why Fiona recommended you." He waved a magnanimous hand over his desk. "Send me the electronic contract. I'll have Accounting cut a check for the deposit before you leave."

I dipped my head in modest acknowledgment and resisted the urge to do a victory dance. "That's wonderful news, Mister—Reg," I stressed. "Event Artistry thanks you for your business." I stood and shouldered my purse, offering my hand to accept his oddly cold (*Reptilian*, I thought again) handshake.

He walked me to the door. "I'm looking forward to working with you, *Daisy*." He winked.

"You'll have the full event outline tomorrow," I confirmed, ignoring his not-so-subtle implications. "And thank you again. I promise Event Artistry will make Millie Maxwell's exhibit this season's must-see event." I strode from the office, shoulders back, head high—the very picture of professionalism. Rounding the corner, I detoured into the women's restroom. I checked for feet in the stalls before letting out a triumphant "Whoo-hoo!"

The door opened, and the brunette walked in, catching me mid-cheer. I froze, arms outstretched. She shot me a bemused glance before ducking into the first stall.

Face flaming, I hurried off to find the accounting department, still mentally celebrating.

I wouldn't have to pack my desk and leave town in professional shame. The contract was mine. Well, Fiona's and Event Artistry's, but still... I'd done it.

I texted my coworker John the good news. He responded immediately with a GIF of champagne glasses toasting.

My smile faded as a second notification appeared, announcing two new voicemails from my mother. As I stared, the screen lit up again: *Smother calling.*

Honestly, the woman was worse than Beetlejuice. Merely

thinking her name summoned her. I could practically hear the conversation through the phone's insistent vibrations: "Daisy, it's your mother. What are you doing in Kansas City? Daisy, it's your mother. Come home where you belong."

I pocketed my phone. I would return her call later.

My family always found a way to infiltrate my life at the most inopportune times. Why should this—the most important day of my life—be any different?

Chapter Two

When your name is Daisy Greene, you get used to flower jokes.

When your name is Daisy Greene and your family owns a flower shop, your life becomes the joke.

Once, when I was five, I overheard a customer remark, "You Greenes are like a family of flowers." My mother had laughed and replied, "Well, three of us are. Daisy is our little cactus."

Over time, I might have forgotten the comment and how it made me feel, but unfortunately, my three-year-old brother heard it too. Despite numerous admonitions from our parents, the nickname "Cactus Butt" was born. And (ironically) it stuck.

So that's me: Daisy Greene, the cactus girl with a flower name mistakenly planted in the wrong family.

I knew from an early age that flower shops were not for me. I suffered from pollen allergies and spent most of the spring and fall seasons with a stuffy nose and red, streaming eyes, my body physically rejecting the environment in which I was expected to thrive.

"It's all in your head," my mother would argue as I scratched and sneezed. "No one is allergic to their life's calling."

Adding insult to injury, I also had no discernible talent for floral arrangement. While my father, known to one and all as "Bloomin' Bert," could turn out gorgeous bouquets and centerpieces, mine were awkward and stiff.

"Feel the flowers," he would say in his gentle way as I struggled to fit stems into a wide-necked vase, my hands clumsy in the heavy gardening gloves I wore to prevent rashes. "They'll tell you where they want to go."

Flowers and I were not on speaking terms. It was no accident that all my arrangements withered and died. The flowers wanted it that way.

I learned to introduce myself and hold for three beats for the inevitable comments: "With a name like Daisy Greene, you should be a florist," or "You must love flowers!" before smiling, nodding, and pivoting the conversation.

My brother—christened Bertram Junior but called "Bud" since birth—was everything I wasn't: easygoing, friendly, and happy to comply with our parents' expectations that we would take over the business one day. Bud never minded the inherent possession and predetermined destiny implied by his name. As soon as he got his driver's license, he became the store's delivery boy. Meanwhile, I was relegated to the back room, wiping fingerprints off vases and updating the photo albums we kept to show prospective clients.

So I smiled and nodded and, upon graduating from high school, pivoted straight out of Denver, Colorado, to the University of Kansas. My brother, never one to challenge expectations, continued to work for the store. Mom retired, but not from her continued attempts to convince me to move home and take Dad's place, thus completing the transition of Blooms by Bert to the next generation.

At least once a week, I received a call that started with, "Daisy, it's your mother. When are you moving back?"

"I like it here," I'd say. Sometimes, I would change my answers: "The day after never," or "I'd love to, but I changed my major to circus performance, and tightrope finals are this weekend." It didn't matter; my family was remarkably deaf when it came to listening to me.

After college, I moved to Kansas City and began working in banquets and catering. I worked for a number of high-end hotels before landing with Event Artistry and Fiona. My career choice suited me on two levels: I thrived in fast-paced environments, and the demanding nature of the business required a lot of evening, weekend, and holiday work, thus offering a convenient excuse from family functions. Even before the pandemic, I hadn't been home in two years, sending instead what John referred to as my "annual excuses gifts."

"What's the big deal?" he once asked. "They're your family. Driving you nuts is part of the job description."

"It's more than that." I sighed, knowing he would never understand. John had grown up in Kansas City, married his high school sweetheart, and lived within an hour of scads of family members. His phone calls with family were filled with laughter and weekend plans, not guilt trips and stubborn silences. "They don't know me, don't see me, don't respect that I want to do something different with my life. I just don't belong in their world."

"Have you tried telling them how you feel?"

"Only every day since learning to talk."

The look on my face must have convinced John because he dropped the subject. But I could still feel his quiet judgment each time I let a call go to voicemail or spent another holiday alone.

I don't need anyone else to be happy, I rationalized whenever I felt a sting of regret. *I can't keep fighting for permission to be myself. Alone, but not lonely. It's easier this way.*

"Alone, but not lonely," I murmured as I climbed into the back of my rideshare, heading back to the office with the good news that the Kansas City Art Museum contract was in the bag. I wouldn't let anything—especially my family—get in the way of my success. The Millie Maxwell exhibit would be the largest solo event of my career. And although Fiona did not know it, the commission would bring my next dream to life—running my own events company.

I had come to Event Artistry five years ago after crossing paths with Fiona at a fundraising event. Bored with my current job, I'd been impressed by the sight of her employees hurrying by, one hand on their earpiece, the other directing orders in an impatient series of gestures, as though the fate of the world hung on their next words.

Acquiring Fiona's email via a sneak peek at the event contract in my manager's office, I'd sent my resume and cover letter that night. Two days later, Fiona herself had called me in for an interview and had offered me a job.

I loved the adrenaline of event planning: the challenge of anticipating and coordinating details for every possible scenario, the thrill of moving unseen behind the action, a puppet master pulling strings. I loved the glamour of staying in the newest, nicest hotels, sampling good food and even better wine. I luxuriated in filtered conference room air, so different from the hazy pollen-filled rooms I'd grown up in. The hours were long, and Fiona was demanding; still, the accolades of clients bolstered my confidence in ways my family never had. During the months of the shutdown, I successfully transitioned several contracts into online events. When in-person events returned, Fiona rewarded me with larger assignments, culminating in today's art museum contract.

Now I was met by my coworkers, all of whom wore pointy party hats and rattled noisemakers, while Martin, Fiona's nephew and our latest intern, busily dispensed drinks.

"Congratulations," he said, pressing a cup of sparkling cider into my hand.

"To Daisy Greene, rising star!" Fiona called. She stood on a chair, her spindly legs and ridiculously high heels making me nervous for her safety. Ever anticipatory, John hovered nearby, ready to make a diving catch, should need be.

No one knew how old Fiona was, but rumors placed her between sixty (good genes) and eighty (good surgeon). She loomed above us, resplendent in a power suit the exact shade of red as her (surely dyed) hair. Radiating energy, she was the biggest presence in the room despite standing barely five feet tall.

She tapped her glass with one talon-like nail before raising it above her teased hair. "Raise your glasses," she called. "To our newest client, the Kansas City Art Museum." Everyone cheered and held their red cups aloft. I did the same, the warm glow of Fiona's praise traveling up my neck and settling on my cheeks.

If only my family could see me now. How could they think I would ever want to give this up?

"As you know," Fiona continued, "Event Artistry is more than a company. We're a family. And success for one means success for all." She paused, and everyone cheered again. A slight movement caught my eye as Tavia, our newest hire, made a face behind her raised cup. I turned my attention back to Fiona as she capped off her speech: "Daisy, we applaud your achievement, and personally, I can't wait to see what you do next. Congratulations. Your future awaits!"

I toasted in Fiona's direction, then around the room, before taking a victorious sip. Over the rim of my glass, my eyes met John's. "It sure does," I agreed.

Everyone returned to their desks and got back to work after Fiona's toast. Our office was a large open room, with two long tables marching down the center to encourage collaboration and provide plenty of workspace for laying out samples or drawing seating charts. File cabinets crammed with paperwork and takeout menus capped each end of the tables. Floor-to-ceiling shelves held all manner of event decor as well as various abandoned coffee cups, fast-food wrappers, and sticky notes denoting which items were currently in use. Fiona's office jutted above the bullpen at the top of the stairs, encased in glass like a skybox at a Chiefs game. It wasn't unusual for an employee to feel eyes on the back of their neck, only to look up and see Fiona staring down at them like an emperor in a coliseum. Behind her office was the restroom and the employee kitchen, the only place in the office suitable for private conversation.

John and I stood in the kitchen beside the Keurig, brewing coffee to cover our discussion.

"Once I have my commission from the museum, we'll have enough to make the down payment on the arts district space," I murmured. The coffee spat and fizzled as it finished percolating. John poured the steaming liquid down the drain and inserted another pod, pressing *Start* again.

"I spoke to my friend at the Kauffman Center. There's a rumor that Lisa Pharnum is touring next summer. He's going to recommend us to manage a fundraiser for her charity..." John trailed off as Martin staggered in, a box of flower vases in his arms.

"Sorry to interrupt. Auntie, er, Fiona wants these washed before tomorrow's luncheon," he panted, inclining his head toward the dishwasher.

John gave me a "We'll talk later" look and took his coffee, whistling as he descended the stairs.

Martin began loading the dishwasher.

"Here, I'll help you," I said, leaning over to start unpacking the box.

"Thanks." Martin was younger than our usual interns, barely out of high school. He still had a sprinkle of adolescent acne dotting his forehead. Fiona was tough on us all, especially her interns; most lasted only a week. Martin had made it six months and had become something of a pet project for me. He was amiable and eager, willing to do even the most menial jobs. I tried as best I could to train him to do things properly (translation: the way Fiona wanted them done). I would miss him when John and I left.

"Thanks," Martin repeated, slamming the dishwasher closed after loading the last vases. I pointed to the forgotten detergent on the counter, and he sighed, yanking open the door and sprinkling powder over the dishes.

"You're welcome," I said. "Believe me, I know it's tough working for a family member."

He gave me a questioning look, and I reddened. I didn't usually engage in office small talk with anyone besides John. The new contract and office celebration had thrown me off. Not to mention my mother's phone calls.

"My family owns a flower shop," I admitted. "My brother and I used to work there."

A flash of memory hit me: Bud and I sitting in the store window, a beam of sunshine painting our bare legs, our blond heads bent together as we watched a ladybug crawl across his hand.

"That's nice," Martin said. "Like something out of a fairy tale."

Another series of memories descended: antique gold lettering lined in black, spelling "Blooms by Bert," a string of brass sleigh bells tied to the front door jingling merrily as I shut the door behind me for the last time.

I shook my head, and the sights and sounds of childhood vanished into the fog of the past. "Not exactly. When you work for family, they expect your life to be about them. What you want doesn't really matter."

Martin snorted. "Sounds vaguely familiar."

As if on cue, a deep bout of coughing broke the silence. "Martin," Fiona rasped over the office intercom, "get in here." She hacked again and signed off.

Martin rolled his eyes. "See you." He took off at a trot, pausing briefly to knock on the skybox door before entering. "Yes, Auntie Fiona?" The door closed behind him.

I filled the detergent compartment correctly and started the machine. Sinking into a kitchen chair and drumming my fingernails against the table, I mentally cataloged what I needed to do: *finalize the museum contract, deliver the deposit to Eunice to take to the bank, check the numbers for Saturday's event, call the flower shop... er... caterer at the hotel.*

Call your mother, Mom's voice reminded me.

Call Mom. Later.

Chapter Three

"Are you ever going home?"

I looked up to find John standing over me, tapping his watch. It was nearly seven o'clock, and the office was empty except for us.

I saved the budget breakdown I'd been immersed in revising and closed my computer. Standing, I brushed the creases from my skirt and pushed my chair in. I gathered my bag and my purse and turned out the small desk lamp.

John wove around abandoned chairs while I trailed behind, pushing each in against the table. We slipped out into the cool evening air, and he waited as I set the alarm and closed the door, tugging once to ensure it locked properly. Together, we set off toward Pavel's, our favorite post-work bar. I tamped down the nagging feeling that I should head home to return Mom's call. This was *my* night, *my* celebration. Denver was an hour behind Kansas City; I had plenty of time.

Pavel's was dimly lit and smelled of spilled beer and stale popcorn. John secured a table while I went to the bar to order, standing on the brass pipe that served as a footrest.

"Hi, Pavel!"

The normally stone-faced proprietor turned, a grin spreading across his face. "Daisy Greene!" He craned his thick neck, looking for John, who waved from a corner booth. "I'll get your drinks."

I waited, arms resting against the sticky bar top as Pavel poured a glass of white wine for me and uncapped a beer for John. He placed our drinks on green paper napkins with a ceremonial flourish. "You want to start a tab?"

I shook my head, handing over my credit card. "Not tonight. I'll settle up now." Pavel returned my card with the bill and a pen, watching pointedly as I added a big tip and scrawled my signature. He winked at me. "You're my favorite, Daisy Greene."

I returned his wink as I collected our drinks. "You're my favorite too."

"What did the realtor say?" I picked up our conversation as I slid into the booth and handed John his beer.

He beamed. "She's willing to give us the discounted rate if we put up first and last months' rent and do all interior renovations ourselves."

I resisted the urge to do a victory dance for the second time that day. It was happening. Ground Floor Events was about to become a reality.

The idea started six months ago, after a grueling Board of Directors retreat for one of Fiona's most demanding corporate clients. Not only had the hotel released part of our room block, but they also gave one of the top suites to the CEO of our client's main competitors. The entire Event Artistry staff had worked overtime to secure alternate housing and meeting space while John and I stayed onsite overseeing logistics.

Fiona, meanwhile, "supervised" from her beachfront condo in Miami, where she was vacationing with friends.

John and I groused about it during our customary debrief/rant session in John's living room. His wife, Zadie, sat beside him on the couch while eighteen-month-old Sabrina sat on his lap. I sat on the floor among Sabrina's toys and abandoned Cheerios, grateful to be off my feet at last.

"You know, everyone thinks event planning is so easy." I sipped the champagne we'd swiped from the previous night's Board dinner. I closed my eyes, savoring the fizz of bubbles on my tongue. "They don't realize it only looks easy because we work our tails off. Fiona doesn't appreciate how hard we work. If I were the boss, I'd make sure my employees felt properly recognized."

I opened my eyes to see John and Zadie sharing a conspiratorial glance over Sabrina's head.

"What? What's going on?"

"I told Zay the same thing last week," John said, a serious look replacing his usual sunny expression. "I think you and I should start our own company. We know how events work. We could train our employees from the ground floor instead of just throwing them into the water and expecting them to swim." He mimed air quotes as he said this. "Meanwhile, you and I could move into managing client relationships instead of logistics."

A thrill of excitement ran through me. I'd dreamed about it, of course, but assumed I was at least four or five years away from going out on my own. With a partner, however… our own company. A chance to build a new brand, establish new clients, be our own bosses.

And best of all? Starting a company was precisely what I needed to prove to my family that I was meant for a life outside of running a flower shop. Finally, something I could point to and say, "See? This is where I belong."

I didn't even need to think about it. I held up my glass in agreement. "Absolutely. I'm all in."

And so, Ground Floor Events was born. We planned on weekends and evenings, meeting at John's house or the back booth at Pavel's. I scouted sites before finding the perfect space in the Crossroads Arts District. It was cramped and needed renovations, but it was within our budget and an ideal location. John discreetly met with our realtor, Maggie, and secured handshake deals with a number of clients wanting to sign with us once we made the break from Fiona.

The last piece of the puzzle was funding. But now, with my sizable commission from the art museum event, we would have enough to make the deposit and cover our startup expenses.

My thoughts returned to the present as John drained the dregs of his beer and checked the time. "Gotta go. This is the first night all week that I'll be home in time to put Sabrina to bed. And I owe Zadie a foot rub." Zadie was three months pregnant with their second child, and John relished doting on her when his schedule allowed.

"At Ground Floor, we'll ensure our employees have a healthy work/life balance," I agreed, making a mental note of the addition to our company values statement.

We bused our glasses to the counter and waved goodbye to Pavel. Outside, the mid-May air carried an unseasonable chill.

John hunched his shoulders and stuck his hands in his jacket pockets. "G'night, Daisy. Great job today."

I smiled at my friend and future business partner. "Thanks. Good night. Say thanks to Zadie for letting me keep you out."

We set off in opposite directions, John to his car and me to my condo just a few blocks away.

Walking up the street, the wind at my back, I raised my face to the sky. Dark clouds were gathering, obliterating the rose-pink dusk; a storm was brewing. I quickened my pace. Rounding the corner, a delicious smell greeted me, carried on the increasing winds. Impulsively, I ducked into my favorite noodle shop, stomach growling. I deserved to celebrate.

Thirty minutes later, I closed the door to my condo with a box of Pad Thai in one hand and a bottle of Prosecco under my arm. I slid the deadbolt into place with a comforting *thunk* before kicking off my shoes into the freestanding bookshelf I'd converted into a mini coat closet.

"Alexa, play classical music," I called and was greeted by soft music. I was home.

I'd purchased my condo as a bank foreclosure and fixed it up with the help of DIY tutorials on YouTube. It had been long hours and hard work, but I'd created a space that represented me for the first time in my life, and I took pleasure every time I walked into the impeccably clean space.

The overall aesthetic of the condo was black and white. I loved the drama of the absence of and combination of all colors into diametrically opposed values. My living quarters were one continuous space, with my bed and a small kitchenette at the back, while my enormous white leather couch took up the room's front half. A bar-height counter and kidney-shaped dining table demarcated boundaries between areas. I'd painted the long wall running the length of the condo a glossy black, making it look like the room stretched on forever. Framed reproductions of Ansel Adams photos hung behind my mattress in place of a headboard.

Best of all, there were no flowers. Not even a fern. Nothing to make my nose itch or my eyes water. And definitely no pets. I didn't have time to care for living things. My work was my pet, my baby, my living thing. I didn't have time to walk a dog. I cringed at the idea of chatting with other dog owners with their big, smelly mutts and small, smelly children. I didn't have time to talk to a plant or monitor its watering cycle. It was—I was—better this way. Easier. I was beholden to no one and nothing.

After dinner, I changed out of my work clothes and into pajamas and my favorite terry cloth robe. I stretched out on the couch and scrolled through my Netflix queue, looking for something to watch. *Nope, nope, seen it, nope.* Giving up, I reached for my phone, noting that my head was swimming pleasantly.

"Alone, but not lonely," I murmured into silence. Alexa had completed her playlist; the only sounds now were the comforting *ticktock* of my kitschy, googly-eyed cat wall clock and faint wisps of street noise four stories below.

I rolled onto my back and rested my phone against my knees as I scrolled social media, liking and saving images from my favorite events venues. I stopped on a suggested post, a photo of a bakery's grand opening. Designed to resemble a Paris boulangerie, the storefront stood framed in white and blue hyacinth bursting out of charmingly rusted watering cans while small, gingham-covered tables sat beside potted lemon trees. The building was painted a dusty blue-gray, while gold lettering on the window proudly proclaimed, "Lucille's." Underneath, smaller cursive script read, "A family business." The familiar font and coloring stirred my memories. My mind's eye blurred momentarily, replacing Lucille and her baked goods with my family's storefront signage, "Blooms by Bert," followed by a line drawing of my dad's signature lime-green Stetson.

I sat up, my head throbbing with the sudden movement. I'd forgotten to call my mother.

Heart (and head) heavy, I pressed the voicemail icon and closed my eyes as the electronic time stamp announced itself, followed by the familiar voice. "Daisy, it's your mother." She always introduced herself, no matter how often I reminded her that she didn't need to. "I know you're very busy." Her emphasis on being "busy" made it sound like a personal failing. "You should call your father. He's not feeling well." She ended her call with her usual sign-off: "Thank you. Goodbye."

Her tone held no inflection hinting at the reality behind the call. In our family, "not feeling well" could encompass anything from heartburn to a heart attack. Mom was an epic over-worrier, constantly fussing over Dad's health and stress levels while passive-aggressively suggesting that he could be doing more. It was impossible to gauge meaning from someone whose logic included statements such as: "Your father works too hard. Of course, if the store were open on Mondays, he wouldn't be so busy the other six days of the week."

The second message played. "Daisy, it's your mother. Your father says not to worry; he feels fine. Thank you. Goodbye."

If Mom were Chicken Little ranting about the sky falling, Dad would have denied the sky existed. "Greenes don't complain," he was fond of saying as he worked fourteen- to sixteen-hour days, placing inventory orders, directing arrangements, and delivering last-minute bouquets on forgotten anniversaries. My father barely rested, rarely sat down, and never, ever complained. I took pride in inheriting his work ethic and hoped one day he'd be proud of me, too.

"Daisy, it's your mother." Mom's third voicemail was muffled as though she were speaking with her hand cupped around her mouth. "Your father insisted I leave that second message. 'Greenes don't complain' and all. I'm taking him to the doctor this afternoon whether he likes it or not," she huffed. I could imagine her drawing her shoulders back and puffing out her chest, a general preparing for battle. "He looks terrible." A pause. "Your father, not the doctor." Another pause. "Anyway, call him when you can. Your father, not the doctor. Okay, thank you. Goodbye."

I thought of my genial, hard-working father and felt the sting of guilt afresh for ignoring my mother's calls. *But*, I reminded myself, *Dad would have done the same thing.* He would understand that I was, as Mom put it, "very busy," even if he didn't condone that I was busy six hundred miles away from home and working for somebody else.

I dialed my parents' landline. It rang out. Strange. I tried the store. My father's voice greeted me from the geriatric answering machine: "Thank you for calling Blooms by Bert, where flowers and families flourish. This is Bloomin' Bert speaking. Our business hours are..." I hung up.

I had no luck with either of my parents' cell phones, which was unsurprising. Mom constantly lost hers, while Dad turned his off at night to conserve the battery.

Which left... Bud.

My heart sank. While I still had regular, if strained, interactions with my parents, contact with my brother had dwindled to friendly waves over FaceTime and the annual birthday text. In my mind, Bud remained frozen in time, perpetually immature, shaggy-haired and Gollum-bodied, slouching through his charmed existence like a real-life Ferris Bueller. His good looks and outgoing personality made him popular at school. His compliant nature at home made him our parents' clear favorite. While I regularly fought for the right to live my own life, Bud never argued.

And yet, even more infuriating than his complicity in our parents' master plans was the fact that my brother was the one I missed the most. The one I didn't call because I was afraid to hear his voice, afraid he might ask me to come back. Because out of our whole family, my little brother was the one I'd probably do it for.

And that made him dangerous.

So, I didn't call. And true to his nature, Bud didn't either. Being proactive had never been his strong suit.

My finger hovered above Bud's number (saved in my contacts as "Absolutely Do Not Answer"). Three calls in one day was a lot, even for Mom, but the fact that neither Dad nor Bud showed up in my call log led me to believe it was a classic case of Mom overreacting. If it was serious, someone else would have called by now.

I slid the phone into my robe pocket. I'd done the daughterly thing and tried to return Mom's call. I would try again in the morning.

I picked up the remote and resumed channel surfing, finally stopping at a baking competition. Sleepy from the wine and uninvited memories, I pulled a blanket off the back of the sofa and snuggled against a throw pillow. I watched contestants wail about their soggy-bottomed pie crusts until my eyes drifted closed, and I fell asleep.

Chapter Four

Buzz. Buzz. Buzz.

I woke, the vibration from my phone pulling me out of my dream. I caught the tail end before coming fully awake: Reginald Davis, surrounded by swirling colors and sprays of hydrangeas, telling me to "Call your Smother."

Buzz. Buzz. Buzz.

I tried to sit up, but my left arm refused to cooperate. I'd rolled onto it in my sleep, and now it was dead weight. Flopping onto my back, I scrabbled at my pocket with my good hand, fingers closing around the phone as it buzzed again. Eyes blurry from sleep, I squinted to read the caller screen:

Absolutely Do Not Answer calling.

Bud.

Groaning, I dropped the phone into my lap, where it fell silent as though chastised for its behavior. Simultaneously, my left arm lit up as the feeling returned. I wiggled my fingers and arm to get the unpleasant prickly sensation over and done with.

Buzz. Buzz. Buzz. He was calling again.

Over and done with, Daisy. Over and done.

I rolled my shoulders like a prizefighter about to enter the ring and pressed *Accept*.

"Hey, Bud."

"Finally! Mom left you three messages."

I cut him off before he could hand the phone to Mom, whom I imagined was hovering nearby. "I heard. Dad isn't feeling well? What is it this time? Did she leave him locked in another hearse?" This had actually happened. Dad sprained his ankle carrying a wreath across a muddy cemetery, and Mom commandeered the hearse to drive him to the hospital. In her hysteria, she locked the doors, leaving Dad alone and trapped as she charged into the emergency room, demanding help. Subsequently, Dad created a minor scene by rapping on the hearse's curtained windows, begging to be released. It had ended up in the newspaper under the headline "Bloomin' Bert Burial Bumble." Mom had it framed.

"Not exactly." Bud paused, letting my comment hang in the air.

I shifted uncomfortably as I felt a low hum of dread begin at the base of my skull.

"Pop collapsed at work this afternoon. He's in the hospital."

"Dad did what?" I shot to my feet, the sudden movement sending my mostly liquid dinner sloshing in my stomach. A wave of shame crested through me, and my eyes filled with tears. Dad was sick, and I was making jokes. "Is... is he okay?"

Bud remained silent. Hot, instant tears slipped over my lower lids and down my cheeks, tracing my chin before falling away. I swiped my hand carelessly across my face. "Bud?"

I could hear Bud's ragged breathing. He was crying, too. I yearned to reach through the phone and hug him. Years of separation didn't matter right now. I couldn't bear to hear my baby brother upset.

My legs gave out, and I fell back to the sofa just as quickly as the adrenaline had fired me to my feet. I reached for the wine and took a swig. Bad choice. I hiccupped, and bile flooded my mouth. Phone in hand, I raced for the bathroom, making it in time to vomit up noodles, wine, and possibly even the pumpkin bagel I'd had for breakfast a lifetime ago.

Dry heaving, eyes streaming, I fumbled with my free hand to flush the mess away. The roar of the toilet echoed against the tiled walls and floor, and I could hear Bud calling my name.

"Daisy? Daze? You okay?"

"I'm fine, Buddy." The childhood nickname, abandoned for more than a decade, fell from my mouth. "Tell me what happened."

My brother took a deep breath, as if summoning his courage. "He's been feeling bad the last few days. Headache, dizziness, not eating much, not sleeping, working too hard. You know, the usual." Bud slipped into a pitch-perfect imitation of Dad. "'No one will care about our business if we don't care about our business,'" he intoned.

Despite the circumstances, I chuckled. Bud's impressions had always been a popular act in school talent shows. Anyone else would have gotten in trouble, but Bud was always a hit, with students and teachers alike calling out suggestions from the audience.

Bud continued, "Mother's Day was outrageous—by the way, I made a very nice bouquet for Ma and signed your name to the card, you're welcome—we had almost double the orders we expected. We even joked about how another holiday like that would kill us." His voice hitched.

"It's okay," I urged, my voice soft. "Go on." The cold from the bathroom floor tiles seeped through my robe. I pulled a bath towel from the rod above my head and wrapped it around my outstretched legs.

"I told Pop to take it easy this week and let me manage everything. Of course he won't because no one can trust me to do anything." Bud paused. In the background, I heard a door slam and a child's voice. "He went to work this morning, promising Ma she could take him to the doctor this afternoon. I found him unconscious behind the counter with a nasty bump on his head. The paramedics said he fainted and hit his head when he fell."

Images of what could have been flashed through my mind. I put the call on speaker and typed "reasons for collapse at work" into my search bar. A list of terrifying results filled my screen, such as stroke, seizure, and heart attack.

"Do they know what caused it?" I asked as I doomscrolled.

"Not yet." Bud sounded stronger, the worst news behind him. "He'll be in the hospital for a few days. The doctors want to observe him, run some tests, and make sure he doesn't have a traumatic brain injury. Depending on what they find, he'll either come home or possibly go to a rehab center."

"What about the store?" In our family, every conversation boiled down to business.

"I'll be there." Bud sighed, and I could hear the exhaustion in his voice.

I took a deep breath and asked the scariest question of all: "What can I do?"

"Come home, Sis. We need you."

I awoke the following morning with a hangover and an impending sense of doom.

Rolling over relocated the sack of bricks in my head from one side to the other, where they toppled and crashed against the base of my skull. My mouth tasted like hot garbage, and the jackhammer behind my eyes made me nauseous.

"Alexa, what time is it?" I croaked.

"It's 6:05 a.m.!" chirped the speaker on my nightstand.

I groaned and burrowed under the duvet, blocking out the sunlight trying to filter its way past my eyelids. The previous day's events began reassembling themselves: "Call-Me-Reg" Davis, the Kansas City Art Museum account, a celebratory drink with John, stops at the noodle house and the liquor store. Okay, that explained the hangover. But what was this sickly nervous feeling hovering at the periphery of my recollections?

I pulled a pillow over my face and pressed it against my temples, hoping to smother the throbbing inside my head.

Smother... mother... Mom. Mom's voicemails. Bud's phone call. Dad. Hospital.

I sat up then fell back immediately as my head exploded into fireworks. Clutching the pillow to my face, I recalled Bud's words: "Come home. We need you."

"Urrrrrgh," I moaned, a string of saliva winding its way along the corner of my mouth. My family needed me. *Needed me*, needed me. This wasn't one of those times when the word "need" was tossed into the conversation to make a point: "We wouldn't *need* to hire anyone if you worked at the store," or Mom's favorite, "If you were here, I wouldn't *need* to check up on you." This was the real deal. Dad was in the hospital, Mom was by his side, and Bud was left to run the store, probably into the ground.

Music blared from my nightstand as my alarm went off. Lightning sparked against my eyelids.

"Alexa, stop!"

I staggered to the bathroom for aspirin. Gulping water straight from the faucet, I swallowed two pills, considered, and then took two more. I reached into the shower stall and turned on the water, breathing deeply as steam collected in the small space.

I stayed under the scalding spray until my skin itched and my fingers pruned. The patter of water against my scalp soothed me, and my headache receded just far enough for me to begin forming a plan.

My priorities were clear: Dad, Mom, Bud, and the store. I needed to go to work, talk to Fiona, and ask for time off. I would call Reg to explain—not a phone call I was looking forward to, given how angry he was about his previous event planner leaving town. But this was different. He would understand. He surely had his own little reptilian family he would slither back to in their time of need.

I recited counterarguments into the steam: I wouldn't be gone long. I could work remotely while John handled the in-person side of things. Reg would hardly notice my absence.

Horribly, selfishly, I wondered if this would affect my commission.

Stop it, I scolded myself. I opened my mouth and let hot water stream into it, trying to wash away the taste of leftover food, wine, and guilt.

By the time I got dressed, my hangover had dulled to an annoying but manageable thudding at the base of my skull. Unable to face the din of the hairdryer, I braided my hair into a loose fishtail that hung wetly against my back. I dressed in my favorite sleeveless black dress and pulled on a black military-style jacket. Eschewing the challenge of heels, I slipped my feet into shoes I usually reserved for event nights, black ballet flats with orthopedic inserts. I donned sunglasses, shouldered my bag and my purse, pocketed my phone, and walked out the door into a day that, at first glance, seemed like any other. Only I knew I was facing a whole new world.

Chapter Five

My phone shrieked as I reached for the Event Artistry door, driving a fresh spike of pain between my eyes.

Absolutely Do Not Answer calling, my screen warned.

"And so it begins," I muttered.

I stepped back from the entryway, holding up a finger to Martin, who, having spotted me from the other side of the glass, juggled the box in his arms to open the door.

"Bud, what's up? Is Dad okay?" I pressed the phone tight against my ear, trying to hear him over the street noise of downtown rush hour. Behind me, I heard the crash of Martin losing the battle between box and gravity.

"Pop's resting. Well, as much as he can, with Ma sitting right next to him. He goes in for another scan this morning." Bud's answers came in short bursts between heavy exhales.

I frowned. "Are you jogging?"

"What?" Panting. Half-laugh. "No, I'm delivering the Walsh funeral. Lots of lilies." More panting. "Lots of stairs."

I squinted against the morning sun. "Listen, I'm at work. I need to talk to my boss and get some things squared away before making plans. I just got this big account, and…" I trailed off as Tavia pulled up to the curb on her Vespa.

Tavia had been with the company only a few months but had already made it clear that she wanted my job. When she first started, she'd worn flowery dresses, and her dark hair had hung long and loose. Today, she sported an all-black jumpsuit and a military jacket that looked suspiciously like mine. She hopped off her moped and skipped to the door, flashing a wolfish grin at me from under a metallic blue helmet. A fishtail braid hung down her back.

"Good morning," she drawled. "Looks like someone was out late celebrating her big news." Envy dripped off each word, even as she continued to smile.

What big teeth you have, Grandma. "Good morning," I said, returning her insincerity with my own. "I'm finishing a client call. See you in a minute."

She sniffed as if disappointed I hadn't taken the bait and threw open the front door, startling Martin, who dropped his box again.

I turned my attention back to Bud. "Are you still there?"

"Yeah. I'm—" I lost the end of the sentence as the phone erupted in a clatter. I clutched my forehead.

"Bud? Hello? What happened?" I could hear muffled voices but got no response. I counted to thirty, still calling out, "Bud? Bud?" before ending the call. I redialed, but the phone rang out until I was invited to leave a message.

I sighed and headed inside. I would call my brother later. Right now, I had to find Fiona. I deposited my things on an empty seat and went to the kitchen for a much-needed coffee. As I waited, I saw Tavia exit Fiona's office and skip down the stairs, looking suspiciously cheerful.

Abandoning the coffee and summoning my courage, I ran a hand over my hair and knocked on Fiona's door.

"Come in!"

Fiona's office reminded me of a Vegas piano lounge. Cramped and smoky, it always seemed dark despite the row of windows behind her desk. Photos of Fiona with various celebrities dotted the room while Fiona herself sat behind an enormous desk sporting a hulking computer and a 1990s-era conference phone resembling a spaceship. In the corner closest to the door sat Eunice, Fiona's long-suffering assistant, wedged behind a desk half the size of her boss's. Eunice sat with her laptop balanced on her knees, typing away, a Thermos of coffee and a can of Febreze within easy reach.

"Sit, sit, sit." Fiona gestured regally, clutching a vape pen between her fingers. "I'm glad you came by. I wanted to speak with you."

I sat on one of the two olive green leather side chairs, folding my hands in my lap. Although Fiona had switched from smoking to vaping, the smell of cigarettes still coated everything in the office like a glaze.

My heart hammered. Why was this so hard? "Fiona, I—"

"I just got off the phone with Reginald Davis. It seems you made quite an impression on him yesterday."

My rehearsed speech died on my lips.

"I have my eye on you, Daisy," Fiona continued, tapping one long, red fingernail on her desk. "I've always thought we were quite alike." She gave one of her throaty, seldom-heard barks of laughter at my shocked expression. "You're driven by success, unconcerned with more... conventional distractions such as children." She waved her hand in a lazy figure eight. "You and I, our work is our life. Our only priority. That's why I gave you the art museum account. This event will open doors for you and introduce Event Artistry to a higher level of clients."

"And I appreciate the opportunity." I found my voice and tried again. "But Fiona..."

"No buts." She pointed at me. "I know you'll give everything you've got to ensure this event goes perfectly. Reginald Davis is the type of client who requires constant attention. He needs to know that you are absolutely, one hundred percent dedicated to this event, no matter what."

Behind me, Eunice had stopped typing, and although I could

hear tinny music emanating from her earbuds, instinct told me that she was hanging on every word of our conversation.

"Event Artistry *is* the most important thing to me. But—"

"So, we understand each other." Fiona waved her hand, and I knew I'd been dismissed.

"Thank you, Fiona." I exited the room on wobbly legs. In under two minutes, I'd received the highest praise and the most direct threat of my career.

Now what was I going to do?

In hushed tones, I explained the situation to John as best I could.

He looked bewildered by my reticence. "You have to go. It's your family."

"But this is the worst possible time for me to leave," I said, voicing my shameful fears. "What if Fiona takes the account away? I'll lose the commission"—I lowered my voice even further—"and our deposit money."

"Ask her to give the account to me. That way, the commission still works in our favor."

I brightened slightly. John could put a positive spin on even the worst situation. It was one of the reasons we worked so well together. I plotted and fretted over every detail, while he maintained an "everything works out for the best" attitude that calmed me in moments when the whole world seemed like it was going downhill.

As if to prove how things could always be worse, Tavia breezed into the breakroom, earpiece in, gesturing as she talked. "Yes, we can accommodate any dietary restrictions." She stopped between John and me, holding up a "wait a moment" finger as though we were the ones interrupting her conversation. "Mm-hmm." Pause. "Mm-hmm." Pause. "Of course. I'll have her call you right away, Mr. Davis." She giggled. "I mean, *Reg*." She signed off with a flirty "Byeeeeee!" She even wiggled her fingers in a small wave.

"Oh, Daisy," she said as if just noticing me. "That was Reg from KCAM. He tried to call you, and when you didn't answer, Eunice patched him straight through to me." Her expression was smug. "He *is* a character, isn't he? I would *love* to work with you on this event."

Behind Tavia, John shot me a look. "Relax," his expression read. I released the death grip on my coffee cup handle and watched the blood return to my whitened knuckles.

Unaware of (or, at least, unfazed by) the "Go away" vibes I was shooting at her like daggers, Tavia leaned against the counter and surveyed us. "So… what is the Dream Team up to this morning?" She flashed a big, fake crocodile smile.

Another reptile. She and Reg would make a terrific couple. The thought made the corner of my mouth twitch. Tavia's eyes narrowed slightly, assessing me.

John smoothed over the moment. "Daisy and I were discussing last month's numbers." He made a sweeping "walk with me" arm gesture. "C'mon, Tav. I'd love to get your thoughts on how we can keep our lighting costs under control." He guided Tavia down the stairs while pointing between me and Fiona's office.

Talk to her, he mouthed.

I will, I mouthed back, grimacing.

I was raising my fist to knock when my phone rang. I answered without looking at the screen. "Mr. Davis, I am so sorry I missed your call."

"Daze, it's me," Bud broke in. "Sorry about before."

I hustled down the stairs and out the front door, ignoring my coworkers' curious stares. "Is everything all right?" I hissed. "What happened?"

"Everything's fine. I dropped my phone while I was straightening a wreath. I had to wait until after the recessional to get my phone back. Stupid open casket."

I gasped. A man passing by turned in surprise. *Sorry,* I mouthed. "Are you joking?" A horrible thought occurred. "But I called you back. Please tell me the body didn't ring." The man turned and hurried on, throwing a final worried glance over his shoulder at me.

"What do you take me for, an amateur?" Bud sounded offended. "I had it silenced." I heard scuffling noises. "I think there's embalming fluid on the phone case. It's sticky and smells like pickle juice."

I ignored this revolting piece of information. "How's Dad?"

"Awake. Groggy. A little confused." He paused. "He asked Ma where you were."

Ouch. I put my hand to my chest as guilt's knife hit home. "What did she say?"

"She told him you were on your way." He paused. "You *are* on your way, aren't you?"

"Yes, yes, of course I am," I promised, even as doubt swirled around me. What would Fiona say? Would she understand? Would she fire me? Or worse, give the job to Tavia? "I haven't talked to my boss yet," I hedged. "There are still some things to work out. I'll call you back in a few hours, okay?"

"Daze?" I could hear Bud's confusion and imagined the furrow between his eyes, which always appeared when he was upset. "Daze, I need you."

"I know." I felt the prickle of tears behind my eyes. "I know." I hung up, not trusting my voice to say "Goodbye."

"You have to talk to her." John's voice in my ear caused me to jump and accidentally press *Send* on the email I was drafting.

"No, no, no..." I scrambled to select *Unsend*. I turned to John, affronted. "Don't scare me like that."

He shook his head, unapologetic. "You're hiding." He cocked his head toward Fiona's office. "It's been two hours, and you've barely looked up." He slid into the chair beside me and put his hand over my computer screen. "This doesn't matter. You should be booking your flight, packing, and talking to your family." His voice belied agitation, an unnatural state for him. I pulled my fingers out of the way as he shut my laptop. "Family is family. Go."

"But what if Fiona fires me? Or takes the account away?"

"She's not going to do that." John shook his head. "And even if she does, so what? You'll get a new job in two seconds flat. You don't get a new family."

"But"—I looked around to ensure no one (Tavia) was listening—"what about Ground Floor? What if we lose the space?"

"I'm telling you. It's not going to happen. And you're stalling."

John, always my better angel, was right. I took a breath and stood, smoothing my dress. "Okay. I'm going." I looked toward the stairs. "Here goes."

"You're not moving."

"I thought I was."

"Nope. You're standing still." He gave me a gentle push.

"Fine. Here I go." I gave John a final miserable glance as I climbed the stairs.

Five minutes later, it was over. I had marched into Fiona's office, knees quaking, and announced that I needed a few personal days to visit my father in the hospital. To my amazement, Fiona sprang to her feet and enveloped me in her spindly arms. It was like being hugged by a bag of sticks. "Of course," she said, patting my back as if soothing a crying child. "Take the rest of the week off."

Gobsmacked, I stuttered out all the arguments I'd expected to encounter: "But what about the KCAM account? And Reginald Davis? You said—"

She cut me off. "I know what I said. But family is family. I'm sure John can manage for a few days." She snapped her fingers at Eunice, who appeared at my side with a box of tissues and a sympathetic expression. I took a tissue and held it, unsure of what was happening. I felt as though I'd stepped into Bizarro

World. Fiona, being supportive of a personal commitment? Fiona, who referred to children as "conventional distractions?" What was happening?

Fiona pressed the intercom button. "John! Tavia! My office."

Tavia? Oh no. Nonononono…

John and Tavia appeared immediately, making me think they'd been crouched outside the door listening. John put on a convincing show of surprise that I was taking some personal days, while Tavia utterly failed to hide her glee at the news that she would be assisting John in my absence.

"It's terrible about your father, Daisy," she said, simpering. "But I'm grateful for the opportunity."

"Of course," I growled, my right eyelid twitching. "I'm pleased my father's illness is working out so well for you." From the corner of my non-twitching eye, I could see Fiona watching us, looking like the cat that got the cream. She knew what she was doing. She was dangling my account in front of Tavia and dangling the threat of Tavia over me. Win-win on her end, but for Tavia and me, there could only be one winner.

And it's going to be me.

"Now," Fiona said. "*I* will call Reginald and inform him of the situation. He won't be happy, but he'll go along if he has my assurances that this disruption is only temporary." She pinned me with a steely look. "And will in no way inconvenience him or Ms. Maxwell." She shifted her gaze from me to Tavia to John, then back to me. "Am I correct in my assumptions?"

"Yes, Fiona," we chorused.

"Okay then. Get to work." She dismissed us.

Eunice put a motherly arm around me. "You go get your things together while I order your ride home. Text me your flight information and your return date." She led me to the top of the stairs. "Don't worry about a thing, dearie. Enjoy your time with your family."

I wasn't sure "enjoy" was the correct word under the circumstances. "Endure," perhaps.

I returned to my desk and pulled up a list of nonstop flights to Denver, blanching at the hefty price tags for same-day reservations. Then, I packed my belongings and carried the Millie Maxwell folder to John, who walked me out.

"Bye, Daisy!" Tavia trilled. I repressed the urge to hiss in response.

John waited with me at the curb until my ride pulled up and held the door as I climbed in.

"Safe travels," he said, giving me an encouraging thumbs-up. "And don't worry about anything. This will all still be here when you get back." He squeezed my arm reassuringly. "Everything's going to be fine. Say hey to the fam for me." He chuckled. "What I wouldn't give to be there for the reunion."

I watched from the window as John and Event Artistry grew smaller and smaller before disappearing completely. I turned around and fell back against the seat.

This was it. In a few short hours, I would be home. I'd called Bud with my flight information, declining his ride offer. I would rent a car at the airport. When it came to my family, having an escape route was crucial.

Back at my condo, I packed with the efficiency born of numerous work-related trips. It occurred to me that I was acting as though I was heading someplace unfamiliar. Most people packed light when they went home, figuring they could borrow whatever they needed. It was imperative to me that I *not* need anything, if only to prove, once again, that I was self-contained and planned to stay that way. I didn't want to feel beholden, not even for a bottle of shampoo.

I zipped my suitcase and placed it by the door. I took the trash to the chute, stopping on my way back at the door across from mine. Frantic barking erupted from the other side of the door as I knocked.

"Oh, hush." I heard shuffling and a woman's voice calling, "Coming, coming." She kept up a low, murmured conversation with the dog, who continued to whine and scratch at the door.

Welcome to Blooms

With a *click* of a lock, the door opened wide enough for me to see a pair of watery blue eyes peer out from beneath a cloud of silver hair. "Yes?"

I smiled, trying to look neighborly. "Hi, Mrs. Rudnicki. I'm going away for a few days, and I was hoping you could pick up my mail for me?" In the narrow space of the open door, a snarling black-and-tan Chihuahua lunged for my ankle. I jumped back, startled.

"Precious! No!" Mrs. Rudnicki scooped up the little dog, who quieted immediately and began licking her face. The elderly woman looked back at me. "I'm sorry, dear. Who are you?"

"I'm Daisy, your neighbor." I gestured at my door. "I live across the hall."

Mrs. Rudnicki frowned. "That apartment is empty. I never hear anyone in there."

I bit my lower lip to keep my face in check. "No, ma'am. It's not empty. I live there." I held out my extra door key as proof. Left by the previous owners, it was a custom key in red-and-gold Kansas City Chiefs colors, attached to a metal football helmet with the team's insignia printed on one side. "Would you mind bringing up my mail? And keeping an eye on the place, in case any packages are delivered?"

Mrs. Rudnicki took the key but still looked unconvinced. "I suppose so. But I'm not sure why anyone would deliver packages to an empty apartment." Shaking her head, she closed the door in my face.

"Thank you," I called, wondering if I'd made a colossal mistake.

I perched at the edge of the couch, willing my phone to ring. I wanted someone to call and tell me that there'd been a miraculous turn of events: Dad was okay, there was no need to come to Denver, and I could go back to my life as planned.

My phone buzzed, and my heart jumped at the possibility of

a hoped-for reprieve. But it was only a notification that my driver would arrive in two minutes.

Time was up. I stood, cast a final look around, and gathered my coat, purse, computer bag, and suitcase. I paused in the doorway a moment longer, then, squaring my shoulders and lifting my head, I turned out the lights and closed the door, locking it behind me.

Chapter Six

Daisy, Age 17

Each year, my high school hosted a career day. And each year, my mother packed a Blooms by Bert apron into my backpack and pressed the latest copy of *American Florist* into my hands. While my classmates spoke of becoming doctors, lawyers, or professional sports players, my presentations consisted of the latest trends in centerpieces and the merits of carnations versus roses in bouquets.

By junior year, I'd had enough. Secretly, I'd decided to be a marketing executive and present the spreadsheet I'd created during student council, outlining a budget proposal and decorating scheme for Homecoming.

For the first time ever, I was excited for Career Day. But when I got to school and opened my backpack, the shoulder-padded electric-blue blazer I'd borrowed from my friend Amy's mother was missing. In its place was the dreaded apron with a note pinned to it.

"Nice try," it read. "Love, Mom."

"Daisy Greene, please report to customer service," a voice intoned over the loudspeaker in the Denver International Airport main concourse.

I stopped. From behind me, I heard several people exclaim in annoyance. An elbow in my back and a not-so-gentle "Ex*cuse* me" encouraged me to step aside and let the flow of traveler traffic stream by and up the escalators to the meeting area outside baggage claim.

I strained to hear over the noise of conversation, machinery, and disembodied reminders that "the doors are closing." Maybe I had imagined it.

"Daisy Greene, please report to customer service."

I hadn't imagined it. A chill ran down my spine. I knew what that meant.

My family, against my vociferous objections, had come to pick me up.

For a moment, I considered getting back on the train. I could do it. I could ride the train back to a terminal, walk up to a gate, and ask to buy the first ticket available to anywhere. I could call with my regrets from Antigua.

Bud's voice cut across my vision of blue sky and warm sand: "We need you, Sis. Come home."

I sighed and stepped onto the escalator, feeling the years fall away as I rose. I was a teenager again, my agency and self-confidence gone, leaving me awkward and self-conscious, always wondering what was wrong with me, why I didn't fit in, why I didn't want the things they thought I should.

"Daisy!" An object came hurtling at me as I approached the customer service desk, enveloping me in a crushing hug and lifting my feet off the ground.

"Bud!" I croaked, my face pressed against the familiar lime-green of his work shirt. He smelled the same: flowers, soil, and sweat. Memories of noogies past flooded me. "Put me down!"

He complied and stepped back, holding me at arm's length. "Heya, Daze. It's good to see you!"

I gawked, doing some quick recalibrations to my mental image. Four years of video calls hadn't done justice to his transformation. In my head, Bud was as I'd last seen him in person—gangly, unshaven, hair hanging over his collar. The Bud before me was clean-shaven with a haircut that would pass military standards. His work shirt strained against his thickened arms and torso. His eyes and smile were the same, though, warm and laughing, and I felt a tug at my heart with the realization that I'd missed being looked at with such affection. Even if it came in the form of my infuriatingly irresponsible brother. "Hey—" I started but was cut off by another billowing figure coming in from my right.

I ducked instinctively, my mind processing what seemed to be a giant bat swooping at my head. Mom squished my face between her palms and kissed me on the forehead with a loud *mwah*. "My baby."

"Hi." I gasped as a cloud of jasmine enveloped me. I pulled my head back, bringing my mother into focus.

Unlike my brother, Mom hadn't changed a bit. Ruth Greene was a woman of generous size and nature. Her (suspiciously blond) pageboy was still shellacked into place, and her blue eyes were large and unblinking. Oversized tortoiseshell glasses dangled from a beaded cord around her neck. Her flowing chiffon blouse featured huge cabbage roses and dolman sleeves, while her wide-legged pants fell in a straight line, making her into a perfect square.

To my dismay, I felt tears in my eyes as all the worries I'd suppressed threatened to break free. Missing nothing, Mom reached forward and pulled me into a hug. "There, there," she murmured. "You're home now. Everything's okay. Your father will be so happy to see you. And to think it only took a stroke to get you here," she continued gently. "He didn't even have to die."

I froze. Behind me, Bud began coughing, which sounded suspiciously like laughter.

Mom's hands moved from my back to my arms, squeezing as she went, as if testing a melon for ripeness, assessing me. "Hmmph," she said.

I rolled my eyes. John once asked me why I flinched whenever someone hugged me.

This was why.

I disengaged from her grasp on the pretense of gathering my bags. Bud beat me to it, shouldering my workbag and gently nudging my grip from the rolling suitcase handle. I followed with nothing to carry except my purse, almost running to keep up with his long strides. He and Dad had gotten all the height in the family. My mother, though short-limbed like me, seemed to sail along effortlessly like a ship cutting through water.

"You didn't have to meet me," I panted as we exited the main concourse and headed toward the parking lot. "I was going to rent a car."

"Nonsense." Mom flicked a dismissive hand as we arrived at Bud's ancient Honda Accord. "Why spend the money? You're home. You'll be with us the whole time. Why would you need a car?"

"For eh"—I stopped myself from saying escape—"mergencies?"

"Phoo," she said, settling into the passenger side. My brother cast a quick grin over his shoulder at me and threw my luggage into the trunk with a *thud*. I hoped it was my shoes and not my computer. Bud climbed in the driver's seat while I took the back seat, shutting the door and bracing myself for whatever lay ahead.

Mom remained uncharacteristically quiet on the drive to the hospital, occasionally humming along with the music but mostly rubbing her hands along her pant legs, a sure giveaway that she was nervous. Bud drummed his fingers on the faux-leopard steering wheel cover. Even from the back seat, I could see the greenish-brown stains under his fingernails and the florist calluses on his fingertips, the next generation of our father's hands.

"I can't believe how much the city has changed," I said to cover the silence. The once-bare commute between Denver and its airport was now populated with housing developments and shopping centers. Neighborhoods had merged into suburbs. "Where did everyone come from?"

"Texas, California, you name it," Bud said, cheerfully honking his horn and zipping around a slow-moving truck before slamming the brakes to avoid running into a Prius, whose bumper sticker encouraged us to "Visualize Whirled Peas." He flung his arm out to stop Mom as she lurched forward, the Honda's stretched-out seat belt more like a vague suggestion than a safety harness. Mom fell back against the seat, seemingly unfazed, and resumed humming. He cast a look in the rearview at me. "You okay?"

"Yeah, I'm fine." I shook my head, then gestured out the window. "It's all so different. The city. You," I added, looking at my brother, who was concentrating on the line of brake lights ahead of us.

"Everything is fine now that you're back where you belong," Mom piped up, not turning around.

I stiffened. "I'm not back. I'm here for a week."

Mom sniffed. "We'll see."

Bud ignored this exchange. "Yeah, a lot has changed." His voice held no hint of resentment or expectation, and I relaxed slightly. "At least Arlene here is the same." He thumped his car's dashboard fondly. The glovebox fell open, hitting Mom in the knees.

I changed the topic. "What's the latest update on Dad?" It was impossible to imagine my ever-busy father lying in bed. He was always working at the store or at home, endlessly occupied.

"Pop's feeling better. Sitting up, eating Jell-O, annoying Ma." Bud veered onto the exit ramp, eliciting a chorus of angry honks around us. I gripped the armrest, expecting to feel the crunch of impact at any moment. Miraculously, we glided to a smooth stop at the intersection. Unfazed, Bud rolled down his window and pointed west toward the mountains.

"Turn signals haven't worked in a few months," he said, as if this were perfectly acceptable driving etiquette.

Same old Bud. "How is Chantal?" I asked.

"She's good. She and LilyRose are back at the house. She volunteered to make your welcome-home dinner tonight." Bud's pride was evident as he spoke about his partner and their daughter. I had to keep reminding myself that my brother wasn't only my brother anymore. He was a father and a boyfriend.

It had come as a surprise when, four years ago, Bud had announced that he and his girlfriend were having a baby. An even bigger surprise was when it became obvious that Bud was not only a father but a good one, abandoning his much-beloved bachelor pad above the garage and moving with Chantal and baby LilyRose into the second floor of our childhood home. Delighted to have someone new to boss around, Mom took up, with great zeal, the role of helicopter grandparent, watching LilyRose while Chantal taught art at the neighborhood elementary school.

For a brief, miraculous moment, I thought the arrival of my niece meant that Mom's energies would henceforth be redirected permanently away from me. How wrong I was. The unforeseen outcome of my brother's belated foray into maturity only increased the intensity of my mother's belief that I was shirking my familial duties by remaining steadfastly single, busy, and far away. Her calls increased in tone and intensity:

"Daisy? It's your mother. When are you going to settle down?"

"Daisy? It's your mother. The cutest little house went up for sale only two blocks from us. I called the realtor, and he's willing to take half a percent off his commission if you pay the down payment in cash."

After months of gritting my teeth and blatantly ignoring her, she got the message and changed tactics, employing my father to make the phone calls instead. When that didn't work, she strong-armed Bud into the role. That was when I'd renamed the contacts in my phone.

"I'm looking forward to meeting them," I said. A lie. As nervous as I was about seeing Mom and Dad, I was even more anxious about meeting Chantal and my niece. I wondered what they thought of me, the absentee sister, daughter, aunt. Somehow, everything had been easier to justify back in Kansas City. Here, I felt like I was starting off wrong-footed, still the cactus girl in an ever-growing family of flowers.

"We're here, Ma." Bud veered into the hospital parking lot and pulled up at the entrance, engine idling. "You and Daisy go in, and I'll park the car." Mom started as if she'd been asleep. She touched her face and hair, confirming both were still in order, and gathered her purse.

Panic rose in my chest. I wasn't ready. I wasn't ready to see my dad in the hospital. I wasn't prepared to be alone with Mom without the buffer of Bud. I wasn't—

"Ready?" Mom was already out the door and waiting on the curb, her blue eyes sharp and watchful. I had no choice. I'd come too far. *Oh, Antigua,* I thought, *I should have run to you when I had the chance.*

The sight of my father lying in a hospital bed stopped me cold. I barely recognized him. Dad's white-blond hair was now entirely white and so thin I could see patches of scalp. His bony neck and arms sprouted from his voluminous hospital gown, making him look like a child playing dress-up. The room was filled with flowers, well wishes from friends and business associates. A surreptitious glance at one of the messages revealed the name of a grocery store chain printed across the bottom of the card. The irony.

Mom steered me forward. "Bertram! Look who's here!"

Dad jolted awake. "Huh? What?" His glasses slid from his forehead to the bridge of his nose, and he blinked, his focus coming to rest on me. "Oh, hello, Petal."

The childhood nickname set my bottom lip quivering. "Hi, Dad." Shaking loose of Mom's iron grip, I gave him a gentle hug. "How are you?" I kissed his papery cheek.

"Oh, fine, fine." I released him, and he sat up straighter, smoothing down the blanket covering his legs. I saw the abandoned crossword puzzle amid the covers, the uncapped pen bleeding blue onto the hospital sheets. Never able to sit still, my father kept a crossword behind the counter at the store and one in almost every room of the house. The sight of it here gave me hope. "Such a fuss over nothing."

"It's not 'nothing,'" I said, taking the chair next to him. "Bud told me the doctors said you're considered high-risk for a heart attack. That you're under too much stress."

"Psshh," Mom said, straightening Dad's bedclothes and whisking the crossword and pen away. I saw Dad's arms lift slightly, like a child reaching for a favorite toy, before falling back, defeated. "*Stress*, they say. What does your father have to be stressed about? We had a couple of rough years after the shutdown, but things always worked out for the best." She booped me on the nose as she passed. A boop was my mother's favorite way to end a conversation. I'd once seen her boop a complaining customer's nose. The man had hurried off, clutching his bouquet, looking confused.

I shook my head. "The best? Mom, Dad's in the hospital."

"Yes, but now you're back, and everything is as it should be."

Something about her emphasis on the word "back" set off an alarm in the back of my mind. "Wait, why do you keep saying I'm back?" I asked as Bud entered.

"Who's back?" he said, sliding up to Dad's bedside. "Oh yeah, he's back. Dad is back." He feigned a punch to Dad's shoulder before turning his grin on me. "And look at all the

Greenes in the same room." He slung an arm around my shoulder. "Cactus Butt and Bud, back together."

"Don't call me that," I snapped. Even to my own ears, I sounded like a sulky teenager, but I couldn't help it. My family brought it out in me. "I'm not ba—" I stopped, cut off as a nurse rolled a cart into the room.

"Now then, Mr. Greene, it's time to take your vitals." She popped a thermometer into Dad's mouth and consulted her clipboard. "Perhaps you'd be more comfortable if your family waited outside."

I saw Mom's eyes narrow. Ruth Greene did not like being sent out of any room she thought she belonged in. "Come on," I said, grabbing my brother's arm. "We'll be in the hall."

Just before the door closed, I saw Mom approach the nurse who'd tried to dismiss her. *Oh well, her problem now.* Speaking of problems, I turned to mine. "Why does Mom keep harping on me being 'back' and everything as it 'should' be?"

Bud's cheerful expression slipped slightly, and his eyes slid away from my gaze. Oh, I knew those signs. I took a step forward. "What did you tell her?"

To his credit, he didn't deny anything. "Hey now, all I said was that you were *coming* back. I never said you *were* back." He shrugged. "Of course, I didn't correct her either—hey!" He yelped as I pinched him on the inside of his arm above the elbow.

"Shhh!" a chorus of nurses shushed us, pointing at the "Quiet please" sign as our heads swiveled toward them.

"What were you thinking?" I whispered, resisting the urge to run out the door. I knew I should've booked that flight to Antigua. "Why would you let her think that?"

"Because you two have been fighting long enough." Bud spread his hands as if it were obvious. "You need to get past it, make amends…"

"Oh my God." I rolled my eyes. "Are you Parent Trapping me?" For a brief, wild moment, I wondered if the hospital and

Dad's illness were part of an elaborate setup to bring me home. Were Mom and Dad in the room now, waiting to yell, "Surprise?"

Bud continued as if I hadn't spoken, "... because we've got bigger problems. *I've* got bigger problems." He looked at me. "The store's in trouble, Daze. I think—"

Dad's door opened, and the nurse hurried out, rolling her cart as fast as she could, shoes squeaking as she disappeared down the hall. Argument abandoned, Bud and I slipped back inside the room to find Mom sitting primly next to Dad, a satisfied look on her face. If she'd had a mustache, she would have been twirling it.

"As I was saying before we were so rudely interrupted," she said, darting a glare toward the door. "With Daisy back, we have lots to talk about, don't we, Bert?"

"Hmmm?" Dad looked up from his recovered crossword book to see Mom staring at him, one eyebrow arched. "Yes, of course, dear."

"However, your father needs to rest now, so why don't the two of you go home?"

Bud was already inching toward the door. I stayed put; there were some things I wanted to straighten out. "What about you?"

"I'm staying here tonight," Mom said, tilting her head toward the overstuffed Vera Bradley bag by the door. "Somebody has to supervise."

I doubted that her version of "rest" and Dad's were the same, but that was an argument for another day. I had bigger problems. "Mom, about my being 'back?' I think there's been some confusion. I'm not—"

"Come on, Sis, let's go." Bud ushered me into the hall before I could say another word or investigate why "lots to talk about" had such an ominous ring. Another hallmark of time with my family was never getting to finish my sentences.

Before we'd taken two steps, Mom stuck her head out the door. "Visiting hours start at ten, but you can come at nine. I'll take care of that one." She glanced down the hall, where the nurse watched us from behind an IV stand. Mom started to close the door, stopping halfway. "Bud, get Daisy something to eat. She looks terrible."

She directed her next comment to me. "And you make sure he remembers the chrysanthemums for the Youngdahl order." She ducked her head back inside, then out again. "Daisy, dear, it *is* good to have you back." She reached out and booped me on the nose. "Finally."

With that parting shot, she disappeared behind the heavy door.

Chapter Seven

Mom always said the first thing that attracted her to Dad was the flower shop. The only child of a single father in the military, my mother had a childhood of relocations and temporary friendships. When her father was transferred out of Colorado, my mother was old enough to stay behind and start a new life in Denver. She met my father when she stopped into the store to buy a bouquet to celebrate signing the lease on her first apartment. As she tells it, "I took one look around and knew that I was truly home."

Dad's upbringing was the opposite of Mom's. He inherited Greene's Flower Shop from his father and rechristened it Blooms by Bert. On the day he and Mom married, his parents gifted them the house he'd grown up in, bought a camper, and set off to travel the country. Sadly, a few years later, they were killed in an auto accident. Then, Mom's father passed from a heart attack. So while their backgrounds were diametrically opposed, the results were the same. Mom and Dad believed in family and stability. "Greenes put down roots and bloom where they're planted," Dad would say, while Mom nodded vigorously beside him. Too bad they couldn't see that the tighter they held us, the more it felt like a chokehold to me.

Our house was in an older neighborhood on the west side of downtown Denver, on a street crowded with colorful two-story Victorian homes and alley parking. Maple trees dripped leaves through the telephone wires. Slowing, Bud navigated Arlene across the gravel, squeezing into a spot between an unfamiliar silver Prius and the shop's ancient delivery van, the fading gold company name and logo clinging to the sliding door for dear life.

I opened my door to its full capacity—one inch—and glared at my brother. "You trapped me." *In more ways than one*, I thought.

"Climb out my side," he said, exiting easily, a twinkle of mischief in his eyes. "You've got people to meet." He was practically bouncing with excitement.

I clambered over Arlene's armrest, groaning as I heard a couple of stitches pop in the seam of my skirt. I managed an awkward dismount from the car, wobbling on one foot while disentangling my shoe from the steering wheel.

Bud joined me, my luggage in hand, and started up the flagstone walkway to the back door, which served as our main entrance. I hung back, taking my first live look at my childhood home in more than four years, marveling that something could look exactly the same while simultaneously appearing completely unfamiliar.

The house was lit up like Christmas. All the windows were open, lights blazed from every room, and soft music floated into the night. I smiled a little, thinking of what my father would say about electricity being so flagrantly wasted. The house was still green with white shutters; however, it looked as though someone had taken an eraser to all the colors, rubbing indiscriminately so that patches of wood shone through. The backyard, once a popular hangout spot for Bud's Hacky Sack friends, was bare of decorations save for a red tricycle parked by the back steps and a plastic climbing structure under a birch tree.

The kitchen door flew open, and a small, purple-clad rocket with braids burst out, running straight for Bud's legs.

"Daddy!"

Dropping my suitcase, Bud squatted down, scooping up the girl (*his daughter, my niece*, my mind corrected) in one smooth, practiced move. She threw her arms around his neck, and he stood, swinging her around and around on the patchy grass as she whooped with laughter. He sang "LilyRose, LilyRose" to the tune of the old Chordettes song "Lollipop."

"LilyRose!" a voice called from inside the house. A moment later, its owner appeared at the top of the steps. She was tall and gorgeous, with close-cropped hair and wide brown eyes that matched her daughter's.

Chantal. Artist and elementary school art teacher. Bud's partner. LilyRose's mother. She and my brother had started dating just before the last disastrous holiday I'd spent at home. We'd waved at each other over FaceTime but had never met in person. I felt my palms go clammy. This was a big moment.

I smoothed my hands over my skirt, and, once again, put on my brightest, most professional face. *Think of it as an account*, I told myself. *You're meeting an important client.*

"Hello!" I called, coming to stand by Bud, who was now dangling a delighted LilyRose by her feet and swinging her like a pendulum.

Chantal moved fluidly down the stairs, her paint-splattered shirt and noisy flip-flops doing nothing to detract from her grace. Her warm smile washed over Bud and the upside-down LilyRose but cooled considerably as she turned to me.

"It's nice to finally meet you, Daisy," she said, her emphasis on the word "finally" decidedly Ruth Greene-esque. She took my hand and gave it a single, strong squeeze before turning back to Bud. "Stop swinging her, or she's going to puke. She ate half a bag of Goldfish crackers while I was working." Chantal stepped back, angling her body to include me in the conversation. "As you can imagine, meals have been scattered."

Bud set LilyRose on the ground in front of me. "GrandPop's sick!" she announced cheerfully.

"I know." I nodded. *My niece*, I thought again in amazement.

She studied me with huge brown eyes. "You're my Aunt Daisy. You live in Misery."

"That's right, I... sorry, what?"

The girl sighed, clearly impatient at having to repeat herself. "Mommy, Daddy, and I live in Colorado. You live in Misery."

"Missouri," Chantal corrected her daughter. "Aunt Daisy lives in Kansas City, Missouri." Chantal's eyes met mine, and I registered that I was being assessed by both mother and child. "She's here to visit GrandPop and Grandma and to help Daddy at the store. Isn't that nice?"

LilyRose looked at me expectantly. I felt foolish, unsure of the appropriate way to introduce myself to a child.

Oh well, I thought, *when in doubt, stick with what you know.* I held out my hand and said in my most professional voice, "I'm pleased to make your acquaintance, LilyRose."

She giggled, covering her mouth. "You're funny."

On impulse, I gave a small curtsy. "Thank you."

"Come on, sweet thing." Chantal put a hand on the girl's back and steered her inside. Bud picked up my abandoned luggage and followed them. Holding nothing but my purse, I brought up the rear, climbing the familiar cracked concrete stairs and running my hand along the wobbly wrought iron railing. I paused on the stoop, took a deep breath, and stepped into my childhood.

Entering the kitchen was like traveling back in time: the smell of the lemon juice Dad used every day to remove the stains from his hands; the scratched wood table, too big for the space, ensured everyone had to move sideways to navigate around it; the off-white wall-mounted phone still hanging next to the swinging hallway door, its stretched-out cord dangling to the ground in tired defeat; and the familiar scratched Formica counters, currently covered in mixing bowls and tomato splatters.

A heavenly aroma made its way to me from the only new item in the room, a stainless-steel stove with a bright green digital display. Chantal bustled between the cabinets and the table, setting the yellow dishes we'd used all my life onto unfamiliar red placemats patterned with large hand-painted daisies. LilyRose trailed a step behind her mother, solemnly placing forks and spoons across the middle of each plate in an X. Five places were set.

I looked questioningly at Bud, who would not meet my eyes. "Lasagna smells great, babe," he said, blowing an air kiss at Chantal as he squeezed by, my suitcase hoisted into the air, my work bag around his neck. "I'll deliver these to Daisy's room and be right back to help."

"It smells delicious," I echoed, following my brother through the swinging door and down the darkened hallway, which was, as ever, a jumble of floral arrangement materials and shoes lined against the wall. I passed by family photos hung on the burgundy-papered walls: pictures of Bud and me ranging from birth to senior portraits, prints of the four of us in coordinated outfits posing against the storefront, Dad towering over us, beaming, while Mom's hand rested on my shoulder as if holding me in place. Next in line was Mom and Dad's wedding photo, which had always been one of my favorites. In it, Mom's hair was an '80s bonanza of hairspray and teasing, outdone only by a bridal bouquet so large it almost obscured the happy couple. Dad loved telling the story of how his enthusiastic father made the arrangement so large and heavy, they both had to hold it during the ceremony.

Mixed in among the familiar photos, a few newer images had appeared, replacing long-forgotten relatives and generic scenery shots. A baby picture of LilyRose—wrapped in a fuzzy lilac blanket and matching beanie—sleeping. A framed photo booth strip of Bud and Chantal dressed in 1920s costumes, laughing at something off camera. A candid shot of Mom and Dad, LilyRose between them, walking through a park. A quick scan confirmed that my college graduation photo was the most recent picture of me on display.

Bud led me upstairs as though I might have forgotten the way. We passed Mom and Dad's bedroom and bathroom at the front of the house, followed by Bud's room and the adjoining Jack and Jill bathroom. I stopped in front of my childhood bedroom door, but he shook his head, pointing instead to the door across the hall, which stood open and waiting.

"You're in here."

"The guest room?" My cheeks flushed as I realized my mistake. LilyRose was in my room. She lived here. I was the guest. "I mean, thanks."

"It's a little cramped," Bud said in apology.

Cramped was the optimistic term. The room held all my old furniture: a twin bed sporting a new plain blue quilt and matching shams, the battered desk where I'd done my homework and journaled about my fabulous future, plus a variety of extra pieces of furniture, and miscellaneous boxes. Wedged into the corner next to an Exercycle sat an overstuffed blue armchair brightly patterned with embroidered flying parrots. As a child, I refused to sit in that chair, afraid the birds would peck me. Bud, all knobby knees and bravado, had come to my rescue, climbing into the chair and farting. "I killed them!" he hollered, and I'd laughed so hard my sides ached.

Bud dropped my satchel and suitcase onto the parrot chair, then turned in a circle as though seeing the room for the first time. "Bit different, huh?"

"It's fine." I tried to keep my voice light. "It makes sense that LilyRose has my room—my *old* room." I corrected. "It's not like I had a bunch of things stored here." *Because I didn't plan on coming back.*

"Sorry," Bud said, dropping onto my bed, hands behind his

head. "I know I've dropped a lot on you in a short amount of time."

"Really?" I asked, sitting beside him and shoving his ancient work boots off the comforter. "I hadn't noticed."

He snorted and pushed up to his elbows to look at me. "I'm happy you're here, Sis. We've got a lot to catch up on, but not tonight. Tonight is going to be fun."

Something about the way he pronounced "fun" caught my attention. I flashed on the kitchen table: five places set. There were only four of us here. "Buuud?" I asked, drawing out his name like I used to when we were growing up and he'd done something to irritate me. "What did you do?"

He shook his head. "Nothing."

I waited, arms folded.

"Nothing, I swear. I… invited a friend for dinner."

"Whose friend?" I narrowed my eyes at him.

He shuddered. "You look like Ma when you do that."

My jaw dropped in horror. "I do not! Take it back!" I pinched him.

"Ouch! You got mean in Misery."

Scowling, I raised my fingers, ready to strike again.

"Okay, okay, I take it back. You do not, in any way, resemble Ma when you make that judgey face. Ow!" He yelled as my fingers found their mark. "Stop! Stop! Jeremy will be here any minute."

I stopped, fingers poised above his upper arm. "Jeremy? As in *my* Jeremy?"

Bud took advantage of my surprise and rolled away from me and off the bed, backing toward the open door. "Well, he'd take issue with being called *'your'* Jeremy, but yes. Hey," he said, anticipating my reaction, "I thought I was doing something nice! This is a big day for you, and I thought it'd be less stressful if we had another friendly face at the table."

"So you thought inviting my ex over for dinner *wouldn't* be stressful?" I covered my eyes with my hand. "Honestly…"

"You're not dating anyone, are you?"

"That's none of your business."

"Which means no."

"I am seriously considering stealing your car and driving home right now."

"Or you could stay and see if any sparks—"

Chantal's voice interrupted, "Bud? Daisy? Our guest is here, and dinner's ready."

Still rubbing his arm, Bud jabbed a thumb toward the stairs. "You can't leave yet. You don't want to miss Chan's vegetarian lasagna."

My traitorous stomach growled, negating the last of my objections. Seeing no other choice, I followed him down the stairs into what I could already tell would be certain doom.

Jeremy. For Pete's sake.

Chapter Eight

Daisy, Age 18

Jeremy Michaels was a California transplant, transferring into my class at the beginning of our senior year. His love of jam bands and skill with a Hacky Sack meant he quickly became part of Bud's social circle despite the two-year age difference, while I'd been smitten with his long, brown hair, kind eyes, and surfer drawl.

We'd gone to prom as friends, and on a few quasi-dates: an outdoor movie, an impromptu trip to Bonnie Brae Ice Cream where we'd met up with a group of his friends (including Bud). One sunny Wednesday morning, he picked me up and we drove to Estes Park to go hiking in Roosevelt National Forest. I hung my feet out the window and sang along with the radio. I wasn't usually a sing-along person, but being with Jeremy relaxed me, smoothed my jagged edges. With Jeremy, I felt less like a cactus and more like, well, myself. Or at least, my potential self.

But time wasn't on our side. He was moving back to California to go to college in Santa Barbara. I was on my way to Lawrence, Kansas. We belonged to two separate worlds.

. . .

On the morning I left for college, he brought coffee and blueberry muffins and helped me pack the car I'd rented. I'd been planning to leave early without a final scene from Mom who was still trying to cajole me into staying ("You want more freedom? How about the apartment over the garage?").

He slammed the trunk of the overstuffed Chevy Malibu closed. "Well, I guess that's it," he said, joining me on the back steps.

I turned to face him, taking in his kind brown eyes, his shaggy hair, and the smattering of sun freckles across his nose. I leaned in and kissed him softly. "Thanks," I said. "And just so you know, you don't owe me any promises. Like, now that we're both leaving."

He sat back as though startled. "I don't?"

I straightened, aware that I'd said something wrong, but wasn't sure what. "I just mean that we had fun this summer," I explained, my face growing warm beneath his scrutiny. "But I'm leaving, you're leaving. And things are different in college."

"They are?"

Nervous laughter bubbled out of me. "God, I hope so. It'd be a real bummer if all this work we did to get into college was for nothing, right? How depressing would it be to find out everywhere else was the same as here?"

Jeremy said nothing, but I saw his jaw clench and lines appeared between his eyebrows. The early morning light, which had bathed everything in the golden hue of a promise just a moment ago, now felt sterile, making me shiver.

I placed my hand on his arm. "Jer?" I asked, knowing it was time to go, but not wanting to leave on a sour note. "We're on the same page, right?"

He turned, putting his hand over mine. His fingers were warm. "Yeah, sure." He gave me a small, sad smile.

He rose and walked down the steps. At the end of the alley, he turned and waved. "Good luck, Daisy Greene," he called.

And that was the last I'd seen of Jeremy Michaels. Until now.

Bud and I entered the kitchen. The lasagna sat in the place of honor at the center of the table, steam wafting from the surface and giving off the most intoxicating aroma. To my left, leaning against the fridge, was Jeremy.

"Hey, Daze." He smiled at me, and the corners of his eyes crinkled.

"Hey, Jer," I said softly, not trusting myself to say more. Here was another reminder of how life had continued without me and how people I'd once known had changed. Unlike our house, which had softened with age, Jeremy appeared more clearly defined. I catalogued the changes, searching for familiar landmarks. His hair remained long and shaggy, but in a way that suggested regular maintenance rather than teenage neglect. He wore a slim-cut shirt and joggers in a fabric too high-tech to be called "gym clothes." He looked like the boy I'd known years ago, and yet, completely new. I wondered how I appeared to him.

The moment stretched on. Finally, Bud cleared his throat. "Hey, you two. I hate to break up this sparkling conversation, but shall we eat dinner?"

Jeremy's ears turned pink. I tore my eyes away from him to glare at my brother, whose fault everything was. "Let's eat," I mumbled.

We settled around the table, where I sat wedged elbow-to-elbow between the two men. LilyRose sang a short Sunday School blessing to the tune of the old Addams Family theme song. It even had the snaps.

"Good job, baby girl," Bud said as he beamed at his daughter. He gestured to Jeremy and me. "Guests first."

We reached for the serving spoon at the same time. A blush crawled up my neck. "You first," I said, embarrassed. "You're the official guest."

"Thanks," he said, scooping a huge portion onto his plate,

strings of mozzarella stretching up from the serving dish. Using my fork, I reached out to break the strands and my hand collided with his.

Food toppled onto the table, splattering his pants with tomato sauce.

"Oh no!" Instinctively, I snatched up my napkin, dunked it in my water glass, and began dabbing at the spots on his lap until it dawned on me what I was doing. I froze, then looked up at Jeremy, who was staring at me, a bemused grin on his face.

Face flaming, I all but threw my wet napkin at him. Muttering that I had a stain stick in my purse, I rushed from the room. Hoots of laughter followed me, along with LilyRose's voice: "What? What's so funny?"

My feet pounded up the stairs as though I could stomp out my mortification. Digging through my purse, I found the spot remover. My phone, abandoned at the bottom of my bag during the chaos of family reunions, flashed notifications: I had thirteen new texts and two missed calls, all from John.

Whoops. I typed a quick message saying I'd arrived safely and would call later.

"You okay?" Jeremy appeared at the door.

"What? Oh, yeah, sure." I pushed my phone aside and held out the stain stick like a crucifix warding off a vampire. "Here. You should treat the fabric before the stain sets."

"Thanks." He took the plastic tube from my iron grip. "I'm sorry Bud sprang me on you like this." He splayed his hands, conciliatory. "He called to tell me you were coming and said you might like to see a friendly face after your… extended absence." Jeremy paused and switched topics. "How's Bert? Bud was light on details."

I dropped onto the bed as the day's exhaustion descended. "He looked so old." My voice wobbled at the word "old," and I pressed my lips together to steady myself. "I've never seen him look so still."

Jeremy perched on the bed next to me. I breathed in, remembering his smell, warm and fresh like he'd been soaked in sunshine. Just like with the lemon juice, I was suddenly eighteen again, happier memories called forth by the familiar scent.

Perhaps Bud hadn't deserved that pinch on the arm.

I smoothed my skirt and folded my hands in my lap. "Sorry." I apologized, not because I was sorry, but because it was something to say. "It's been a long day."

"I can imagine."

"It's strange being here. I haven't visited in ages, even before the pandemic."

To my relief, he didn't look horrified by my confession. His mouth scrunched up as he considered what to say. I remembered him making the same face years ago. It was still cute. "I get it," he said, nodding. "I came for a visit nine years ago, met my wife, and never left again. Life can change direction in a moment, can't it?"

He saw my eyes dart to his bare left hand. "Divorced. Two years ago. But we have a son, Ethan. He's seven." He pulled his phone from his pants pocket and showed me his lock screen—a photo of him and Ethan on a playground, pulling silly faces for the camera.

"You always wanted a family," I said, remembering. "I'm happy for you. I mean, I'm sorry about the divorce, but I'm happy you have a son."

He nodded. "Danica and I are lucky—we're good at co-parenting. And I like her new girlfriend. She's the calm one when things get too emotional. Dani and I were too much alike, so we didn't work. We both need a Type A woman to keep us on track." Now, it was his turn to look at my bare hand. "How about you? Family? Kids?"

"God, no," I answered, then backtracked. "I mean, I'm married to my job, my one true love."

"So there's no one… special?" His ears pinked as he asked.

I cleared my throat, uncomfortable. "I don't really have time to date. There was someone a few years ago, but they wanted marriage and a family, and I didn't." It was my stock answer, meant to stop the well-meaning questions from friends looking to set me up. It had the additional benefit of being true. Lyle wanted to take the next step, and I hadn't been ready. Still wasn't. Thirty-two years with my family would do that to a person.

There was a long pause. I scratched my nails across the quilt.

"Well, it's good to see you, Daisy." Jeremy cleared his throat, stood, and held out his hand. "C'mon, let's go have some lasagna. Bud swears it's good, even if it is vegetarian."

Stuffed from Chantal's dinner (which was, as promised, delicious) and emotionally drained, I pleaded exhaustion after the meal and escaped to my room, insisting I would do all the dishes in the morning. Bud came up with me, carrying a half-asleep LilyRose to bed. We said goodnight in the hall before going our separate directions.

After washing my face and brushing my teeth, I called John, wanting the comfort of shop talk.

"H-hello?" he answered. Shoot, I'd forgotten the time difference. It was midnight in Kansas City.

"I'm sorry," I said softly. "I was returning your calls. Let's talk tomorrow."

"No." I heard the covers rustle, a slight exhalation followed by movement. "I'm up. I'm glad you called. How is it?"

"Everything okay?" Zadie murmured in the background.

"Shhh… it's Daisy. Go back to sleep," he whispered to his wife. To me, he said, "Hang on a second."

I sat in the parrot chair, pulling loose threads from the busted seam of my skirt. I would need to fix that before I went to bed. I could hear the muffled sounds of Jeremy, Bud, and Chantal chatting companionably below me. Looking around the room, I tried to sync my memories and reality. It seemed ridiculous to me now that I'd imagined my house and family all frozen in time during my absence. As if everyone had remained the same while I'd grown up and gone on with my life. I'd been as blind to their reality as I'd accused them of being to mine.

"Hey." John's voice pulled me back. "How's your dad? And how are you? What's it like being home?"

I looked around again, trying to describe how it felt to be in a place that was so familiar and yet totally foreign. How it felt to be relegated to the guest room of my childhood home, and how naive I'd been to assume it would be otherwise. I'd made myself the guest.

I gave up trying to be eloquent. "He's good. I'm fine. It's weird. Nothing changed, yet everything did."

"Hm." I recognized his tone as the one he used when trying to be diplomatic with demanding clients. "I guess that's to be expected, right?"

"I guess so." Not wanting to elaborate, I switched topics. "How was the rest of your day?"

"Good." John perked up, as I knew he would. "Tavia has a great idea for lighting the main reception area."

My worst fear was coming true. I was being replaced. "I've been gone less than twelve hours. When exactly did she have this great idea?"

"Hey now." John's voice lowered, conciliatory. "We won't make anything official without your input. But you'll like it, I promise. I'll send you a picture tomorrow."

"Great." I gritted my teeth. "I'm sure I'll love it."

"So"—John yawned—"any other news?"

My mom thinks I'm moving home permanently, and my ex came to dinner.

"Nope."

"Well, you're there a week, right? There's bound to be some excitement soon. And I wouldn't worry about things being weird. There was always going to be a period of adjustment. Tomorrow is another day, Scarlett."

"You can say that again." We said our goodbyes and hung up.

John was right. Today might have gotten off to a rough start, but I would set the record straight tomorrow. I had plenty of time to make sure Dad was okay, help my brother, and convince Mom that I had a life I liked back in Misery... uh, Missouri.

How hard could it be, really?

Chapter Nine

Daisy, Age 28

"Is this a joke?"

I stared at the shirt and apron sitting jauntily amid the Christmas wrapping paper. "Blooms by Bert" stared back at me in embroidered white lettering.

Beside me, Bud opened his gift, a twin of mine. "Hey, thanks," he said, pulling the faded Grateful Dead T-shirt over his head and tugging on the lime-green polo. "You went for the moisture-wicking polycotton blend. Nice."

His sincere delight annoyed me. Once again, he was the perfect child, Mr. Go Along, Get Along, and I was the prickly cactus, the ungrateful recipient of my parents' gifts.

I set the shirt and apron aside. "Excuse me," I muttered, taking care to walk, not run, from the room. A heavy silence trailed in my wake, followed by low voices.

Three against one. As always.

In the kitchen, I gripped the counter and squeezed my eyes shut, willing the tears that pricked the backs of my eyelids not to fall. *Keep it together, Daisy. Simply thank them and move on.* For something to do, I filled the coffee maker and set a fresh pot to brew. The familiar noise of the ancient machine soothed me. I relaxed against the counter, smoothing my hands down my flannel pajama pants as my heart rate settled. Three more days.

Until now, it had been an uneventful trip. I'd flown in late Monday night, and yesterday had been filled with endless projects such as tree decorating and holiday meal preparations. I'd gone shopping with Bud to pick out a gift for his new girlfriend, Chantal, steering him away from Walmart and toward Nordstrom. Dad had been at work late, fulfilling last-minute holiday orders. Conversations remained light, all of us skimming along at surface level to avoid unpleasant detours down familiar roads ("When are you coming home?", "Why don't we see you more often?", "When will you give up this event planning nonsense and join the family business?"). I'd been lulled into thinking—hoping—this might finally signal a fresh start, the beginning of my family's acceptance that I didn't want what they wanted, that I wanted to do something different with my life.

And then… this. An apron and a work shirt.

It was Career Day all over again.

Mom burst through the swinging kitchen door. "What is the matter with you?"

The coffee maker spat and sizzled as if in agreement. Stalling, I poured a cup of coffee, purposely choosing an innocuous chipped blue mug from the cupboard rather than one of the store mugs lining the counter. Turning to retrieve the milk from the refrigerator, I saw Mom holding it. Her expression was one of honest confusion, and despite my resolution moments ago, my frustrations flared.

"What's the matter is that you aren't listening to me." I took the milk and poured it with a shaky hand, overfilling the mug in my haste. Milky brown liquid ran onto the counter. Before I could react, a dishtowel appeared, already dabbing at the spill.

"Thank you," I snapped, taking the towel from Mom's grip and wiping the counter. "I like my job." The decade-old argument bubbled to the surface. We both knew our lines; I could hit the highlights without preamble. "I like my life in Kansas City. It is *not* a phase," I said, cutting her off. "It's my choice. You can accept it or not, but it's my life. And I don't appreciate the constant reminders of how I'm disappointing you."

Mom moved to the stove, picked up the teakettle, and crossed to the sink to fill it with water. Her movements were slow, methodical, and familiar. Only the slight wobble as she set the kettle on the burner hinted at her thoughts.

"Your father and I kept this store going for you," she said. "Your grandparents—may they rest in peace—gave it to him, and we've kept it going all these years to pass on to you and your brother." She turned, and I saw tears in her eyes. My mother didn't cry. For an instant, my resolution wavered. It would be the work of a moment to capitulate. To do as she asked. To accept the apron.

"I moved so much as a child," Mom continued. "My father's relocations took us all over the country. But once I met your dad and saw this store, I knew it was a chance to finally settle down and create a home. Stability. Everything I never had. I don't understand why you don't see this as the gift it is, Daisy. What kind of person turns down a gift?"

There it was again. The sense of otherness, of being different, that kept me from giving in. My brother was one of them, so he lived in their house and worked in their store. If I gave in now, I'd be stuck, rooted forever, spending the rest of my life as the cactus in the flower bed. Mistaken, mismatched, misplanted.

"Stop saying it's a gift; it's a flower shop, not a foot spa." I spun angrily on my heel and left the room, annoyed I hadn't come up with a more clever comeback. I stalked into the family room, where Dad was studying his new crossword book with great concentration, and Bud stared out the window as if entranced. I glared at them both. "Stop pretending you weren't listening."

"We weren't," Bud objected, his eyes wide with innocence.

I pointed. "The blinds are closed, and Dad's book is upside

down." They looked at each other sheepishly. "I'm sorry I disappointed you, Dad. I'm sorry I can't be more like Bud, happy to take orders and do whatever you want." I felt, rather than saw, Mom enter the room. I continued, "But I don't want to work in the store. I know it was Grandpa's gift to you, and you wanted to give it to us, but it isn't the life for me. It's not who I am." I turned to face Mom. "And the fact that you can't understand that makes it difficult for me to be here."

"We do hear you, and we do understand, Petal," Dad said, just as Mom said, "We want what's best for you."

"No, you don't. You want what's best for you." Seething, I hurried from the room before my tears undermined my determination.

The day continued downhill from there. Dinner consisted of strained chitchat between Mom and me. Bud tried his best to mediate while Dad retreated into his crosswords. When Fiona called with a last-minute client request, I interpreted it as a sign that it was time to go. Bud had already left for Chantal's, the cashmere sweater I'd picked out and painstakingly wrapped for him stuffed under one arm.

My parents tried to talk me out of leaving all the way to the airport, but I held firm. I needed to get back to where things made sense. Where *I* made sense.

"Safe travels, Petal," Dad said, hugging me before tactfully walking away to pick up a couple of coffees for the drive home. Mom and I watched him go, his cowboy hat a moving beacon among the masses of holiday travelers.

"Thanks for everything, Mom. It was a nice holiday."

"We love having you home." She emphasized the last word.

I tried again to state my case, a final push to make myself heard. "I know, and I appreciate everything you and Dad have done. But you're asking me to change my whole life, and I like it the way it is."

Mom paused before answering. "If that's how you feel, then I guess there's nothing more to say."

"I guess not."

That was where we'd left it and where we were still, each waiting for an apology that neither of us could give.

We gradually acclimated to the distance. Mom never stopped hinting, but I found it easier to handle her "helpful" suggestions about available rentals in the neighborhood from the other end of a phone call. Of course, I'd missed things: Bud and Chantal's burgeoning relationship, LilyRose's birth, holidays, celebrations. But the initial sting of regret faded, and soon our new normal was established.

Until now.

While I'd had to revise my mental pictures of my brother, my father, and my hometown, the flower shop of my memory remained perfectly preserved in real life: the exposed brick walls, the antique armoire loaded down with silk flowers and hurricane glass centerpieces, the reach-in filled with carnations, roses, gerbera daisies in garish colors, baby's breath, and assorted greenery. The chalkboard menu of prices along the back wall, though updated and expertly lettered, still harbored the ghosts of old pricing, which peeked out from behind the stark white calligraphy like naughty children. Even the slight twinge in my nose, hinting at long-dormant allergies, greeted me like an old friend.

The sole change was the window display, which hosted an explosion of hydrangeas in vibrant pinks and blues set against a painted silk banner. "This is pretty," I said, touching the banner and admiring how the fabric fluttered in the light breeze created by my movements.

"It is," Bud agreed. He propped the front door open with a rusted Radio Flyer wagon, setting the ribbon of sleigh bells jingling, the soundtrack of our childhood. "Chantal does all the window displays now. Sometimes she brings in her artwork or school projects for the background." He pointed at the banner. "She had her first graders help with this one."

"It's great," I said. "You should be doing more things like this."

Bud snorted. "Believe me, I'm trying. I want to expand the store and use the space for events and classes." He moved around the room, sketching out ideas in the air. "Chan could lead floral painting and wine nights. We could host DIY bridal bouquet classes in this area," he said, indicating where a display of forlorn potted plants sat in front of the window. "And over here," he said, pointing to the silk flower display that Mom had always insisted we carry for reasons unknown. "Would be the Home and Garden section where we'd feature local vendors, decor, planters, and cards."

I stared as he continued, fascinated. When we were growing up, Bud had worked at the store because it was expected, the path of least resistance. I'd thought he was doing it to one-up me. But now I could see he was in his element. His expression, always sunny and smiling, deepened in concentration and focus as he talked about the possibilities.

"Wow," I said, genuinely impressed. "You have everything figured out."

"All I need is for Ma and Pop to listen." He looked at me. For the first time, I could see the small worry lines radiating out from his eyes. "That's where you come in. They've always listened to you."

I scoffed. "Are you kidding? They never listen to me. I practically had to go into witness protection to get out of working here."

"Yeah, but they let you go, didn't they?" Bud shrugged. "That's their version of listening."

"Well… I'll help as long as I'm here. What can I do?"

I knew I'd made a tactical error when the words left my mouth. I'd given away my negotiating power up front.

"Funny you should ask." Bud pulled a crumpled notebook

paper from his back pocket. I had a brief vision of my brother in high school when homework assignments and permission slips received the same treatment. So, not everything had changed.

"First, I could use your help organizing Pop's office." Bud led me to Dad's office, a cramped room on the other side of the wall from the chalkboard display. "He's always been possessive about the back office, but this past year, he's been absolutely secretive." He lowered his voice as though the flowers could hear us. "I don't think it's good news, Sis."

My eyes widened. "Really?" I whispered too. "I can't imagine Dad letting the finances get out of hand."

Bud flopped down in the guest chair, motioning for me to take Dad's place behind the antiquated computer. I hesitated before sitting. It felt disloyal somehow to sit in Dad's spot. "Quarantine destroyed our numbers. All those event orders canceled; all our foot traffic gone." He sighed. "Online orders kept us afloat, barely. But we had to let everyone go. It's Dad, me, and Aunt Agnes now. And Chan helps out after school."

"Did I hear my name?" Chantal appeared at the door, followed by LilyRose, who scrambled into Bud's lap. Chantal dropped a kiss on Bud's head.

"Daze and I are developing a plan of attack," Bud said, tickling LilyRose with the word "attack." The girl screeched with laughter.

I offered Chantal my most capable, professional smile. I wanted her to like me. "I'll help sort out orders, make calls, and do whatever you need that doesn't involve touching actual flowers."

"Daisy's allergic to everything." Bud grinned. "Especially weddings."

My body tensed. I kept smiling but felt my expression harden. I knew what was coming.

"One time, Daisy helped Mom make a delivery to a bridal party, and she broke out in hives."

"That's awful." Chantal grimaced.

Bud was giggling now. I clenched my fists. *Here comes the punchline.*

"But the best part of it is, you know what the flower she's most allergic to?" He paused for dramatic effect.

"What?" LilyRose was enthralled.

"Daisies!" he said, making a silly face. "Daisy is allergic to daisies." Father and daughter threw back their heads with laughter. Chantal shot me an almost sympathetic look.

"Are you quite done?" I asked my brother stiffly. "Because if we're reliving old memories, I seem to remember you and your high school girlfriend, Penny, sneaking in here and…"

"Time to go!" Bud shot to his feet, bustling LilyRose toward the door.

"Come on, sweet thing," Chantal said as she took her daughter's hand. "Daddy and Aunt Daisy have work to do." She beamed at Bud before her eyes shifted to me. I saw the challenge in them. *Don't let him down,* they said.

I shut myself in Dad's office, re-familiarizing myself with the layout. On his desk sat piles of purchase orders and invoices. I shuffled through the papers, wincing at the meager bottom lines. Bud hadn't exaggerated; business was slow. In the corner of each event invoice was a file number written in Dad's neat block lettering. I spun to face the filing cabinet, pulling open a drawer at random. I thumbed through receipts, wholesale orders, and old timesheets. Each of the other drawers was similarly stuffed, except the bottom drawer, which was locked.

I texted Bud, who was out in the alley helping unload the day's deliveries: *What's in the bottom drawer of Dad's file cabinet?*

A moment later, Bud stuck his head around the door, a bucket of gypsophila in his hands. "Dad's file cabinet? No idea. He never lets me in here."

"Well, the bottom drawer is locked."

"Search me. I'll ask next time we go to the hospital." Bud

hoisted the bucket, sloshing water onto his shoes, and squelched away toward the showroom's reach-in cooler.

"Well, aren't you a sight for sore eyes?" A wizened figure replaced my brother's hulking form.

"Aunt Agnes!" I jumped up and ran to give the store's oldest employee a hug.

Aunt Agnes wasn't really our aunt. Dad inherited her with the shop when he took over from his father, and she was such a fixture in our lives that Bud and I bestowed the honorary title of "Aunt" on her. Age and background a mystery, she made a fascinating addition to our family tree. You could never predict what would happen when Agnes was around. Once, in high school, I was dusting the silk flowers when a tall silver-haired man appeared in the store, crying, "Agnes! My love! I've found you at last!" I'd been unceremoniously ushered from the room, and soon after, the man had left looking crestfallen. I'd begged for details, but she refused to say anything other than, "Maybe when you're older."

"Good gracious, child." Agnes laughed. "You'll squeeze me to death."

I loosened my grip. "I'm sorry. It's so good to see you." Like the store, Agnes seemed frozen in time—her steel-gray hair carefully coiffed into a helmet of tight curls, her large, black-framed glasses magnifying her eyes to enormous proportions, her tiny frame ensconced in head-to-toe purple, her signature color.

"Well, let's look at you." Aunt Agnes similarly sized me up. "Too skinny, too pale, working too hard." She reached out and pinched my cheek. "Still not having nearly enough fun, are you?" Her eyes were sharp behind the thick lenses.

"Work is fun," I said defensively. "I don't need anything else."

She sniffed, dismissing my objections. "Seeing anyone special?"

"Did Mom ask you to ask me?"

Her eyes widened, the very picture of innocence. "Why, of

course not, dear." Her over-emphasis on denial assured me that this was precisely what had happened. "She simply mentioned that you'd come back *alone*..." She trailed off, clearly waiting for me to elaborate.

"Oh, for Pete's sake, I'm not ba—"

The office phone rang, saving me. Agnes picked it up. "Blooms by Bert, how may we help you?" A pause. "She's right here, Ruth." She held the phone out to me, winking.

Beetlejuice, I'm telling you.

"Hi, Mom, what's—"

"Daisy, it's your mother. Are you at the store?"

I rolled my eyes. "Mom, *you* called *me*. You know where I am."

"You and your brother need to come to the hospital right now. We need to decide what to do with your father's remains."

My gasp caused Agnes to jump, bumping into Bud, who was carrying a box to the showroom. Flower food packets went flying. "What do you mean, remains? Mom, is he..." I couldn't say it.

"Of course not!" She sounded offended, as if this wasn't all her doing. "Teddy brought by some medical forms you need to sign, that's all."

Teddy was Dad's best friend and had long been roped into doing whatever odd job was asked of him. Over the years, he'd worked as the store's accountant, estate lawyer, and handyman. I had no idea if any of what he did was legal. Still, I figured the less I knew, the better my plausible deniability defense would hold up in court. My eyes wandered to the locked file cabinet drawer.

"But Dad's okay, right?" I pushed, willing my pulse to return to normal. Great. One day into my visit and *I* was ready to collapse. Maybe the hospital offered family rates.

"He's perfectly fine. He's right here, eating Jell-O. Say hello, Bert," she commanded.

"Hello, Bert," Dad said and chuckled.

I sighed and made a blast-off motion to Bud, one palm sweeping across the other into the air. It had been our signal since childhood for Mom's tangents and usually resulted in us dropping whatever we were doing to cater to her latest whim. He grinned and resumed collecting flower packets with Agnes.

"Okay, we're on our way. Don't do anything until we get there." I enunciated each word, concerned she might donate our father's living, breathing body to science in the next twenty minutes.

"You don't have to shout. I'm not deaf."

"We'll be right there," I repeated, hanging up and turning to Bud. "We need to go to the hospital and make sure Mom doesn't harvest Dad's kidneys while he's still using them."

Bud looked at the pile of paperwork on the desk. "What do you want to do with this?"

"I'll go through it later." I closed my laptop and grabbed my purse. "We'll figure this out, Buddy. We'll make them listen. Dad's not going anywhere, and I'll tie Mom to a chair if necessary."

Bud grinned. "You know, I think I've still got Penny's handcuffs…"

"Please don't finish that sentence."

On the way to the hospital, I gathered the courage to say the words that had been hanging in the air between us since I landed: "I'm sorry I haven't been here these last few years. I really am."

Bud shrugged. "It's cool. I know how hard Ma pushed you. All the comments, the hints, that apron…" He trailed off, and I could tell he, too, remembered that last disastrous Christmas. "The funny thing is, I'm the one who wants the store. I'm the one who stayed. But they don't trust me. They think I stayed because it was easier than leaving. By leaving, you somehow proved that you were the one with the motivation. The worthy successor to the kingdom. If I'd known that's what it would take, I would've moved out years ago."

This was perilously close to what I'd always assumed of Bud. "I'm sorry," I offered again as much of an apology for my behavior as our parents'.

"Thanks." He shot me a small smile. "Like I said, I think I could save the store—classes, partnerships, rebranding—but Dad won't let me in, won't let me try. You know him." Bud straightened his posture and pushed an imaginary pair of glasses up his nose. "Our business is a family tradition," he said, pointing finger guns in a perfect impersonation of our father. "Bloomin' Bert sells flowers. Not gimmicks." He dropped the act and became himself again. "Well, if we don't figure out something soon, we won't even be able to sell flowers."

"I'll help. However I can, I'll help." I was shocked to hear those words fly out of my mouth and even more shocked to realize I meant them.

Chapter Ten

My certainty in our mission began fading as we rode the elevator to Dad's room. What would it take to make Dad see that Bud was trustworthy? What would it take to make Mom realize that I wasn't, in fact, back for good?

Bud nudged my shoulder. "Don't sweat it, Sis. I'm sure they'll be totally chill."

"Really?"

"Nope." His eyes twinkled. "But they're usually yelling at me, so this will be a nice change."

"Oh great. That's really encouraging."

"Here to help."

"Why start now?" But I was smiling as I said it.

How ironic was it that Bud and I were finally working together just to prove that we wouldn't work together?

"Hey, Ma. Hey, Pop." Bud breezed through the doorway of the hospital room like he was walking into a party and flopped into the chair opposite Dad's hospital bed. Without missing a beat, he picked up the TV remote and turned on the wall-mounted set. Within moments, he and Dad were immersed in deep conversation over the highs and lows of the latest Rockies game.

I lingered in the doorway, taking in the situation. Mom was seated at a small round table in the corner of the room, hands clasped, looking for all the world like she was calling a meeting of the Five Families. Dad lay in bed, eyes glued to the screen as he took bites of something that might have been oatmeal from a Styrofoam bowl. Outside, the Rocky Mountains, still sporting trace amounts of snow at their highest peaks, were bathed in morning sunshine.

Quit stalling, I chided myself. I pulled back my shoulders, raised my chin, and stepped into the room.

"Hello, Petal," Dad said as I kissed his cheek.

"How are you feeling?" I asked, trying not to stare at the wires and needles running from his body to the monitors.

"Oh, I wish everyone would stop making such a fuss," he said, wiping his mouth and putting his empty bowl on the rolling bed tray. "I got a little overtired. I'll be back to work in no time."

I glanced at Mom, who began pulling papers out of her enormous, quilted bag like some kind of administrative Mary Poppins, and then over to my brother, who was tapping out a message on his phone. It was up to me to start the conversation. I took a deep breath. "Dad, you are overworked and overstressed. You need to start transitioning the store over to Bud." I coughed pointedly at Bud, who startled to his feet and pocketed his phone. "Mom, Dad needs to take a step back. Bud has some great ideas for the store—"

She cut me off. "Psshh. Now that you're back, we'll have plenty of time to go over that."

My right eye twitched. "I'm not back."

She rattled the papers, drowning out my objections. "First, there are some medical forms we need for insurance." She held out a pen.

"Ruth," Dad cut in, "I'll take those. Please get those for me, Petal."

I slid the papers away from Mom and placed them gently on my father's lap.

"You've got so much to do, honey," he said, tucking them inside his crossword book. "I'm just lying here. I'll take care of filling them out."

Mom looked like she wanted to say more but then thought better of it. "Now, Daisy, you'll take over for your father and the day-to-day operations. Bud can focus on what he's been doing—order fulfillment and deliveries. After you've settled in, we can talk about a permanent title for you, like Manager of Business Affairs."

I could see Bud's shoulders slump from the corner of my eye. My heart went out to my little brother. *Speak up*, I thought as much to myself as to him. *Fight!*

I turned to Mom. "I'm only here for a week," I reminded her. "Bud, tell Mom and Dad your ideas for new revenue streams—"

Mom waved her hand, the bell sleeve of her cobalt blue shirt flaring out. "You can't go home with your father in this state. Let's call you Acting Manager and start setting up customer calls."

"Mo*ther*," I said, horrified to hear the adolescent whine creeping in on the second syllable. "Bud should make those calls. The customers know him. Plus," I added, "there's no need for an acting manager when you have a permanent manager available." I shot a look at Bud, raising my eyebrows in a "You want to get involved here?" way.

He got the hint. "I already talked to most of them, Pop. We won't have any lapses in service. Chantal will help me with the wedding this weekend and update photos on the website."

Mom ignored him and continued addressing me. "When you talk to them, let them know that there will be no gaps in service. In fact, maybe we need to offer a discount for the inconvenience."

Having found his voice, Bud cut her off. "A late delivery is an inconvenience, Ma. This is Pop we're talking about." He turned to Dad. "Pop, this is your legacy, and I respect that. But the doctors say you can't keep working at this pace. This was your one warning. Let me run the day-to-day stuff. I *want* to do it."

Dad's eyes flitted to Mom and then back to Bud. Maybe it was the meds, but he seemed conflicted, as if he had something to say. I chanced a glance at Mom who was shaking her head as her mouth was already forming the word "no" that would end the conversation.

"How about this," I said, jumping in when the silence continued a moment too long, "I'll help Bud for as long as I'm here. Which is a week," I emphasized. "Meanwhile, think it through, and let's discuss this again later."

A look passed between Mom and Dad. Finally, they both nodded.

"Great," I said, dragging Bud from the room. "We'll see you later. Get some rest, Dad."

"What was that?" Bud asked as we exited the hospital. I realized I still had his sleeve in a death grip.

"They agreed to think about it. It's a start." It occurred to me that for the first time in my life, I had employed Bud's go-along, get-along strategy while he'd been ramping up for a fight, me-style.

"Yeah, well, what if they 'think about it,'" he said, miming quotes, "and come back with a resounding no?"

"We won't let them."

"We?"

"Like I said, I'm going to help you." I released my brother's sleeve and took his hand, squeezing it to make my point. "I'll help you convince Mom and Dad that you should take over. We can do it, Buddy. We can save the store." I imagined the dramatic swell of the orchestra as I made my proclamation: cymbals crashed, a bass drum went *boom boom boom,* and an imaginary audience stood in ovation.

"While I appreciate the enthusiasm, Cactus Butt, you're crushing my hand."

I crashed back to reality, my triumphant soundtrack petering out with an anemic kazoo wheeze, *eeeeee...*

Never mind the big musical moment, I thought. I would spend the next week helping my brother prove to our parents that he was ready to take over the store. Once they saw that he was the only one for the job, I could go home and focus on the art museum and the new business with John. My mind raced ahead. Maybe I could even visit again without the pressure and nagging about when I was going to "come home where I belonged." I could get to know Chantal and LilyRose. I could finally have a relationship with my family that didn't revolve around guilt and disappointment.

There was no time to waste. By helping Bud, I would finally be free.

I shut myself in Dad's office, hoping to avoid the rising cloud of pollen as Bud and Agnes fulfilled the day's orders—my throat was already suspiciously scratchy—and checked my messages. There was a text from John asking me to check my email, and a short voicemail from Reg confirming that Tavia had my full support on her proposed event improvements. I bristled at the phrase "improvements" and wondered who had used the term first.

I called Reg, breathing a sigh of relief as my call rolled directly into his voicemail.

"Hello, Mr. Davis, this is Daisy Greene returning your call. I assure you that we have your event well in hand. I am in regular contact with the office and current on their activities. I look forward to resuming the lead when I return. Meanwhile, I will schedule a conference call with my team to review all event logistics."

Satisfied, I pressed *One* to send my message and disconnected the line. "Conference..." I muttered, tapping the phone against my chin. "I wonder..."

Brushing Dad's piles of paperwork aside, I hauled my laptop out of my bag and powered it on, tapping my fingers impatiently on the keys as I connected to the store's Wi-Fi (I was annoyed to see that the password was still C@ctusButt99).

I pulled up my search engine and typed in "flowers expo Denver May." The third result was for a bridal expo happening this weekend. A *zing* of excitement shot through me. *Perfect.*

Bud appeared at the door, startling me. "I'm starving. You ready to get some lunch?"

"Look!" I pointed proudly to the expo website. "I've solved your problems."

Bud peered at the website, lips moving as he read. "Oh, yeah. I heard about this."

His demeanor was not the immediate praise and adulation I'd expected. I frowned. "Don't you think exhibiting is a good idea?"

He looked up at me, surprised. "Well, sure. It's a great marketing opportunity. But we don't have the budget for a big fancy display. Plus, we've got the Howland-Hunt wedding on Saturday. And Agnes will be here at the store." He raised an eyebrow. "Unless you want to..."

"Oh." Now it was my turn to sound dubious. "I mean, I-I..." I stuttered, then remembered Chantal. *Don't let him down.* "Of course I want to. I run events for a living. You make up a nice bouquet and give me a few talking points. I'll handle the rest." My confidence grew as I talked. "What would be the best outcome for you? Two wedding contracts? Three?"

Bud snorted. "Two more weddings on the books would be great, Sis. And would help shore up the argument to Dad that the store can manage without him." I could see a blush of pink on the apples of Bud's cheeks, which always happened when he got excited. "We've got wedding flowers coming in tomorrow. I'll call our wholesaler—that's Cecil; you'll meet him; he's great—and ask him to include some extras for a centerpiece. Chan will make a showstopper for you." He gave me a hug. "Thanks,

Daze. I knew I could count on you. We'll get through this and then compile a revised budget for Pop. He won't be able to say no. Now," he said, closing my laptop screen, "let's go to lunch."

We returned to work after a quick lunch of empanadas from a nearby food truck. The first thing to do was to reserve a booth space. I hummed to myself as I skimmed the map of available booths. Not surprisingly, the best locations were taken. However, a few small spaces remained. It would have to do. I filled out the online form, leaving the application open while I brainstormed some ideas for new marketing copy. There was no way I was donning Dad's cowboy hat as "Bloomin' Daisy."

My phone buzzed; it was John. I picked up on the second ring, answering in case Fiona was listening in, "Event Artistry, Daisy Greene speaking."

"Hey, Daisy Greene." John's voice echoed; he was on speakerphone. "I'm here with Tavia. We have that lighting idea to run by you."

"Hi, Daisy, it's Tavia," she bellowed as though John hadn't spoken. "I can't thank you enough for this opportunity. I know you're busy"—was I imagining her slightly condescending tone?—"I'll make this brief. I was looking at your sketch of the main exhibit hall, and I think if we utilized some fabric screens and LED strips, we could solve your decor and lighting budget overage. I did something similar for an event with my previous company," she added with a modest chuckle, "and it worked beautifully."

John chimed in, "I sent you some pictures," he assured me. "We won't finalize anything without you, but I think it looks great. The way the light reflects off the screens really vibes with Ms. Maxwell's art."

Vibes with the art? John didn't say things like that. I made some noncommittal noises before launching into my own news. "I heard from Reginald Davis this morning. Is this the idea he mentioned in his message?"

"That was me," Tavia volunteered, missing (or possibly

ignoring) the rebuke in my voice. "I was so excited about my idea; I couldn't wait to call him."

Ever the peacemaker, John jumped in, "It's unconventional, but when you see it, I know you'll agree that it's a brilliant solution. Tav has skills." He emphasized the "s," making it sound like "skillz."

Tavia giggled. "You're too much."

"I'll tell you who's too much," I muttered.

"What's that?"

I cleared my throat. "Let's proceed with caution for right now. And don't finalize anything until I've seen photos."

"Of course!" Tavia trilled. "I was telling Reg this morning what an honor it is to stand in for you, even for a few days—"

John cut her off. "Thanks, Daisy. We'll talk to you soon. I hope your Dad is feeling better." He hung up before I could address the problem of Tavia speaking to Reg directly (and, I worried, frequently). John was too trusting. I needed to get back to work as soon as possible before that sneak embedded herself permanently in my role.

"Aunt Funny!" LilyRose appeared at my side, startling me with the new nickname and making my hands jump against the keyboard. Reflexively, I closed my screen. "I made you a picture in Mommy's art class today." She held out a warped, slightly damp piece of construction paper. She pointed to a small smiley face on top of a sparkly purple triangle. "That's me." She pointed to a larger, frowny face on top of a black triangle. "And that's you."

"That's, um, lovely," I said, holding the paper by its edges. "Why am I frowning?"

"I don't know." She shrugged. "But Daddy says it looks just like you."

"Did he? And what are these gray swirls around me? Clouds?"

"That's Misery. Where you live," she reminded me.

"I see. Well, thank you." I started to open my laptop. Lily-

Rose watched, an expectant expression on her face. "Er, why don't we hang this on Grandpop's wall?" I suggested and was rewarded with a big smile. I crossed to Dad's bulletin board and, borrowing a pushpin from the corner of a group of documents marked "To File" in Dad's neat block handwriting, stuck Lily-Rose's picture in the center. "Ta-da!"

"Ta-da!" she repeated, complete with jazz hands, before scampering out of the office. I looked at my laptop, then back at the picture, the frowny-faced circle surrounded by Misery. Sighing, I followed her into the main showroom.

Agnes, Bud, and Chantal were gathered around the desk, talking in low voices. They broke off as I approached.

"Hi," I said, feeling like an intruder. "How's the planning going?"

"Great," Bud said, slinging an arm around my shoulder. "I was telling them about the wedding expo."

"It's a good idea." Agnes looked at me, her voice softening with concern. "But, honey, do you think you can manage it?"

"Absolutely." I worked to project more confidence than I felt. "I grew up around this place, you know. I'm sure it will all come back to me."

Chantal nodded in my direction. "I'm sure it will." She turned to Bud. "LilyRose and I are heading home. I want to get in some studio time before dinner."

I jumped at the change of subject. "Are you working on an art project?"

Chantal paused, shooting a side look at Bud and Agnes. "You could say that. Come on, LilyRose, let's go home."

LilyRose jumped down from where she'd been sitting in the front window rearranging flowers. For a moment, time swam backward, and I remembered sitting in that window as a child, pretending to be part of the window display, waving at people as they passed by.

"Bye, Daddy, Aunt Agnes, Aunt Funny."

"Thank you for my picture, LilyRose." I hoped I sounded sincere.

"Bye, baby girl. Love you a million," my brother called, blowing kisses.

"Are you good for another half hour?" Bud turned back to me. "I've got a few things to finish up."

I looked around the store, seeing its depleted stock and lack of customers. I couldn't imagine what would take half an hour to do. But I was in this to help, so I smiled and nodded. "Absolutely. That will give me time to order a banner for the expo."

Bud looked worried. "Sis, we don't have the money…"

I waved him off. "Don't worry. My treat. Here to help, remember?"

He visibly relaxed, then punched me in the arm. "You're the best, Cactus Butt." He headed to the back room, whistling "Sugar Magnolia," hands in his pockets, work boots clomping in time with the tune.

"Your parents will be happy to hear that you're helping out," Aunt Agnes said, looking at me with affection. "Your mother especially is pleased that you're back." She patted my arm, then followed Bud.

"I'm not—" I started, then threw up my hands. What was even the point?

That evening, desperate for something that made sense, I called John.

"How's life in the Upside Down?" he asked.

"How much time do you have?" I settled into the parrot chair, my legs tucked under me, a glass of water balanced on the chair arm. A single distorted bird's eye stared up at me through watery depths.

I recapped the day, starting with an update on Dad's health, the doctor's warning about cutting back on stress, the shop's financial woes, and finally, coloring in details with Bud's ongoing quest to take over the store and Mom and Dad's reluctance to relinquish control.

John listened in an uncharacteristic silence. A few times, he muttered things like "What?" and "Are you serious?" but I treated his questions as rhetorical and kept talking.

"You should see it," I said, shaking my head. "Bud has all these great suggestions, but Mom and Dad are so stuck in their ideas of how Blooms by Bert should be that they can't see what it *could* be. They're basically holding it over our heads that we have to agree to run the store together before they step down. It's downright diabolical." I continued, voice escalating, "This is why I stayed away. I'd never have gotten to have my own life here."

I realized I was ranting. I trailed off, taking a sip of water. My throat felt dry and itchy after a day in the store. "I'm sorry," I relented. "I know I'm not the only one under stress here. How's work? Any more suggested improvements from Tavia?"

John laughed. "Give her a break. She's excited, and she wants to impress you." He lowered his voice. "I do have an update on Ground Floor, though."

"Why are you whispering?"

"Am I? Habit." His voice returned to normal. "Maggie got a message from the building manager. There's another company interested. We need to sign the lease agreement and put down a deposit to secure the space. I sent you a text earlier today." A note of accusation crept into his last sentence.

I scrolled through my phone and saw the missed message. "You did. I'm sorry. I got distracted."

John sighed. "I know you did. It's okay. I'll email you the agreement. Just complete your part of the financials, sign it, and return it to Maggie."

"I will," I promised. "I'll do it as soon as I wrap up this expo thing. I fly home on Tuesday. Let's meet with her in person once I get back."

We chatted a few more minutes, John catching me up on

office gossip and family anecdotes before saying, "Sorry, Daze. I need to go to bed. I had a long day." He yawned as if to make his point.

"Of course," I said, checking the time and realizing it was after 11. "Thanks for calling. Give my love to Zadie and Sabrina."

"Will do," he said, yawning again. It came out as "Wih-doo."

I hung up and sat, thinking. I'd had a long day too, but instead of being drained, I felt energized.

From below, I heard noises: a door opening and shutting and the sound of running water in the kitchen. I went downstairs to investigate, treading softly past LilyRose's closed door. Expecting to find my brother or Chantal, I was surprised to see Mom standing at the stove with her back to me. The teakettle spat and hissed on the front burner.

"What are you doing here?"

"Oh!" She spun around to face me, hand to her chest. "You startled me." In the quick about-face that was her trademark, she regained her composure. "Why wouldn't I be here? I live here." Mom pulled the kettle off the stove and poured the water into a waiting mug. "Tea?" she asked, not waiting for my answer as she reached into the cupboard and pulled down a second mug. I straightened the tablecloth, which was sliding off the table as if someone (Bud) had sat on it during dinner.

"I thought you were staying with Aunt Agnes." I swept the crumbs from my chair before taking a seat.

"She had plans tonight. I didn't want to be alone." Mom placed a Blooms by Bert mug in front of me.

"Thanks." I sat forward and breathed in. English Breakfast, her favorite. I preferred green tea, but it wasn't worth an argument. *Go along, get along, get out.* I dunked the teabag a few times. "How's—"

"Your father is better." She pulled up her chair and regarded me over the lip of her mug, already sipping, even though the water was still steaming.

I wasn't sure if I believed her. I started to reply to the contrary, but then I caught the look on Mom's face: the tightening around her eyes and mouth, the rigidity of her shoulders. *She's scared*, I realized. How could I have missed something so obvious, so apparent? She needed to say Dad was better. More than that, she needed me to believe it. Or at least pretend to. I thought of Chantal's comment about how I could help. Here was something else I could do. I could give Mom this moment of controlling a narrative that was, for once, out of her control.

"That's great, Mom." On impulse, I reached across the table and took her hand.

She looked surprised but squeezed my fingers in return. "The doctors are optimistic that he'll make a full recovery," she said. "He'll be back to work in no time, don't you worry."

And just like that, the moment dissipated. I couldn't believe this. Positive thinking, yes. I could support that. But I had to speak up for Dad before she had him working his way into another medical emergency. I spoke slowly, measuring my words. "That's the thing, Mom. I am worried. We all are. Dad's health needs to be the priority here. He needs time to rest and recover. Stop talking like he'll be back behind the counter by Memorial Day."

By the way her spine stiffened, I could tell this was indeed what Mom expected. She covered the moment with a regal throat-clearing. "Well, it won't be forever. It's only until you are up to speed. Agnes can do the weddings, Chantal can make window arrangements, and Bud can continue with deliveries."

"Mom." I clenched my fists. "Dad needs a full lifestyle change. Less stress, more rest. Aunt Agnes can't handle all the weddings. You might as well put her in the hospital room with Dad." I brought my hands up, spreading my fingers wide. "Listen to me. Let Bud take over the store. He wants to step up. He has ideas for expanding the business." I let my words hang, my hands still hovering mid-air. I was Eva Perón, on the balcony of Casa Rosada; I was Maria Von Trapp, climbing ev'ry mountain. *This is my moment,* I thought. *Please let her hear me.*

Mom shook her head, and my hopes came crashing down. Cue the kazoo wheeze. "That's ridiculous. Bud can't run the store alone."

I took a sip of tea and counted to five while wrangling my agitation under control.

"Yes, Mom, he can. He will. I'm going back to Kansas City. I'm starting an events business with my friend."

She waved her hand as if my words were flies at a picnic. "Nonsense. We're a *family* business. We need you here."

Were Mom and Dad so blinded by the idea of family traditions that Dad would continue working until he collapsed? I looked at her sipping her watery tea, her face stoic. Only her eyes gave anything away; they roved across the tablecloth, over the wall behind me, scanning the room. She was avoiding eye contact, so I couldn't read the truth. She wanted me home and insisting that I run the store with Bud was her way of getting me here.

But I have my own life to live, the voice in my head argued. I thought of five-year-old Daisy overhearing herself referred to as a cactus, high school Daisy wearing the store apron on Career Day, and eighteen-year-old Daisy with her acceptance letter to college. It took me years to untangle myself from this web of expectations, nonexistent boundaries, and not-so-subtle insinuations about my rightful place.

"Mom," I repeated, "I have a life in Kansas City. I have hopes and dreams and plans of my own."

Mom rose from the table, mug in hand. "Of course you do, sweetheart. And I want you to have hopes and dreams and plans. I just want you to have them here." She booped me on the nose. "Don't stay up too late."

She left the room, and I listened to the familiar creaks as she went upstairs. A moment later, bedsprings groaned above my head.

Joanna Monahan

I sipped my tea, thoughts swirling. I had five days to help my brother and convince our parents that I belonged in Kansas City, not here. Not to mention a sneaky coworker to watch, a high-maintenance client to please, an event to manage from afar, and a new business to start. I sighed. When had everything become so complicated?

Oh, that's right. The moment I answered the phone.

Chapter Eleven

Friday morning found me tiptoeing around the kitchen, relishing the peace of being the first one awake. As the percolating coffee filled the kitchen with a lovely smell, I scanned my missed texts. There was one from John saying he'd sent the paperwork, and another reminding me it was due by Sunday. From an unknown number: "Don't delete. It's Jeremy. Call when you get this." I smiled and saved the number in my contacts. I slid my phone into the waistband of my pajama pants and padded to the back door. I'd missed my hometown's sunrises.

I nearly tripped over LilyRose, fully dressed and seated on the steps, a pink Disney Princess suitcase between her legs. I remembered Bud telling me she was spending the night with Chantal's brother's family in Boulder. To my memory, they were picking her up mid-afternoon, not daybreak.

"Hello," I said, carefully maneuvering around my niece and her luggage and taking a seat on a lower step. I sipped my coffee, *mmm*-ing in pleasure. A man of few vices (other than work), Dad believed in buying only the best coffee. LilyRose eyed me, then leaped to her feet and raced inside, the screen door slapping behind her. I listened, amused, as I heard various doors opening and closing and the screech of chair legs across the linoleum.

LilyRose reappeared, a turquoise plastic mug grasped in her palms. She plunked down, reclaiming her seat, sending milk over the edge of her cup onto my shoulder. She blew across the top of her drink.

"*Mmm,*" she said, taking a sip.

"*Mmm,*" I agreed, tapping my cup to hers.

Raised voices broke our companionable silence as Bud burst through the door. He was dressed in his delivery uniform of khakis and a lime-green work shirt, with a black and red flannel thrown over top in deference to the crisp Colorado morning. Mom trailed behind in her housecoat.

"Ma." Bud ran a hand over his hair. "I don't need a lecture on how to set up the wedding. I've done this before, you know."

"Yes, but never on your own."

"Remember how you wanted me to tell you when you were being bossy?"

"Yes, but—"

"This. Here. Now. Bossy." Bud caught sight of LilyRose. "Oh, hey there, baby girl." He leaned down to kiss his daughter on the head before nodding to me.

LilyRose eyed him with suspicion. "Are you yelling at Grandma?"

I smiled into my coffee, admiring her ability to cut right to the heart of things.

"What? No, darlin'. Grandma and I were just talking. Loudly." Bud plopped down between us, sending more coffee spilling down my pajamas. "What are you doing awake so early? Uncle Byron isn't picking you up until noon."

"We're enjoying our morning coffee," I answered, winking at my niece. "At least we were until you two came charging through here like a herd of buffalo."

LilyRose nodded. "You were loud."

Mom pulled her robe around her and sniffed. "We weren't loud. We were talking."

"It sounded like you were bossing."

I choked on my coffee, spraying it across my lap. Bud looked proudly at his offspring.

"Well, if I was," Mom said, shooting a glare my way, "I was doing it with love."

"Good save, Ma," Bud said. "Nicely done."

"Hmph." Head held high, she swept into the kitchen, closing the door forcefully behind her.

Bud turned back to us. "Now, this is what I like to see," he said, throwing an arm around our shoulders and sending the last dregs of liquid sloshing to the concrete steps. "Two of my favorite people in one place."

"And what does that make me?" Chantal appeared on the top steps. In jeans and a denim work shirt, she looked cover-model ready. I pulled self-consciously at my faded Jayhawks hoodie, now sporting a Rorschach-worthy display of stains.

"Hey, I said 'two' of." Bud leaped to his feet and gave Chantal a loud, showy kiss while their daughter shrieked.

So much for my peaceful morning. Wherever the Greene family went, chaos followed. I gave up and headed inside to get ready for work.

Bud and Agnes assembled bouquets while I worked in the cluttered back office. Despite the closed door, a newly purchased air purifier, and an arsenal of medicine, the influx of fresh flowers set off my allergies the moment I walked in. My throat itched, my eyes were streaming and red, and the small humidifier beside my laptop did nothing to unstuff my nose. Every few minutes, I wiped moisture from my laptop screen with the sleeve of my shirt.

My phone *ping*ed. I glanced over to see a text from John. I reached for my phone, then hesitated. Much as I wanted to talk to him, I needed to focus. The faster I worked, the faster I could get home. I returned to my spreadsheet where I was inputting Dad's handwritten expense reports, pausing only to shake my hands and release the cramping in my fingers. I would respond later.

A burst of laughter from the workroom broke my concentration. My phone buzzed with another text from John. I ignored it. Moments later, my phone chirped, signaling a video call.

I gave up. "Hello?" I croaked through blocked sinuses. It came out as "Hedo?"

John's face appeared, bathed in blue neon light. "Finally! Why are you ignoring me?"

I pulled a tissue from the box on my desk and blew my nose lustily. "I didn't bean to. It's so loud I can't hear byself thing."

John laughed. "You sound great, babe." He imitated me: "Lige Barilyn Bonroe, all sultry and breathy."

I started to reply with a scathing remark that was lost as a sneeze exploded, and I dropped the phone.

"Dabbit." I crawled under the desk, years of dust and dormant pollen sticking to my knees and hands. I wiped my hands across my shirt and pulled myself back into my chair. "What's ub?" I said, rubbing at a rogue fern leaf plastered across my phone screen.

John panned his phone around the room. I caught glimpses of blue, yellow, and green strips of LED lights decorating the walls of the Event Artistry kitchen. "What do you think?" he said, swiveling the phone again. Tavia appeared briefly onscreen, dressed in jeans and a T-shirt, a strand of lights wound around her neck like a Hermès scarf.

"Hiyeee!" she called as the camera panned by. "Hope your dad is feeling better."

"Thangs." I ground my teeth.

John reappeared. "Since you didn't respond to my email, Tavia set up a small display of what we want to do with the lighting." Holding the phone, he walked closer so I could see the lights bouncing off the white stretched fabric canopies. Tavia maneuvered the lights, overlapping colors to create a cool underwater vibe (I thought the word before I could stop myself). I had to admit, it looked great.

"Incredible, right?" John asked, reading my expression. "I'll take your silence as a yes." He lowered his voice. "Don't worry. You get full control back next week. Meanwhile, check your email." He hung up.

I sighed, slumping in my chair, my hand over my eyes. My head pounded, not just from the allergies.

"Daisy?" A voice called from the hallway. Before I could answer, the door opened, and Jeremy appeared in joggers and a warm-up jacket, looking bemusedly at me. I straightened, smoothing my skirt down and my hair behind my ears before sneezing violently.

As if by magic, the box of tissues appeared under my nose.

"Thangs." I took one, swiveling away to wipe my nose and run a knuckle under each eye to catch any stray mascara.

"Parent reflexes," he said. "There wasn't anyone out front, so I let myself in. Hope that's okay."

"Dobody? Where'd they go?" I stood and strode past him. The workroom was empty. Agnes and Bud were gone, although the room was now magically filled with centerpieces: twenty vases filled with roses, sweet peas, ranunculus, and begonia leaves, cream-colored ribbons trailing down the sides of the vases. The showroom portion of the store was similarly vacant, even though the front door stood propped open with the wagon that Dad had once pulled Bud and me around in. Someone had dropped their fast-food bag in it. I pinched the bag between my thumb and forefinger, avoiding ketchup smears, and tossed it into the trash can by the desk. I pulled the wagon inside and shut the door, ensuring the hand-lettered sign on the doorknob read: "Open, Please Come In."

Jeremy prowled around the shop. Dust motes swirled as he

ran his hands over the fusty silk flowers, sparkling like sequins in the mid-morning sunshine.

I felt a flush of shame on behalf of the store's outdated interior and lack of customers. *It's only temporary,* I wanted to say. *We're fixing it.* To cover, I busied myself behind the sales counter, straightening the stacks of order forms and reorganizing the bouquet cards so the birthday and anniversary messages faced outward.

"Wow," he said, finishing his inspection and resting his arms on the counter as if ordering a drink. "This brings back memories, doesn't it?"

I gave a small snort, causing my nose to start running. I wiped at it with a napkin. "Sorry," I said, my cheeks warm. "You say beborries, I say allergies."

He laughed, his eyes crinkling. I suddenly remembered him at prom, looking so handsome in a midnight blue tux. "I texted you earlier but never heard back."

Belatedly, I remembered his "don't delete" message.

He continued, "Are you free for lunch? You look like you could use some fresh air."

I had a million things to do: pick up the new banner, print price sheets, pack the car, go through the filing cabinet, and come up with the perfect argument for getting our parents to give the shop to Bud. Oh, and get back to Kansas City before that conniving Tavia swiped my job.

Still... all of that could wait. What I needed right now was a friendly face.

"Let be get by purse." I turned the door sign to "Closed, Please Visit Us Again" and locked the door.

Jeremy's eyes drifted downward. "Um... Did you know you have two yellow handprints..." He made chest-level circling motions with his index fingers.

I looked down. Sure enough, two pollen-y handprints waved back from where I'd wiped them across my black shirt.

Fabulous.

After 48 hours of immersive family time, lunch was a relief. It was a pleasure to talk to someone who didn't take my life choices as personal insults.

We sat on the patio, one of only three other sets of diners. Guitar music drifted out over the speakers.

"I used to visit during Christmas and birthdays. But I got tired of justifying why I wasn't coming home more or moving back. And apologizing for having a demanding job. And then, of course, the shutdown." I sipped my iced tea, reveling in being able to smell and breathe again. Once away from the shop, my allergies vanished with miraculous speed. "I find family togetherness easier from a distance."

Jeremy looked skeptical. "Don't you miss them?"

"I do, and I don't." I struggled to find the words. "It seemed easier not to come back at all than to spend a whole visit defending my choices." The truth was it had been exhausting. Every moment I was home seemed to remind my parents that most of the time, I wasn't there. I believed we were all relieved when I stopped coming, and they could guilt me from afar. It was neater.

"How about you?" I asked, pivoting the conversation away from my family dynamics. "Have you ever considered leaving again?"

He shook his head. "No. I'm established here." He'd told me over appetizers about his cycling fitness business (which explained why he was in such great shape). "And certainly not as long as Ethan is here."

"I'm sorry," I said, chastened. "I didn't mean to insinuate you would leave your son." I kept forgetting that Jeremy was no longer Prom Date Jeremy but Parent Jeremy.

"I know you didn't." He peeled the label from his beer bottle as he talked. "Besides, I like Denver. My family's here. My career is here. I've got mountains, music, and friends." He grinned, tipping the denuded bottle toward me. "I've got great beer. Why would I go anywhere else?"

I clinked my glass to his, returning his smile. "But weren't you curious about what you could do or who you could be if you went somewhere new?" I pressed.

"I don't have to go anywhere to try something new. I'm happy where I am and with who I am."

I envied his confidence, his assurance of who he was and where he belonged. I could feel my age-old fears creeping in. *Something's wrong with you,* they said. *You're not like everyone else.*

"I'm jealous," I admitted. "I couldn't wait to leave so I could finally figure out what I wanted. I never felt like I could live my real life here." *Alone, but not lonely.*

"Real life, huh? Family can do that to you. Especially yours." Jeremy smiled, letting me know that he understood before changing topics. "Did Bud tell you my dad is dating again? Genny Meyers. Ava's mom."

"No way." Ava had been a classmate of mine. Bud had had a wicked crush on her throughout our adolescence.

"Really." Jeremy drained the rest of his beer. "I think he's going to pop the question soon. I saw him looking at engagement rings on his phone." He ducked his head. "It's hard to admit, but he's doing better on the dating front than I am." He looked up at the word "dating," making deliberate eye contact with me.

The hairs on the back of my neck stood up. Casually, carefully, I set down my glass. "I'm sure you're doing fine."

"It's hard, you know, trying to date as a single parent." He caught our waitress's eye and mouthed, "Check?" He turned back to me. "It's either she doesn't want kids, or she already has kids, or she wants more kids, and no matter which one it is, our schedules never line up. Lately, I can't seem to work up the energy for any of it."

Jeremy smiled at our server as she dropped off the check, simultaneously waving my hand away when I reached for it.

"I've got this. You're the guest in town." He scooted out of his side of the booth, standing and offering a hand to me.

I noticed our waitress watching Jeremy as he paid his bill, only looking away when I caught her staring. If he was having trouble dating, it wasn't due to a lack of options. But I couldn't help being just the tiniest bit happy about it.

Returning to work, I found the front door propped open again, the wagon now filled with the leftover stems from the morning's wedding arrangements. Inside, Chantal and Agnes were behind the counter, looking at images on a laptop and laughing.

"Dude!" Bud appeared from the workroom I was pushed aside as my brother bro-hugged Jeremy, slapping him on the back.

"Hey." Jeremy sidestepped Bud's further affections. "Hi, Chantal. Hello, Agnes."

Agnes tittered like a schoolgirl. "Well, aren't you a sight for sore eyes, honey? We haven't seen you in forever." She batted her lashes behind her thick glasses.

I moved to the counter. "What are you looking at?" I asked Chantal.

She turned the computer screen to face me. "I'm posting some new pictures to social media."

I burst out laughing. The first photo featured Agnes dressed in an audacious makeshift headdress of white tulle and purple ribbon, looking demurely over a bouquet featuring the lilies and roses that now graced our front display.

The next photo showed Agnes clutching two bouquets at chest height, dropping a cheesy wink. "What a pair," read the caption.

A video, titled "Pressed Flowers," featured Bud lying on the sidewalk in front of the store bench-pressing all 90 pounds of Agnes, who held a bouquet to her chest. Both Bud and Agnes were laughing.

"These are fantastic, Chantal. I love them." A loud throat-clearing sounded. "And Aunt Agnes. You look amazing."

Bud and Jeremy joined us at the counter. "I was just telling Jer Bear that we need to go out tonight. I saw in Westword that Neal/Neale is headlining a gig at Herman's. Whaddaya think? You in?"

Jeremy looked at me, eyebrow cocked quizzically, even... hopefully?

I hesitated. Lunch was one thing. A night out was another. I remembered Jeremy's story: "I came for a visit and never left."

Chantal came to my rescue. "No, Bud." she said, making a "zip it" gesture. "Sorry, Jeremy," she amended, "but I am not sharing my child-free evening with a crowd of sweaty drunks." She pinned Bud with a look. "And neither are you."

"Right you are, my precious, my pearl. Jeremy, old bean"—Bud adopted an over-the-top British accent—"we'll have to postpone our festivities. The missus and I will be at home this evening." He bowed low and kissed Chantal's hand while she shook her head, smiling indulgently.

Jeremy turned to me. "What do you think? Do you want to hang out tonight?" Despite his casual tone, his ears turned pink.

I thought of John, missing him. Having a friend in my corner would be nice. But I had a job to do. "I'm sorry, but it's a 'no' for me too. I need to finish getting ready for tomorrow."

"Want some help? We could order in."

"Thanks, but no. I'm better on my own." *Alone, but not lonely.*

"Got it." He squeezed my shoulder. "It was good seeing you today. I hope we can do it again before you go back to your real life."

"Thanks for lunch. It was fun." Feeling awkward, I gave a little wave as Jeremy exited the store. He didn't look back. For a moment, I considered running after him, telling him I'd changed my mind, that I'd enjoy his company. It would be the truth.

No, I would stick to the plan. Help Bud, help myself. No need to get any more involved than that.

Chapter Twelve

Bud left for his afternoon delivery run while Chantal finished up the centerpiece for my exhibit.

"It's gorgeous," I said, admiring the floral urn. In addition to flowers, she'd added an assortment of plums, cherries, and blackberries on skewers and stub wires, the dark colors striking against the all-white blossoms. "I can't thank you enough." I hesitated, then hurried on. "Would you like to go get a cup of coffee? I feel like we've hardly gotten to know each other."

She shook her head. "Thank you for the offer, but I really need to get home and get in some studio time while the house is quiet." Though a rejection, her tone was softer than it had been. Maybe we were making progress.

"Still working on your big project?" I asked.

She nodded but didn't elaborate. "I'll put your centerpiece in the workroom cooler. You can pick it up in the morning." She waved goodbye to me and then Agnes, who was helping me sift through photos to update the store's lookbook.

"Bye, honey," Agnes called as Chantal breezed from the room. She held up a photo. "Should I include the pictures from your high school graduation?"

I peered over her shoulder. There I was, in all my high school glory, bubble-skirted and gladiator-sandaled, flanked by Mom on one side and Dad and Bud on the other. Behind us, looking like a creature rising out of the earth to flatten a city, was an enormous centerpiece of gypsum and fronds. Dad had been employing an overeager horticultural student at the time, and she'd had an unfortunate fascination with topiary. "God, no." I tried to toss the picture into the trash, but Agnes, displaying surprising agility, blocked my shot and reclaimed it, smoothing it back into place.

"How about your parents' wedding?" she asked, pointing to another photo. "Those are some of your father's signature arrangements."

I looked. Mom and Dad stood cheek to cheek, arms wrapped around each other, beaming at the camera and looking impossibly young. With shock, I realized I was now the same age as they were in that picture. While the picture in our hallway was from the same series, it was obvious that this one had been taken later in the evening, well after the festivities began. Mom's veil was crooked, and Dad's bow tie hung loose around his neck.

"They look so happy," I murmured, touching the edge of the picture. *Did you know?* I asked the smiling couple. *Did you know you would have two kids, run a business for thirty years, and wind up in the hospital, overworked and overstressed? If you'd known, would you still have done it?*

"What do you think?" Agnes pressed, pointing to the background.

I looked past the grinning couple to where she pointed. Behind my parents' heads was a green metal arch with ivy and flowers woven through, two silver bells hanging in the center. To the sides of the arch stood faux marble columns, the same ones currently displayed in the window, holding silver urns of neon orange, yellow, and fuchsia-tipped carnations. The joyful mix of colors, textures, and ribbons made me smile.

"Yes. That's a keeper."

Agnes reached across the workspace for a glue stick, and as

she did, her elbow collided with Chantal's sleeping laptop. The home screen sprang to life, revealing a cacophony of teal and maroon swirls with a slash of gold bisecting the image. I squinted, trying in vain to discern the rest of the image hidden behind the login pop-up. "Aunt Agnes, what is this?" I motioned to the screen.

She made a big production of adjusting her glasses, wiping them on the hem of her shirt, and peering intently. "That's one of Chantal's murals. She's been talking about the idea of painting the sides and back of the building. Making it a place for people to take... what are they called... lonelies?"

I laughed. "Selfies," I corrected. I pulled a sticky note from the pad by the wall phone in the workroom and jotted down "selfie station."

"That's a terrific idea for increasing foot traffic," I agreed. "Lots of cities have official walking tours of the most photo-friendly spots in town." I stuck the note in my pocket as a reminder before asking Agnes the question that had been plaguing me since yesterday. "Speaking of lonely, where are all the customers?"

"Oh, you know, everybody orders online now or picks up one of those premade bouquets at the big chain stores." She shuddered. "We haven't been getting the foot traffic since we reopened. Our original client base is getting older. We do more funerals than weddings, and it doesn't take an MBA to know that that ain't a good sign."

I pulled up a stool. Agnes was an untapped source of information. "Would you ever want to leave the shop?"

"Me? Oh, honey, no. I'm happy here. Your granddad gave me a job when only a few people would hire a young, single woman with no employment history. And of course, I love your folks, you, Bud, and Chantal, and little bitty LilyRose." She lowered her voice and motioned me closer. "But your Mama and Daddy, honey, they need to slow down. Let the younger generation do more. It's different for me. I like the quiet days; I show up, I work, I go home. Bert is here all the time, worrying about money or fussing about an order, stressing when he has to let someone go. And Ruth worries about everybody: you, Bud, Chantal, baby girl, your dad, herself. She worries for six."

"How come they didn't let you go? I mean, when they had to lay people off?"

Agnes hooted, slapping her knee. "Oh, honey, I don't work here for money. I come here for something to do."

I sat back, thunderstruck. "They don't pay you?"

"Well, no. They don't have the money to pay me."

"But how do you pay your bills?"

Agnes shook her head. "Don't you worry about it. I'm all taken care of."

As if on cue, the sleigh bells on the front door jingled, and moments later, an elderly gentleman in a three-piece suit entered the workroom. "Hello? Agnes, darling?" Behind him trailed a Corgi, who stopped to investigate a potted fern before raising a leg.

"Oh no!" I cried, rushing forward to save the plant. "Bad doggie! No!" The Corgi lowered its leg and gave me a thoroughly disdainful look.

Agnes and the dapper man laughed. "Clementine, you naughty girl," the man said in a clipped British accent. "You promised you would stop that." He shook a reproving finger at Clementine, who did not look in the least bit sorry. He turned to me and, to my astonishment, bowed and extended his hand. "Cecil Dooley at your service, Ms. Greene."

Seeing no other option, I took the proffered hand. He grasped my fingers and, before I could snatch my hand away, dropped a whisper of a kiss over my knuckles.

Agnes moved to my side and took my arm, steering us into the showroom. "Cecil and Clemmy came to take me out for a late lunch," she whispered as though we were schoolyard confidantes. "It's our Friday ritual. You don't mind, do you?" She looked up at me.

"I, uh, of course not," I said, still trying to recover my composure. "Take the afternoon off. It's not busy, and Bud will be back soon anyway." Now that I knew that Agnes wasn't being paid, it felt wrong to ask her to stay.

She beamed. "You're a peach. I'll be back in the morning to open." She hurried behind the counter to retrieve her ancient tapestry purse.

From the doorway, Cecil gave another bow. "So pleased to have met you at last, Ms. Greene." He held the door for Agnes, who blew a jaunty kiss at me over her shoulder, and then followed her out, Clementine jogging behind him. As the door closed, Clementine turned and bared her teeth. I could swear she was laughing at me.

I worked until seven, printing pricing sheets, checking the banner, and revising my talking points. Meanwhile, my nose was stuffy, and I'd maxed out the medication I could safely take. I finished packing my table decor, leaving all the boxes at the back door. Bud promised to move them to his car in the morning when he came to load the delivery van, and Mom would drop me off on her way to visit Dad.

"Visit Dad…" I murmured, feeling a twinge of guilt. I'd been so wrapped up in the store's drama that I hadn't seen Dad since yesterday morning.

I checked my watch. Visiting hours went until eight. I made up my mind and ordered a ride.

"Well, this is a nice surprise. Hello, Petal."

"Hey, Dad. You're looking much better today."

He was, in fact, looking better. He was sitting up taller in bed, and the color had returned to his cheeks. Of course, that could be a result of his recovery or the fact that Mom wasn't here.

As if reading my mind, Dad chuckled. "You just missed your mother."

"I wouldn't say I missed her," I said, wheeling the doctor's stool over to his bedside and perching on it.

"Now, now," he said, gentle rebuke in his voice. "Your mother is only trying to do what she thinks is best."

I sighed. "Is she? Or is she trying to do what she thinks is best for her? Because from where I sit, Dad,"—I motioned to the monitor beeping above me—"this doesn't look like what's best for you."

Dad set his pen and crossword aside and fixed me with a hard stare. I shifted in my seat, uncomfortable. "Your mother loves you very much," he said, raising a finger to cut off any response I wanted to make. "She and I worked hard to create a legacy for our children."

A memory floated by from that ill-fated Christmas: *Stop calling it a gift. It's not a foot spa.*

"I know, Dad. And Bud and I appreciate everything you did for us. But"—now I was the one with my finger raised to stave off objections—"don't you see that what you want and what we want are different? My talents aren't in floristry." I pointed to my red-rimmed eyes. "I can't be in the store for more than a few minutes before I start to sneeze." I snuffled for effect. "Bud has spent his whole life trying to prove that he's the one—the only one—interested in running the store on his own. Not even on his own," I corrected myself. "Because he has Chantal. And Aunt Agnes. And they have great ideas to take the store in new directions." I thought of the three of them laughing over their photo shoot. Chantal's murals. Bud's ideas for classes. "Stop fighting for what you thought you wanted and accept what you have. One child who wants to follow in your footsteps, and one who wants to blaze her own trail." I swallowed the lump forming in my throat.

For a long moment, there was silence. Then Dad raised his hand and patted mine, the plastic of his finger heart rate monitor clicking against the bed rail. "You are so like your mother," he said fondly.

"Don't say that," I said, stiffening.

"It's a compliment, Petal. You and your mother are very much alike. You are passionate, dare I say adamant, about the things you believe in." He chuckled. "Do you remember the time you helped your mother deliver wedding flowers and broke out in hives?"

I rolled my eyes. "Because Mom didn't believe me when I said my arms itched." I could still feel the hives forming under my thin cotton shirt as I carried arrangement after arrangement to the reception hall.

"She felt terrible about that," Dad said, patting my hand again before reclining against the pillows. "That's when she insisted we start carrying silk flowers in the store. So you would have something you could care for."

This was new information. "That's why we have silk flowers? For me?" I asked, incredulous. "I had no idea."

Dad nodded, his eyes dropping closed. "She did it for you," he said, his voice dreamy. "So that you wouldn't feel left out."

I sat, stunned, as my father drifted off to sleep, his rattling snores as familiar to me as the sound of Fiona's voice over the intercom. I stood, straightened his bedclothes, and moved his pen and crossword to the side table within arm's reach. I refilled his water bottle and turned down the lights.

"Good night," I said, kissing his forehead. "Sleep tight."

Chapter Thirteen

Daisy, Age 13

"Mom, my arms itch."

"No, they don't."

"They do." I pulled up my sleeve and thrust my arm under her nose.

"Well, I don't have any aloe in the car," she said, batting my arm away while never taking her eyes off the road. "Just think about something else."

"Dad always has aloe," I muttered. I scratched and stared out the passenger side window miserably. There was probably only half an inch of snow on the roads, but the wintry winds caused it to move in pulsing waves across the highway. The yellow divider lines peeked out here and there, winking at me and my predicament.

"What'd you say?" Mom changed lanes suddenly and a horn blew behind us.

"Nothing." I yanked the sleeves of my cotton work shirt over my hands, balling up the cuffs in my fists to keep my fingernails from raking the bumps along my skin. Under the thin material, my arms continued to tingle and burn.

"At last." Mom veered the delivery van into the hotel lot and parked under the entrance awning. Disappearing through the automatic lobby doors, she reappeared moments later with a luggage cart. Together, we began unloading the boxes of hurricane glasses and votives, which would sit in the middle of our centerpiece rings. "You'll have to carry the rest," she called. "I told Bud to pack them in those leftover wreath boxes, but you know your brother..."

She didn't need to finish the sentence. Rolling my eyes, I threaded four centerpieces on my left arm and three on my right. My sleeves slid up, the points of the eucalyptus leaves exacerbating my already sensitive forearms.

"Mom, my arms."

"Daisy..." She sighed. She slammed the van's back door and pushed the luggage trolley up the walkway. "It's all in your head. No one is allergic to their life's calling."

There was nothing left to do but follow her. I didn't worry about locking the van. Mom left the keys in the ignition half the time. The van was so old and disreputable that no thief would waste their time stealing it.

Later, when we arrived home, Dad took one look at the angry red rash covering my arms and whisked me off to the bathroom, breaking off a leaf from the aloe plant in the hallway. He dabbed ointment on my arms and placed mismatched oven mitts on my hands to keep me from scratching.

"There you go, Petal," he said, kissing my forehead. "All better."

"Daisy's allergic to weddings!" Bud cackled as I returned to the family room. I batted at him with quilted hands while Mom hollered wearily for us to knock it off, but the proclamation stuck. Just like "Cactus Butt," my wedding allergy passed into family lore.

"What do you mean I don't have a booth?"

I stood at the exhibitor registration table, staring blankly at the woman telling me things I didn't want to hear.

"I'm sorry," she said, giving me a cursory glance before returning her attention to her computer screen. The glow reflected in her glasses, making her look robotic. "I don't have a booth for Blooms by Bert."

"How about Bloomin' Bert?" I asked, grasping for logical solutions. "Or Daisy Greene?"

She shook her head again. I gripped the handle of my hand truck, trying to hide my frustration. I'd filled out the vendor application. I was sure of it. Or had I? I tried to remember that first day in the shop. Aunt Agnes, Mom's call, my allergies, then Chantal and LilyRose stopped by... wait a minute. LilyRose's painting. I'd been working on marketing copy when she came in. I'd shut down my laptop and...*oh no.*

"Okayyyyyy," I said, plastering what I hoped was a winning smile on my face to cover the mortifying realization that this situation was my fault. "Is there an open space available for purchase?"

She went back to tapping her screen. "There is, but you'll be paying the day-of rate."

"How much—never mind." I handed over my credit card, averting my eyes from the total. Next to me, an attractive man in a well-cut suit was rifling through his exhibitor paperwork. Our eyes met, and he gave me a small, sympathetic smile.

"Booth 1119," my nemesis broke in, returning my card and pointing down a long, dark corridor. She ripped my exhibitor's badge off the printer beside her and tucked it into a plastic sleeve. "Have a good show."

I took my name badge and wheeled off in the direction she'd pointed. *Oh well,* I thought. *Things can't get any worse.*

They could.

I stared around the conference room in dismay. A few

vendors were setting up, but the room was largely empty. The space, an offshoot from the main exhibit hall, was clearly the overspill space, held in reserve for cases such as mine.

That's okay, I told myself as I located my booth number taped to a bare 8×10 table. *You've seen worse. Lemonade from lemons.* I'd just have to make sure my booth looked extra spectacular. I had Chantal's centerpiece, and I'd rush-ordered a new store banner that would cover quite a bit of the hideous blue and silver draping that made up the walls of my space. It wouldn't be the best display I'd ever done, but it was the best I could do with limited time and resources. It would be enough to draw people in and get them interested in seeing more. That's when I would offer a free in-store consultation. I was confident I'd leave today with at least half a dozen appointments in the books. And if half of those booked weddings with us, the deposits should see us through the next few weeks, giving Bud and Chantal enough time to implement some of their other changes.

Once Mom and Dad agreed to let them take over the store, of course. After all, how could they argue with the results of a successful event?

Feeling brighter, I unpacked the first box, spreading the lime-green tablecloth I'd washed and pressed last night over the table. I opened the second box to find the mirror, lights, and hurricane vase that would make up the centerpiece base. The store's business cards and the new price guides came next.

A deep voice rumbled over the loudspeaker directly above me. "Attention, exhibitors. There is half an hour until the exhibit hall opens. Please make sure the aisles are clear."

Half an hour would give me enough time to walk around and scope out the rest of the show. I could pass out cards and make a few strategic inquiries about partnerships with other vendors. Last night, I'd perused the exhibitor list, looking for any names that Bud had mentioned working with regularly. Painfully few were listed. It would be cold calls all the way.

I knelt and opened the final, largest box, the one holding Chantal's centerpiece.

"What…" A sea of green rubber stress balls stared up at me. My mind raced, trying to comprehend what I was looking at. "No, no, no…" I stuck my arms into the box, frantically fishing, as if Chantal's creation might be hidden underneath a layer of foam promotional items reading, "Don't stress! Call Bloomin' Bert."

"Nooo!" I cried, dumping the box upside down in frustration. Green spheres rained out, followed by Dad's cowboy hat.

"Need some help?"

I looked up. The man from registration stood to the side of my booth. He held the knuckles of one hand against his mouth as if trying to hold back a grin. His brown eyes, however, sparkled in amusement.

Surprised, I lost my balance and fell backward against the table onto my butt, splay-legged, sending stress balls further afield. One rolled over to the man's feet, and he bent over to retrieve it. Openly laughing now, he offered his free hand to me.

"Thank you." I took it and stood, smoothing my hair and attempting to regain composure. "I'm Daisy. I think I saw you at registration."

"Victor," he said, handing me the ball. "I'm sorry, I don't usually eavesdrop, but I overheard your conversation and thought you might need some help." His eyes traveled over the scene surrounding me.

I glanced around. My booth looked like it'd been hit by a hailstorm. Stress balls were everywhere. The tablecloth was askew from where I'd fallen, sending all my neatly stacked business cards and price sheets to the floor. My brand-new banner lay half unfurled in the corner as if attempting to slither away to some other more impressive exhibit.

I turned back to Victor. "Oh no, this is exactly the aesthetic I was going for."

He frowned, confused.

"I'm kidding. Totally kidding." I held my hands up in surrender. "This is a catastrophe. I would love some help. Thank you."

I snuck glances at Victor as we worked in tandem, returning the errant giveaways to the box. I guessed him to be around my age. His dark hair, worn slightly too shaggy to be considered fashionable, fell into his eyes each time he leaned over, and each time he pushed it back. I wondered if he was even aware of the gesture. The pale salmon of his suit jacket cast a glow against his skin that was out of sync with the fluorescent lighting of the Conference Room that Time Forgot.

"Blooms by Bert," Victor said, returning with the last remaining stress balls. "Your store is over on Federal, right?"

I nodded. "That's us. Well, them. My parents. And my brother. And his girlfriend. My family owns the shop."

"That's nice. I work for my family too." He produced a card from his shirt pocket. "Blissfully Wed, that's me."

I took the card and ran my finger over the raised gold lettering. "You're a wedding planner?"

He laughed. "I am. I inherited the business from my mom, who inherited it from hers."

"Lucky you," I said, giving him a sympathetic grin, letting him know I understood how it was to get roped in by family.

He gave me a strange look. "I like to think so."

Whoops, seems like I miscalculated. Sometimes it was hard to remember that not everyone had the same reaction to working with family. To cover the moment, I gestured to the booth. "I'm actually a corporate events planner. I'm in town helping out for a few days. There was a mix-up," I hurried on, not wanting him to think today represented my best work. "My brother must have taken my centerpiece by mistake."

Victor surveyed my pathetic array of materials. "Well, it's certainly not the most conventional display I've ever seen." He paused. "Do you have anything else in those boxes?"

"Just my dad's cowboy hat. And I don't think I can pull that look off." I dropped a few of the stress balls experimentally into the empty hurricane glass. "Do you think we can make something out of this?"

"You know," he said, giving me a sideways glance, "I think we can."

Working quickly, Victor set the mirror and the hurricane vase on the table. He filled it with stress balls, ensuring the store name and logo faced outward on each one, then strung fairy lights around the table. I bartered with a nearby stationer for some blank card stock and a Sharpie in exchange for a market bouquet. I wrote up a sign: *"Wedding Flowers Got You Stressed? Call Blooms by Bert!"* I rearranged the store cards and a blank piece of paper for email addresses and made a second sign that read: *"Join our mailing list for a chance to win a bridal bouquet!"* I pulled up my laptop and opened the company website, chuckling at the new home page image: a closeup of Agnes holding one of Chantal's bouquets and smiling coquettishly into the camera.

Just as we finished attaching the new banner to the back wall with zip ties, the overhead speakers crackled to life again. "Exhibitors, the floor will be opening in five minutes. Five minutes, exhibitors."

Startled, Victor checked his watch and motioned toward the main exhibit hall. "I'm sorry, I didn't realize it was so late. I need to get back to my space. My assistant will be wondering where I've been."

I tried not to let my disappointment show. I had a sad booth space, a makeshift centerpiece, and a big ugly hat. And yet the last twenty minutes working with Victor had been fun, like problem solving with John.

"Of course. Thank you so much for helping me. I never would have gotten it done without you."

"It was nice meeting you, Daisy," he called, walking backward. "I'm in booth 927 if you can stop by." Victor turned and hurried away, sweeping his hair back as he left.

As if it had been waiting for the right moment to interrupt, my phone began to buzz too. *Absolutely Do Not Answer* flashed at me. I cast a final look toward the doorway before answering. I had a few choice words for my brother. "Bud?"

"Hello?" He sounded like he was in a cave. "Daze… are… there?"

"Hold on!" I shouted over the echo. "It's a bad connection."

Figuring I had a little time until the brides found their way to the Land of Misfit Exhibits, I hurried down the hall to the closest exit, which turned out to be the loading dock. Around me, delivery trucks idled and people shouted orders. I plugged my free ear with my finger. "Do you have my centerpiece?" I hissed.

"What?" He sounded confused. "What centerpiece?"

The nerve! I could hear Mom's voice: *You know your brother…* I briefly visualized wringing Bud's neck. "You know, the one Chantal made me? The one for the expo? The one that was supposed to be the big display piece in my booth?"

Silence. Then: "The one Chantal put in the merchandiser to keep the flowers from opening too quickly?"

My mouth opened and closed, my next snarky comment dying on my lips. A boy in his late teens dressed in a hotel server's uniform of black pants and a white shirt rushed by carrying a box of dishes. "Excuse me, ma'am," he said as he passed. He reminded me of Martin carrying one of his endless boxes at Event Artistry.

Bud was right. Chantal had told me where she'd put the flowers, and I'd forgotten. This was my screw-up. Again.

Around me, workers unloaded boxes and stacked them by double doors. A pallet forklift beeped as it backed up. I moved, not wanting to add "run over by machinery" to this day's ever-growing list of stupid mistakes.

"Sis? You still there?" Bud sounded concerned but also like he might be laughing.

"Yeah, I'm here. I'm just… You're right." My heart softened toward my little brother, who maybe didn't deserve the bad rap we all gave him. "She did tell me. This is my fault. I'm sorry."

"S'all right, memory loss is probably a side effect of wedding allergies." He was definitely laughing. "Did you forget to take your meds this morning, Cactus Butt?"

Just like that, my heart was stone again. I changed topics, wanting something justifiable to be annoyed about. "And what's with all the stress balls?"

"People like free things. I thought you could give them out." I could practically hear his shrug. "Try juggling them. That always draws a crowd."

"You juggle—" I stopped myself. What was the point? Inside, I could see the first of the most adventurous brides making their way toward the overflow hall.

I was out of time. I might have a terrible booth, but I certainly couldn't have an unattended terrible booth.

"I have to go," I said, then paused. "Wait, you called me. What do you need? Did you forget something?" If things were going this badly for me, I could only imagine what scrape he'd gotten himself into. Honestly...

"Nah." His voice went quiet, the laughter gone. "Everything's good here. I just called to wish you good luck. I really appreciate everything you're doing to help out. Love you."

Five merciful hours later, it was over. I'd gathered several dozen emails and given away all the hideous stress balls. I'd even donned the hat as a conversation starter. Most of my traffic had been sympathetic brides who'd had the bad luck to catch my eye. I vowed I would make it up to them. I'd already mentally composed my follow-up mailing: *Thank you for visiting Blooms by Bert! Show this email for 20% off your next in-store purchase. I assure you, we have flowers!*

I was packing up the last of my boxes (the only upside of an empty booth, it took no time to dismantle) when Victor returned, carrying two bottles of water. I whipped the cowboy hat off my head and threw it into a box.

Welcome to Blooms

Victor handed me one of the waters and leaned back against the table, groaning. "My feet are killing me. That was exhausting."

I uncapped the water and took a long drink, nodding in a way I hoped made it seem like I'd been similarly busy. "Thanks for this," I said, saluting him with the bottle. "Did you have a good show? Did you have the couple who wanted a Game of Thrones wedding?" I felt a little guilty poking fun. The couple had been one of my earliest visitors, drawn in, I suspected, by the desperation in my voice when I asked if they had chosen a florist for their big day. "They wanted to know if I could create a topiary dragon that breathed actual fire." I didn't mention handing them a business card and promising I'd see what I could do.

Victor groaned. "No, but I had the Harry Potter bride who asked if I could arrange for her to fly in on a broomstick. And if I knew of any Quidditch fields for the reception."

I grinned. "What'd you say?"

"I told her I would try but that I was most familiar with Muggle weddings." We shared a laugh, and I felt the pleasant buzz of camaraderie. Today might have been a bust workwise, but meeting Victor certainly made it better.

"Well." He stood and stretched again. "I'd better finish packing up."

"Wait," I said, hoping I didn't sound too eager. "Do you need some help? I'm done." I gestured to my paltry few boxes. "And maybe afterward I could buy you dinner? You know, to say thanks for helping me?"

I knew I'd made a mistake as soon as the words left my mouth. Victor's eyes grew soft, and his smile slipped. "Oh, that's really nice of you, but—"

The phone in his hand buzzed, and he glanced down at the screen. "I can't," he finished. "My fiancée is waiting for me." He stepped forward and offered his hand. "It was nice meeting you. Take care, Daisy."

Joanna Monahan

I shook his hand even as a flush of embarrassment curled its way up my neck and across my face. I wanted to explain that he'd misunderstood my intentions, but he had already turned his back to me, texting as he walked away. I crumpled the business card I'd hoped to hand him and dropped it on the table. Limping along on sore feet, I wheeled my boxes out of the booth and set off for the long walk to the parking lot.

Chapter Fourteen

"Hail the conquering hero!" My brother met me at the back door, holding a box of takeout. He slurped lo mein noodles off chopsticks as he held the door open for me. "We stopped and picked up dinner. I hope you still like chicken and broccoli."

"Thanks," I mumbled, angling past him, attempting to hide the bag of takeout I'd also picked up on the way home. Unlike Bud, I'd ordered only enough for myself. It hadn't occurred to me to call and ask if I could bring anyone else anything. Yet another mistake. This day could not end soon enough.

I slid into the closest seat, dropping my phone on the table and sliding my takeout under the chair. Bud flopped down across from me. Above us, the ancient plumbing wheezed with the sound of running water, which I translated as Chantal giving LilyRose a bath.

I nibbled at dinner while Bud gave an exhausted but elated account of how well the wedding setup had gone. "Chantal even booked a style shoot with the reception venue on Tuesday. I'm sure we'll get at least one new event out of this. The venue manager couldn't stop raving about the flowers. You should have seen the centerpieces. They looked just like the one you…" He trailed off. "Well, you know. The one you were going to…" He stopped again, then switched tactics, smiling brightly. "So, how'd your day go? How many contracts did you get?"

My phone buzzed, saving me from making a full confession. I reached for it, but Bud was faster.

"Hello, Ms. Greene's phone," he said in his posh British accent, which I now realized he'd cribbed from Cecil. "Why yes, Mr. Davis…"

I waved my hands and shook my head. "No, no, no," I mouthed.

"… Daisy is right here. Just a moment, please." Bud held out my phone. "It's for you."

Glaring, I snatched the phone from his hand and pressed *Mute* before retreating from the kitchen.

Once in the privacy of my room, I ran my free hand over my hair and down the front of my rumpled dress before unmuting the call. "Hello, Mr. Davis. It's a pleasure to hear from you."

"Daisy." His voice wormed its way out of the speaker. "How nice to speak with you. I was afraid you'd run off on me too."

"Of course not." I forced a laugh. "I'll be back in just a few days. Meanwhile, John and Tavia"—I felt my eye twitch—"are available to take care of everything you need."

I heard tapping and imagined him seated in his office at the art museum, drumming his fingers against the desktop. "Tavia is certainly motivated." Was that a note of amusement or annoyance? "But I hired Event Artistry because of how highly Fiona spoke of *you*. Imagine my dismay at your continued absence." He paused, and I listened as he took a long sip of something.

My heart sank. Was I about to lose my client over a few days' absence? I considered my options—begging? lying?—before landing on brazen optimism. "I respect your concern, Reg," I said, mentally gagging at the simpering tone of my voice. "And I appreciate your faith in me. You must know that I would never have left under regular circumstances." I weighed whether to play the family-crisis card again but decided against it. "Meanwhile, John has my complete trust and has kept me in the loop on all event proceedings."

"So you're happy with the direction the event is going?"

My senses tingled; something was up. I dodged the question with a half-truth. "If I were hosting an event like this, I would hire John."

A sip. A sigh. "I suppose I can manage a few more days without you," he relented. My shoulders relaxed. "But I'll expect to see you soon."

"I'll be back to work on Wednesday. And I'll call John to check in right now."

"Excellent." A pause, a sip. "Good night, Daisy."

"Have a great evening." I ended the call and looked around, expecting to see the bullet I'd narrowly dodged embedded in the wall behind me.

I rang John.

He picked up immediately. "Cheese and crackers, Daisy," he huffed, sounding out of breath. "You are hard to get a hold of."

I sank into the parrot chair, knees to my chest, massaging my sore insteps along the cushion's embroidered fabric. "What do you mean? I'm right here. I called you."

John muttered something under his breath, and I heard a door slam shut. He was definitely on the move.

"What's that?" I asked, keeping my voice light. "I couldn't hear you over that 5k you're running."

Words came in between blasts of static. "I'm... stairwell... hotel... banquet."

"John, I can't understand you."

"Climbing... hold... a minute." A metal *ca-chunk* sounded, which I recognized as the safety bar on a fire door, followed by the sounds of the city. "Okay, I'm outside now." John was out of breath, but at least I could hear him. "I'm at the awards banquet, and the service elevators aren't working. I've been running up and down stairs delivering boxes of plaques."

I sat up in surprise, the reason for my call momentarily

forgotten. The Garr Company's annual awards banquet had completely slipped my mind. I couldn't believe it. I felt homesick, as if I'd been gone a month instead of four days. I should be with my coworkers at the banquet, not spending the day standing alone in a sad booth hawking imaginary flowers like a deranged Eliza Doolittle.

"How's it going? Did the hotel serve that amazing baked brie again? Is the accounting department drunk and doing a cappella yet?" I yearned for details, a taste of home to wash away the day's bitter failures.

"Daisy." John clearly wasn't in the mood for chitchat. "I've been calling all day. First off, Tavia has gone rogue. Do you know she's auditioning bands? Live bands, Daisy. The first group she dragged me to did death metal covers of Shania Twain songs. Their big number was 'Man, I Feel Like a Subhuman.' I'll never regain full hearing in my left ear. And," John continued, "Maggie says you haven't sent in your financials. What's going on? You haven't responded to my texts, my calls, my emails. Are you having second thoughts?"

"What? No!" The expo, Tavia, the office space lease. Everything was going to pieces around me. "I swear I didn't get any messages…" I trailed off, swiping through my phone log. Seven missed calls and an accusatory little red five next to my voicemail icon. I checked my texts. There sat John's name in bold. I scrolled through his messages, which ran the gamut from "friendly reminder" to all-caps panic. "Oh. Oh, no. I'm sorry. I see them."

"Yeah." John exhaled. "Finally."

"I'm sorry. I really am. I've been… busy." Busy flubbing a marketing event that should have been a slam dunk. Busy sneezing my brains out in a cramped office. Busy doing everything I could to get out of here and get back to the life that clearly needed me.

"I know." John's voice softened. "And I wouldn't bother you, except it's not just your career we're talking about here, and we're in a time crunch. Can you please sign the papers?"

"Absolutely. I'll do it tonight." I reached for my laptop and powered it on. "Meanwhile, what can you do about Tavia? She's going to blow this whole event for us."

With the issue of the missing paperwork resolved, John sounded more like his usual confident self. "I'll work on reining her back in. Her work ethic is solid. I'm afraid I praised her creativity just a little too much after she fixed our lighting issues. It'll be easier to keep her in check when there are two of us again."

"I know, I know," I said, resisting the urge to say I'd told him so. I was in no position to comment. "I'll send her a message and remind her that she's helping you, not leading the whole project. Just hold off on any more of her great ideas. I'll be home soon."

"Can't wait. It's not the same without you." His voice echoed, and I could hear footsteps. He was on the move again. "Anyway, how's your dad?"

Crisis averted (or at least postponed), we chatted for a few minutes before Tavia's voice interrupted. "John! I've been looking all over for you. The accountants commandeered the mic and are singing showtunes. Fiona says it's your year to play bouncer."

"Duty calls," John said tersely and hung up.

Setting my phone on the floor, I opened my email and found John's message with the contracts attached. I began scanning the verbiage.

"Hi, Aunt Funny." LilyRose appeared in the doorway. She was dressed for bed in a long cotton nightgown featuring one of the fleets of doe-eyed cartoon characters that she liked and that I didn't recognize. She held a book in one hand.

I waited for Chantal or Bud to materialize behind her, but no one appeared. LilyRose bounced on the balls of her feet, obviously wanting to be invited in.

I closed my laptop and set it aside. *I'll be right back, John.* I smiled at my niece and patted the seat cushion.

In three long leaps, LilyRose bounded across the room and squeezed beside me on the chair. I shifted as her book jabbed me in the thigh.

"Guess what?" she asked, pulling her knees up to her chin and pulling her nightgown over her legs.

"What?"

"Daddy said you can read me my bedtime story tonight." LilyRose waved her book at me.

"Oh, did he?" I looked at the cover. "*Hansel and Gretel*? Are you sure this isn't too scary?" My limited knowledge of appropriate bedtime routines consisted of John and Zadie reading books to Sabrina about helpful anthropomorphic dogs or singing songs in French to make her bilingual.

LilyRose shook her head. "No! I like the witch." She lowered her voice, confiding, "When I grow up, I'm going to live in a house made of cookies."

"Sounds delicious." I nodded. "Okay, let's do this."

LilyRose clambered onto my lap and settled her head under my chin. I opened the book and began to read: "Once upon a time…"

LilyRose fell asleep before the witch's untimely demise in the baking oven. Thinking to move her to her room, I found I couldn't stand; her unconscious body seemed to have doubled in weight. My phone lay on the floor, just out of arm's reach. Effectively trapped, I stayed still and waited for help, listening to my niece's soft, whiffling snores. The weight of her, plus the just-out-of-the-bath scent of lavender and thyme, soothed me. The sour taste of professional failure began to fade as my body relaxed. My mind started churning out possible solutions to the expo debacle: *Send out the follow-up email offering a twenty—no, thirty—percent discount on any in-store purchase, contact the confer-*

ence manager about purchasing an attendee list, create an online DIY bouquet course for budget-conscious brides, scour the exhibitor list for potential partnerships, offer services for upcoming advertising shoots...

"Are you stuck?" In an almost exact reenactment of his daughter's entrance, Bud appeared in the doorway, obviously delighted at the scenario before him. He held up his phone and snapped a picture.

I gestured helplessly. "I didn't know what to do. I didn't want to wake her."

"Never fear! Dad to the rescue." Swooping into the room, my brother expertly transferred his sleeping daughter from my lap to his arms. She shifted, protesting, but did not wake.

The loss of warmth sent a chill through me, the hair on my arms rising as if a breeze swept through the room. I tried to stand, only to find that my legs had fallen asleep.

Bud offered his hand. I took it gratefully and pulled myself up. My legs and feet tingled as the blood rushed back in. "Thanks."

"No problem," he whispered. "I'll just put her to bed."

"I'll help you." I forced my leaden feet to follow him down the hall. In the soft glow of the nightlight, I pulled back the lace coverlet and tossed aside a decorative pillow shaped like a succulent.

"Thanks." Bud laid LilyRose down and gently covered her sleeping form with blankets. He pressed a kiss to her forehead. "Night, baby girl. Daddy and Mommy and Grandma and Aunt Daisy are just downstairs."

"Mmm." She rolled over and burrowed deeper until only the top of her head was visible.

I crept from the room after my brother, gently closing the door behind us.

In the kitchen, Mom and Chantal sat at the table, drinking tea and chatting companionably. My dinner had been cleared away, as had, I noticed with embarrassment, the takeout box I'd hidden under my chair.

Cutting the conversation short, Mom stood up briskly. "Well," she said, "I'm heading to bed." She moved around the room, kissing Chantal's cheek, then stepped to Bud's side and pulled his face down to her level to do the same. She hesitated as she came to me before swooping in for a swift, one-armed hug. "Good night." Cradling her mug, she swept from the room, leaving the three of us regarding one another.

I waited for the stairs to creak before breaking the silence. "Um, I don't know how to say this…" Looking at my feet, I recounted the day's events, from the nonexistent booth to the forgotten flowers to the inevitable conclusion of no new contracts.

It didn't take long, but it felt like forever. "I did get some emails for our newsletter," I concluded, trying to end on a positive note. "I think I can still turn this around. I'll send out an email thanking them for stopping by and include a coupon."

I summoned my courage and regained eye contact. Bud had a strained smile on his face. Chantal's expression was stoic, unreadable.

"So that's it…" I trailed off. No need to bring up the bridal bouquet I'd raffled off. Or the bouquet for the stationer. Or the exorbitant booth fee. I'd fund those out of my own account.

Chantal spoke first. "I'm sure you did the best you could." She gestured to a chair with an authority so Fiona-esque I was already sitting by the time her hand returned to her mug. "Bud and I were talking on the way back from the Springs. We appreciate your efforts." She paused and sipped her tea, allowing the moment to sink in. "But we know what we want to do and how we want to run the store. Where we really need your help is getting your parents to listen to Bud."

"They don't listen to me any more than they listen to him." I gestured toward the faint echoes of Mom's footsteps above. "That one thinks I'm moving home permanently. And Dad's literally working himself to death because he thinks Bud can't handle the store alone." I shook my head. "I know I screwed up today, but I probably have a better chance of booking a hundred new weddings than I do of getting our parents to listen to anything they don't want to hear."

Bud put his hand on Chantal's, locking fingers with her. "No offense, Sis, but speaking of not listening, you're not hearing what we've been saying all week. We need your help, but not like this. We know better than you do how to turn the business around."

I started to protest before realizing he was right. He—they—did know. I'd been acting just like Mom, bulldozing my agenda over them and not listening to what they were asking of me. I sighed, embarrassed by my behavior. Bud, for all his antics, was the one acting maturely.

"You're right. I'm sorry. I get it. And I agree." My mind flashed upon Dad's reaction that first day in the hospital and then to our most recent conversation. "You know what else? I think Dad is ready to retire. He said almost as much to me last night."

Bud nodded. "I think he is, too. He's never been good at standing up to Ma." He shrugged. "You're the only one who's ever managed to get through to her."

He looked at me, and I could see the lines around his eyes again. My brother was exhausted. He needed my help. It was time for me to put my ego aside and listen to what he really needed.

"Let's start with Dad," I said, pulling my phone from my pocket and tapping notes as we talked. "I'll go to the store in the morning and finish inputting expenses while you and Chantal outline what it would take, in labor and financial terms, to make the necessary changes."

Bud nodded. "Can you make a spreadsheet? That's how Dad likes to look at information."

A spreadsheet! Here was something I could do. Everyone at Event Artistry knew that spreadsheets were my love language. "Absolutely. We can get a binder together and draft some short-

and long-term projections." I stopped. "That takes care of Dad. But what are we going to do about Mom?"

Bud looked at Chantal, who nodded as if to say "*go on.*" He looked back at me. "Once we're done planning, your job is to distract Mom long enough for me to talk to Dad and convince him this is the best thing for the store. For all of us."

"You want me to distract Mom?" I blanched.

"After he's home. Take her to lunch. Maybe shopping. She mentioned the other day how she's always wanted to try goat yoga." Chantal's mouth twitched as she tried to suppress a smile. Beside her, Bud turned away, feigning interest in the pantry door.

I balled up a takeout napkin and threw it at his back. "You're not fooling anyone. I can see your shoulders shaking." Despite myself, I started to giggle. Bud gave up his charade and collapsed, head on his arms, his whole body shaking with laughter. Chantal patted his back, smiling fondly.

"Okay," I said when the laughter eventually wore down. "I'll do it." I pointed at Bud. "But work fast."

"You got it," he said.

Chantal stretched and yawned. "Now that that's all settled, I need to get to bed. It's been a long day. Good night, Greenes."

"Good night," I called to her retreating back.

"That's my cue," Bud said, standing and pushing in his chair before depositing Chantal's mug in the sink. He paused at the doorway. "Unless you want me to stay up with you?"

I deferred. "Go to bed. I'm not tired."

Instead of returning to my room, I stretched out on the couch in the family room with the remote in hand, searching for something mindless to quiet my racing brain. I surfed through the library of recordings, past princess cartoons and a flower arranging reality series, before settling on one of Mom's ubiquitous baking competitions. I pulled the wool blanket off the back of the couch to cover my legs and watched ten contestants frantically decorate wedding cakes. Wedding cakes reminded me again of the disastrous expo, which made me think of Victor. I cringed, remembering his face when I suggested dinner. "My fiancée," he'd said.

Oh well. It wasn't like I'd ever see him again. Just a few more days, and I was going home.

I drifted off to sleep as the bakers received the judges' verdict. The paperwork John mentioned flitted across my consciousness, then disappeared, replaced by warm brown eyes and a friendly smile.

Chapter Fifteen

Daisy, Age 32

Do you know that feeling you get when you realize that doing the right thing will be much more complicated than doing the easy thing?

I hate that feeling.

I spent years telling myself that by asserting my independence, I was pruning my family tree for its own good and that cutting back communications would inspire new growth. That our relationships would evolve, coming back stronger than before. But in just a few short days, I'd learned that all I'd done was take a living thing and deny it the nutrients it required to flourish. I'd abandoned my brother and hurt my parents with my absence. I thought my decision would free us to develop into who we were meant to be. But all I'd done was stunt our growth.

Without adequate food and water, a flower cannot bloom. In the same way, our relationships had wilted on the vine, deprived of tender care and loving attention.

It was time for the Greene siblings to blossom.

Bud, Chantal, and I arrived at the store first thing Sunday morning, armed with coffee and laptops. I popped two allergy pills, donned a mask, and tackled the piles of orders and invoices in Dad's office while Chantal and Bud sketched out their ideas.

Afterward we gathered in the back room. I played stenographer while Bud and Chantal discussed their ideas for updating the store. For the first time, I felt like myself in the conversation. I loved this phase of planning, when anything was possible. The only difficulty was remembering that it was my family's future we were discussing, not some high-profile company event with an unlimited budget.

The goal was to bring a complete transition plan to Dad. If he was, as we suspected, secretly ready to step back from the store, he would be the best (and, we agreed, the only) person able to break the news to Mom. However, the proposal had to be airtight, combining tradition and new ideas to uphold the "family" portion of the phrase "family business."

"We don't want to change the feel of the store," Bud said, toying with his coffee cup. "We want to bring all the great things up to date. We want Ma and Pop to see that there are more ways to build business than simply events and individual sales to the same customers. We want to cast a wider net, create a community, become a meeting place."

I nodded, typing furiously. In a way, Bud was describing exactly what John and I wanted for Ground Floor: to build a community, a brand of cooperative corporate culture. I pushed this interesting realization aside for further inspection at another time.

He went on: "There's too much competition for the old ways to keep working. We can't keep up with online florists, we don't have the staff to fulfill wire service requests, and grocery stores are getting the bulk of our impulse buyers."

Chantal added, "And the specialty flowers Bert orders don't sell in quantities that justify ordering them. I can use them in bouquets, but they're usually a couple of days old by then and only sell because we discount the entire arrangement. We need to stick to basics: focal flowers, structural foliage, and a few supporting accents." She lifted her head a fraction and shared a conspiratorial look with Bud. "You order simple, and I'll design fancy. We'll all do our part to train employees. You know, once we have some."

My cheeks grew warm, as they always did when I got excited about a new project. "So, we can't compete nationally, and we can't compete with specialty inventory." I nodded to myself, my fingers tapping at my keyboard. "Your niche is creative arrangements. That's what makes you a destination point."

"A hidden-gem local vendor," Bud corrected. "Ma and Pop have traded on tradition and nostalgia for too long. No more cheesy 'Bloomin' Bert' ads." Bud mimed shooting finger guns at me. "Shopping small and responsibly sourced are the buzzwords now. Grandpa and Pop were ahead of their time in that regard. We need a draw for customers to come in and see that we're what they're looking for."

I nodded. "That's where the classes come in, right?" I looked up at Chantal. "That's a lot on you."

She waved her hand, dismissing my concern. "We're starting small. One night a week. We're targeting bridal parties, book clubs, and retirees." She ticked off each group on her fingers, then tapped her temple. "I've got it all mapped out up here."

"That's great," I said, impressed. "I'd be happy to put together a handout template. Something you can give participants at the end of class to take home. A few simple instructions and some care tips, maybe with a coupon attached?" I caught movement from the corner of my eye—Bud swiping one hand across the other into lift-off.

"Did you just make the blast-off signal?" I demanded, affronted. "About *me*?"

Bud looked sheepish. "You are acting kind of Mom-like."

I sucked in a breath between clenched teeth. "You take that back."

"Can't." He grinned. "It's true."

"Now, now. She's trying to help, right?" Chantal nodded in my direction. "A handout template would be great."

A small thrill ran through me. Maybe, just maybe, I'd taken a step toward redeeming myself.

"Can you send me the high-res logo?" I asked my brother, gladly dropping the worrisome topic of my Mom-like behavior.

"Sure." Bud stood and retrieved his phone, wiping a stray flower petal from the screen.

My home screen lit up as his message was delivered simultaneously to my computer and phone, which lay face up on the table between us. "Absolutely Do Not Answer," Bud read from the notification screen. He looked up, hurt. "You have me listed in your phone as 'Absolutely Do Not Answer?'"

I lunged for the phone, catching it as Bud shoved it away like garbage. "Bud, I'm sorry. It's really…" I saw his crumpling face, the telltale furrow of his brow. I cast a "help me" glance to Chantal, who was staring at me stony-faced. Whatever ground I'd gained with her was quicksand disappearing under my feet.

I stood and crossed to Bud. He backed away, arms crossed. "Hey. I apologize. That was a jerk thing to do."

"So why do it?" He looked at me, and for a moment, I saw the child he'd been. The little brother who'd always had my back, no matter what.

"Self-protection," I admitted, ashamed. "I can say no to Mom and to Dad. But I can't…" I forced the words out, despite the sudden lump in my throat. "I can't say no to you." I reached out and touched his arm. "You know, it wasn't that I didn't want to talk to you all these years. I did. I do," I amended. "It was easier not to because then I was safe. I was afraid that if we kept talking, you might ask me to do something life-altering."

"Define 'life-altering.'"

"Oh, for instance…" I tapped my chin, pretending to think.

"Calling me to say Dad's in the hospital, and can I fly home to help you save the flower shop?"

Bud almost smiled. "Like that would ever happen."

"Right? That kind of stuff only happens in Hallmark movies." I grasped his chin gently, forcing eye contact. "I really am sorry. I'll change it right now." I deleted "Do Not" and showed Bud his new title: "Absolutely Answer."

"I understand, you know," he said as I slid my phone into my laptop bag. "Cutting us off is how you kept yourself safe. I know how you are. How Ma and Pop are. I also know you don't really mean it. Just like you don't mean everything you say about how you don't want to be here."

He straightened his shoulders and shook them like a dog drying off after a swim. "I'm gonna go pick up lunch. We need to wrap up and get home. Ma's got a chore list a mile long waiting."

Dad had passed his latest stress test and was being released in the morning. I'd woken this morning, still on the couch, to see Mom measuring the family room with plans to turn it into a temporary bedroom.

I stopped Bud at the door, my arm across the open doorway. "Thank you for understanding," I said, my voice wobbling. "You're a better brother than I deserve."

He started to respond (probably something snarky like "I know"), then stopped. "We're family," he said instead. "It's not about deserving. It's about choice. When we needed you, you chose to come. That's what I see." He winked and ducked under my arm. "Back in a bit," he called. A few whistled notes of "Truckin'" floated back to me as he started the car and reversed out of the lot.

Chantal and I regarded each other. I could feel her assessing me.

Think of her as a client, I told myself again. *An account to win.* But no, that wasn't right. This was personal. I had to stop thinking of my family as problems to solve and start paying attention to what they needed and how I could help them.

Just like I'd always wanted them to do for me.

"Chantal..." I started.

"Look, whatever you want to say to me can wait." She tapped her hand against the table, like a judge with a gavel, delivering a sentence. In addition to sporting faint remnants of paint, I saw that the edges of her short, squared-off nails were stained brownish-green, like Bud's and Dad's. By contrast, my manicured French tips seemed like a judgment, another sign of my outsider status. I forced myself to make eye contact and give her my full attention, even though I knew what she had to say would be hard to hear.

Time to listen, Daisy.

"You're thinking you want to make things right, to be friends with me, make my daughter laugh, and feel like you've accomplished something. But that's not how this needs to work." She leaned forward. "I'm here every day helping Bud, helping your parents, trying to make a difference. You can't swoop in here, share some laughs with your brother, fill out a few spreadsheets" —she waved her hand over my laptop—"and go home thinking we're all good."

"That's not what I—"

She cut me off. "You've been gone a long time. I don't need to know the whole story. I see how your family is. They're nosy, bossy, think they know what's best, always." She raised a hand, palm up, in a graceful "what can you do" gesture. "But that's being a parent. That's the job description." She pinned me with a stern expression. "Your job here is to be a better sister. Bud needs you. Needs you to have his back, help build him up." She paused briefly as though making up her mind before continuing. "Every one of you underestimates him. And Bud"—she glanced toward the door he'd just exited, a ghost of a smile tugging at the corner of her mouth—"can't seem to stop acting the way you all expect him to. He doesn't think he's allowed to want more, to be more. I seem to be the only one who knows he has it in him to succeed."

Her words hit home. I'd never thought of it before, but she was right. I'd left because my family hadn't expected more from me. Bud had stayed for the same reason. But now we both wanted the same thing: to be more and do more. My throat tightened as a hundred images of my brother tumbled by. Moments when I could have stood up for him. Helped him. Encouraged him.

"You know what I see when I look at Bud?" Chantal asked. She didn't wait for an answer. "Potential. Potential and heart. He's a good man, father, son, and I bet he was a pretty good brother."

I flashed to the memory of Bud farting into the parrot chair, shouting, "I killed them!" I nodded.

"I'm sorry." I found my voice, wishing for better, more meaningful words. "I'm sorry I wasn't here. To help with the store. To help encourage Bud. To meet you and LilyRose. To talk to our parents." The dam broke, and words flowed faster. "I am sorry for the years I spent running from my problems instead of facing them. I'm sorry I left you and Bud alone to deal with Mom's stubbornness and Dad's refusal to change. I should have been here to help. You shouldn't have had to do it alone."

I remembered Mom calling, inviting me to come home and join their isolation squad during the shutdown ("God, no" had been my answer). I'd laughed about it later while on the phone with John, who, I recalled, hadn't found it funny.

Chantal waved her hand, simultaneously acknowledging and dismissing my apology. "I get what you did and why. Your folks are good people, but they want to run your life, not let you live it. It's unfortunate for everyone that they're doing the same thing to Bud. If they let go of what they think they want, they'd see they've got everything they need."

I felt her words down to my core. All my life, I'd had their expectations pressing on me, weighing me down. Who I was and what I wanted hadn't mattered. I'd been slotted into a specific role and expected to like it. So had Bud.

The time had come to break the cycle. It was time to break free. It was time to be more. For both of us to be more.

I squashed the urge to repeat my apology. Chantal was right. Bud needed my help, not my regret. "I can't change what happened before, but I promise from here on out, I'll do everything I can to help." I met her eyes, accepting the challenge I saw there.

"Deal," she said.

We weren't friends yet, but at that moment, we became allies.

As my first order of business (and penance), I spent the rest of the afternoon taking orders from Mom, moving furniture, and clearing paths in preparation for Dad's return home. Bud, Chantal, and LilyRose left for a birthday party for one of LilyRose's classmates.

Chantal gave me a meaningful look as they left. "Good luck," she called with a hint of wry humor.

By dinner, Mom and I had rearranged the family room furniture to accommodate the queen bed from their bedroom.

"There's an extra metal bed frame in Bud's old apartment above the garage," Mom said. "Take some work gloves from the front hall. Lord knows you're probably allergic to metal." She shooed me off before I could argue that I couldn't move a queen-size frame downstairs and across the yard by myself.

The sun dipped low along the foothills, casting long shadows across the grass as I tugged Dad's too-large work gloves on, muttering. I had just wrestled the lock off the second-floor entry when I heard a voice call, "You want some help?"

"Jeremy?" I squinted in the dying light. "What are you doing here?"

He jogged up the rickety stairs, two at a time, looking as though he'd come straight from work in his black bike shorts and a thin white cycling jersey. "Bud texted asking if I had some time to swing by. He thought you might need a hand." He relaxed against the railing, which creaked worryingly. Instinctively, I reached out and pulled him forward.

We stood for a moment, only inches from each other, my hand clutching the thin fabric of his shirt. His breath quickened, though from the stairs or the proximity, I couldn't tell. "Jeremy, I..." I trailed off, wanting to apologize for brushing him off the other day, but unsure of how to start.

"It's fine, Daisy," he said, understanding. "We're on the same page." He gently peeled my fingers off his shirt. "Now, what does Ruth want us to do first?"

Over the next hour, we moved and assembled the bedframe and then wrangled my parents' mattress down the stairs and into place. We fetched and carried various items from the nightstand and upstairs bathroom to the main floor. Mom kept busy by running the laundry, topping off our ice water, and generally popping in to give me meaningful looks when she thought Jeremy wasn't looking. "Meddling" wasn't exactly my idea of "quality time," but it would do for now.

We finished the evening with a plate of toasted bread, each topped with a fried egg and a side assortment of leftovers: avocado, sundried tomatoes, and sliced olives. Between the three of us, we finished off a pitcher of lemonade so sweet it made my teeth ache.

For dessert, Mom produced a plate of lemon squares from the freezer. "You two enjoy," she said. "I'm going to check in on Bert before visiting hours are over. Make sure those nurses are doing their job." She gave Jeremy a grateful smile. "Thank you for coming over. I sure appreciate your help. And I know Daisy does as well." She left, calling over her shoulder to leave the dishes in the sink for her to wash when she got home.

"She doesn't mean that," I told Jeremy. "'Leave the dishes' is her way of saying 'don't forget to do' the dishes."

He laughed. "I remember." He pushed back from the table and began stacking plates. "I wash, you dry, right?"

We finished the dishes, then returned to the table, Jeremy swapping lemonade for one of Bud's Fat Tire beers. He offered me one, but I waved my hand. I was exhausted. A drink would only put me to sleep. I was fading fast as it was.

Jeremy pulled a bottle opener from his multitool keychain. "I hope this isn't nosy," he said, popping the cap off his beer. "But what are your plans for Bert's in-home recovery?"

I sighed. "He'll have exercises to do," I said, heart sinking at the realization that this would be another set of worries dropped onto my brother once I left. "I don't envy whoever pulls the short straw in that regard. He's a terrible patient." I could practically predict what would happen. Dad would feign complete compliance with the doctors and nurses. Then, once he got home, those rehabilitation exercises would be lost amid the piles of store paperwork, never to be seen or thought of again. *Until next time*, a small voice in my head warned.

Jeremy played with his bottle cap, walking it over his knuckles like a magician with a coin. "You know, I could work with him. I'm certified. I do physical therapy sessions for some of my older cycling clients."

The eighteen-wheeler that had just rolled onto my chest rolled right back off. "Do you mean it? That would be fantastic. I know we would all appreciate it." *I* would appreciate it, I wanted to say, but once again, the words refused to come. I was really bad at this. Whatever "this" was.

"You bet," he said, tipping his bottle against my half-empty glass. "Take tomorrow to get settled, and I'll come by Tuesday morning to see how he's doing and walk him through his first workout."

My phone buzzed. John was calling.

"Sorry, I need to take this," I said as I accepted the call. "Hello?"

Jeremy drained his beer and stood, pointing at the back door to indicate that he was leaving. I nodded and waved, mouthing "Thank you" before turning my attention to John. "What's up?"

"Well..."

His hesitation jogged my memory. There was something I'd forgotten to do. What was it?

He continued, "Maggie says she hasn't gotten your paperwork."

I smacked my forehead. "I forgot. I'll do it right now." I raced from the kitchen up the stairs to my room and pulled my laptop from my bag. "You have no idea how busy it's been around here. First, there was the expo disaster, and today we've been getting ready for Dad to come home..." I trailed off as I scrolled through the forgotten paperwork, hastily filling in blanks.

"Look, Daisy. Are you sure you still want to do this?" John sounded like he was pacing. He probably was. I'd once watched him make his daily step count during a conference call with a particularly problematic client.

Only now, the problematic client was me. I bristled, once again picturing Bud making the "blast-off" signal to Chantal.

"I am. I do," I assured him, fingers flying over the keyboard. "I've been distracted, that's all. I told you. That's how my family is. Once you enter, there is no escape. Like the Bermuda Triangle. Or IKEA." A few more clicks, a scribbled signature on the touchpad, and I hit *Submit*. "There. It's done. We're all set."

"Great." John sounded vastly relieved. "I'll call in the morning and tell her it's in."

"I'm sorry, John," I said, wondering how many times I'd apologized this weekend. "I'm overwhelmed. But we're working it out. Bud will talk to Dad, and I've got"—I paused, searching for a suitable description—"a friend looking in on him starting Tuesday. Just a few more pieces to put in place, and I'll be back."

"Promise?"

"Cross my heart."

Chapter Sixteen

Daisy, Age 10

"Gently, now." Dad's hands guided my fingers, clumsy through gloves, as I inserted delicate flower stems into a narrow vase. Biting my lip in concentration, I tried to copy the shape of his example. The result looked more like an accident than an arrangement. Across the workbench, I could see my brother sticking flowers every which way into his vase. And yet, somehow, the outcome was still better than my careful approach—free, vibrant, joyful.

I threw down my last stem in frustration. "I'll never get this," I said, embarrassed at the prickling sensation at the back of my eyes warning me that tears were imminent. "I just can't do it."

"Shhh now, Petal," Dad soothed, removing his hat and wiping his brow with his forearm. "Flowers are about emotion. Whatever you're feeling, that's what will come out."

"Well, I feel like this is a big, fat, stupid waste of time," I said, pulling off my gloves. "I'm not cut out for this. I'm not like you."

"That's right, Pop," Bud agreed, pushing his vase across the table to stand beside mine. Side by side, mine looked even shabbier. "Ol' Cactus Butt here couldn't arrange her way out of a paper bag with a flashlight and a map."

"Ugh." I glared at my eight-year-old brother and shouldered my backpack. "Who wants to work with flowers anyway? When I grow up, I'm going to do something important. And I promise, it will have nothing to do with flowers." I swept from the room, willing myself not to cry as I left my father and brother staring after me.

"Careful, Pop."

Bud held his arm out for Dad, who brushed him off and gripped the railing as he climbed the concrete stairs to the back door. He stumbled on the third step from the top, and the rusted iron wobbled as he struggled to regain his balance. Mom and I rushed forward, abandoning the bags we'd unloaded from the car.

Don't fall, don't fall, don't fall, I thought as I sprinted, closing the distance between myself and the man who used to swing me onto his shoulders in a motion so smooth it felt like flying. I wondered if I should have asked Jeremy to start today. I could have used a friendly face—not to mention someone more equipped to handle the stress of this moment.

The doctors agreed that Dad's progress was encouraging but slow. He had a slight tremor in his hands, and his right side seemed to move a second later than his left. Predictably, he refused to use the walker unless forced.

Batting away all offers of help, Dad made it up the final two stairs. Mom and I followed nervously, prepared to catch him should he lose his balance.

Bud held the screen door open as Dad stepped over the threshold and into the kitchen. We'd pushed the table and chairs to one side to make room for the metal walker, which stood like an uninvited party guest inside the doorway. One of LilyRose's drawings, a smiling yellow sunflower, hung on the kitchen door. Stenciled across the top in Chantal's neat block letters was "Welcome home, Grandpop." I looked closer. Someone had penciled in an extra "o" in "Grandpop."

"I've got it, I've got it." Dad waved Mom and me back as he continued the arduous trek across the kitchen. "You all act as if I'm..." He stopped, out of breath, supporting himself against the counter.

"Sick? Invalid?" Bud patted Dad's back while rolling his eyes at me. "Hate to break it to you, man, but..."

Mom slapped Bud lightly on the arm as she passed. "Don't sass your father. He's had a rough day. He needs his rest." She took Dad's arm, undeterred by his protest of "Ruth!" and practically dragged him down the hall.

Forget the walker. We should have strapped roller skates to his feet.

Bud watched them disappear before turning to me. "You coming? Or are you planning to make a break for it now that Dad's home?"

"Ha ha," I said sourly, partly annoyed that Bud had seemed to read my mind. Although my flight didn't leave until tomorrow evening, I'd already begun packing. "Help me with the bags."

We hauled the two overstuffed duffels inside and dropped them in the hallway next to the family room. I made a show of taking the heaviest bag as if that proved my intention to be helpful. Mom had shut the pocket door, but we could hear her through the thin walls.

"Now, Bert, you relax. Don't even think of lifting a finger. We'll have you back on your feet in no time."

"Ruth, I—" we heard Dad begin.

She continued chattering, cutting him off. "Sit back, no, wait, let me put another pillow behind you." We heard a muffled "ooof" and a half-cough as if Dad was either forced into sitting or lying down against his will.

Bud made the blast-off gesture, and I nodded in agreement. When Mom ratcheted up the Smother levels, the best course of action was to let her wear herself out. Until then, Dad would be forced to enjoy his mandatory relaxation.

We abandoned the luggage and tiptoed back to the kitchen. Bud pushed the table and chairs into place and moved the walker to the hallway. The stress of the day had me craving comfort food. I searched the freezer for the Moose Tracks ice cream Dad always kept on hand. Moving a frostbitten, family-sized bag of cheese ravioli, I found a fifth of Absolut instead.

Hm. Interesting.

I glanced at the wall clock. It was four p.m., which meant it was happy hour in Kansas City.

Close enough.

Ice cream abandoned, I pulled the bottle out. Taking two mugs from the counter, I poured a generous shot into each.

"Here." I plunked one in front of my brother, whose eyebrows shot up in surprise. "I think we deserve this."

Recovering quickly, Bud lifted his glass in salute. "Here's mud in your eye."

"L'chaim," I said, raising my mug.

We drank, and I refilled the glasses.

"To Grandpoop's triumphant return," Bud said, inclining his head toward his daughter's drawing. Mystery solved.

"To surviving Mom."

"To saving the store."

"To new beginnings."

A pleasant warmth wound down my throat and curled up in my stomach like a purring cat. Across the table, my brother grinned as he poured another shot into our mugs. We toasted each other between sips, everything from tomorrow's successful style shoot to a World Series title for Bud's beloved Rockies.

A contented hum began in my head as the stress of the last week melted away. Dad was home. Bud and I had made up. All that was left for me to do was distract Mom long enough for Bud to talk to Dad alone tonight.

I could do it. I would do it.

Bud rose as if to put the bottle back in the freezer. "Time to face the music. You ready?"

"No!" I protested, my tongue suddenly thick. "One more."

I mean, a little extra sibling bonding time never hurt anyone.

The kitchen had taken on a rosy glow. I felt good. No, better than good. I was happy. So happy. I loved everyone. I smiled to myself. Everything was good. No, better than good. Everything was perf—

"What in the world are you two doing?" Mom's voice cut through the haze. I froze, spitting the drink I'd just taken back into my glass.

Bud giggled from under the table (when had he fallen off his chair?). "We're drinking, Ma. Pull up a self and help yerglass."

I stared, trying to decide which Mom to look at. "He'sh right, Ma," I said, burping mid-sentence. "We're toashting Grandpoop's health." I held my mug aloft.

Grasping the tabletop, Bud pulled himself to kneeling. "We want him to be reeeeeeall healthy."

Mom reached over and snatched the vodka bottle off the table.

"Heeeey," I protested weakly. I tried to grab her arm(s) and missed all of them.

Mom poured the rest of the vodka down the sink, then marched to the cupboard and took down two jam jar glasses. She filled them with tap water and thrust them at us. "Drink this."

Bud took one, sipped, and made a face. "Thish vodka went bad. Mine's bad." He tried to hand the glass back, but Mom pinned him with the glare she'd been using on us since childhood. Powerless against such tactics, Bud stopped complaining and drank his water.

I sipped experimentally. The cool water felt good on my throat. I wondered how much I'd had to drink. As if in response, the room suddenly dipped and rolled. The rosy glow vanished.

I closed my eyes, hoping that would help.

Nope, closed was worse.

I opened my eyes.

Mom's hand appeared. "Take these," she ordered.

I tried and failed twice before plucking two aspirins from her palm. I dropped them in my mouth and took a huge swig of water, almost choking. *Can throats be drunk?*

"Uggggh." I laid my head on my arms. When I felt Mom's arms around me, lifting, I didn't fight.

She led me to my room and tucked me into bed like a child. On her way out, she paused in the doorway. "If you're going to throw up, try to make it to the bathroom. The trash can in your room was a gift from Great-Aunt Marge."

I burrowed down, my head between the pillows, the smooth cotton soothing against my forehead. I listened to Bud's thudding footsteps and vociferous objections as Mom put him to bed. She did not close his door gently.

Having been scolded and sent to my room, I did what any self-respecting 32-year-old would do: I passed out.

I awoke to the sound of a vacuum cleaner. A moment later, the door burst open, and Mom came in, dragging her ancient Electrolux canister vacuum around the edge of my bed. She wore yellow plastic gloves and a grim expression. A spray bottle of apple cider vinegar was tucked into her elastic waistband.

Groaning, I propped myself up. "Mom, does that have to happen, like, right now?"

She forced the vacuum head under the bed frame with a jolt. "Oh, I'm sorry," she said in a clipped tone. "Did my life interrupt your busy day-drinking schedule?" She jerked the vacuum back and forth, jarring the bed with each impact. "It's interesting how you (*thunk*) seem to have so much time to spend (*thunk*) goofing around with your brother and so very little time (*thunk*) to spend helping your father keep (*thunk*) his (*thunk*) store (*thunk*) open. Personally. I couldn't imagine a better time to clean your room."

I fell back and pulled a pillow over my head. "What time is it?"

She yanked the pillow away and spritzed apple cider vinegar at me. "Seven."

I waved my hands as the mist landed on my arms. "You couldn't let me sleep more than two hours?"

She almost cracked a smile. "Seven in the morning. It's Tuesday. Get dressed and come downstairs. Your father and I want to talk to you." She wheeled the vacuum out of the room. I heard it roar to life a moment later, followed by a yelp.

Bud was awake.

Bud and I sat on kitchen chairs at the foot of our father's makeshift bed in the family room. Mom stood beside him, arms crossed, yellow kitchen gloves still on. The overwhelming smell of vinegar signaled she'd been rage-cleaning.

"Now," Dad said, "what's this I hear about the two of you drinking all my vodka?"

"What were you thinking?" Mom said at the same time. "On his first day home, no less."

I shifted in my chair. Bud stared at his feet. I wondered if he was still tipsy. I was having difficulty staying upright.

Mom continued, "Your father and I are disappointed. The two of you are supposed to be a team—part of our team, as a matter of fact—Team Greene. Need I remind you?"

"No, ma'am," I mumbled. Beside me, Bud grunted and held his head.

Mom put a gloved hand on Dad's shoulder. "Not only did you abandon your duties helping your father and me, but your duties at the store as well." She *tut-tut*ted. "I would expect this behavior from your brother, but not you, Daisy. Not from you. I need your word that I can trust you to do what needs to be done. Whether it takes a week, a month, or a year."

A year? I started to protest, "But, I—"

The steel in Mom's eyes stopped me.

Dad cleared his throat. "Daisy, your mother and I," he said and glanced pointedly at Mom, who arranged her face into a blank stare, looking somewhere past my left ear, "we understand that you have things that are important to you in Kansas City."

Mom broke in again. "Bud can't run the store on his own. You need to—"

"Yes, I can!" Bud exploded. "Chan and I have ideas on ways to expand the business. Take it in a new direction. Make it profitable again. If you would just listen—"

At the same time, I said, "Why can't you guys understand? Bud wants this. He wants the store. I don't. I need to get home—"

Mom pointed at Bud. "We are listening." She pointed at me. "You *are* home. End of discussion. Now, shoo, both of you. Your father needs to rest."

The defeated look on Bud's face broke my heart. I sighed, stood up, crossed to Dad, and kissed his head. "I'm glad you're home. And I'm sorry." Ignoring Mom, I looked at my brother. "Let's go."

In wordless agreement, we headed out the back door and sat together on the concrete stairs. The morning was crisp, and a few remaining stars twinkled over the Front Range.

"Well," I said, "that could have gone better."

"Yeah." My brother sighed. "Luckily, we still have a few more days to fix it."

"*You* have a few more days," I corrected. "I'm going home tonight."

"Haha, very funny." Bud nudged my knee with his.

"Why is that funny?" In the back of my mind, a faint alarm sounded. Something was off. "I'm not kidding. My flight is at 6."

Bud turned to me in slow motion. "You don't remember?"

The alarm's volume increased. "Remember what?"

"Oh, wow. That's wild." Bud chuckled, playing with the cuff of his hoodie. "You changed your flight. Said you wanted to stick around a few more days. Something about karma and alliances. I didn't really follow all of it."

I felt what little color I had in my face drain away. This was impossible. I wouldn't. I couldn't. I whipped out my phone and pulled up my airline reservations.

I had.

Instead of leaving tonight as planned, I was flying out on Sunday morning, five days from now.

I looked at Bud. "How could you let me do this?"

He held his hands up in surrender. "Hey, I tried to stop you. You told me to mind my own business."

"And for the first time in your life, you listened to me?" My mind slid over the previous evening, attempting to catch more details. Still, it remained as slippery as a shot of vodka going down smooth.

Another thought occurred: I had to call Reg. And Fiona. And —my heart sank—John.

Bud observed me, his expression morphing from bemused to concerned. He patted my knee. "Well, time to get to work." He heaved himself to his feet. He started down the steps, then paused. "If it helps, I'm glad you're sticking around. Not that you can help it, Cactus Butt. Get it? *Sticking* around?"

He dodged my kick at his shins. I could hear him laughing all the way to the car.

Two very terse phone conversations with Fiona and Reg later, I was standing in the kitchen waiting for the coffee to brew.

Chantal and LilyRose blew into the kitchen, dressed for school. LilyRose danced around the table, singing a (painfully loud) song about letters stuck in a tree. She stopped and peered up at me. "What's the matter, Aunt Funny? Are you sick?"

"Aunt Funny has a headache," I told her, trying not to grimace at the sound of her spoon clinking against the cereal bowl.

"My daddy had a headache, too," LilyRose observed before returning to her breakfast.

"That's right. Aunt Funny and Daddy are the same sick today." Chantal shot me a withering look over her daughter's head. Not only was I partially responsible for squandering Bud's opportunity to talk to Dad, but I'd also cheated Bud's family out of his presence last evening. I added "guilt" to my growing list of today's regrets.

"We'll both feel much better soon," I said, looking at LilyRose but directing my words to Chantal. "I promise."

"Let's hope so. Come on, baby girl." Chantal helped her daughter clear her dishes and put them in the sink. "It's time for school."

My phone buzzed, and John's picture appeared. I picked up immediately. There was no sense in putting off the inevitable. "Hey."

"Hey." John sounded dejected. "We lost the office space."

"What? Why?" I asked, ignoring the thrumming in my head. "I sent in the paperwork."

"Yeah, but Maggie got a cash offer on Sunday." He sighed. "And since she didn't have a signed contract from us, she took it."

I sank into a kitchen chair. "This is my fault."

John said nothing. He didn't need to. We both knew the truth.

"So, listen—" I began.

"You're not flying back tonight, are you?"

"How'd you know?"

"I haven't worked with you all this time and not learned how to read you. I could tell something was up. Plus," he added, "Fiona's stomping around and yelling at Martin even more than usual."

I didn't have the energy to apologize again. "I'm coming home Sunday. I promise. No more changes."

"Okay. Sure. Whatever you say." Sarcasm dripped down the line.

"Do you want me to call Tavia to explain?"

"Oh, I'm sure she's the only one who has no problems with your change of plans." John gave a mirthless laugh. "She's working on menu planning today. I took over all the print materials. She got a little, let's say, flamboyant with the invitation mockups."

I covered my face with my hand. "On a Met Gala scale of Rhianna to Lady Gaga, how flamboyant are we talking?" He didn't answer. "Send me one," I begged.

"I think it's better if I don't."

"John…"

"I'll handle it. Forget I said anything." Resignation colored John's voice.

I offered the only olive branch I had left: utter mortification. "If it makes you feel any better, I'm staying specifically to distract Mom." I paused. "Goat yoga may be involved."

John snorted. "Okay, that helps a little. At least we're both dealing with tough clients. Hey, you want me to send Tavia out to help?"

"Not for all the meat dresses in the world," I swore. "I have to go. Hang in there, John. I really appreciate all you're doing."

"I'm pretty wonderful," he agreed. Some of the tension eased, although I sensed forgiveness was still a long way off. "Look, Daisy. I know you're going through some things, but I need you back. Get your stuff handled and come home, would ya?" He signed off with a cheerier, "Bye."

There was a knock at the back door as I hung up with John. I sighed, missing the peace and quiet of my (according to my neighbor, Mrs. Rudnicki, uninhabited) condo.

"Daisy!" Mom called from the front room. "Can you get that? I've got to help your father with his *toilette*."

"Got it," I called back, wincing.

She continued, "If it's the neighbor kids selling candy, make sure to get the kind without raisins and nuts. Your father broke a tooth last time."

Rubbing my hand over my eyes, I opened the door, excuses at the ready. "I'm sorry. We don't want any…" I trailed off at the sight of Jeremy on the porch, dressed in workout gear and carrying a large duffel bag.

"Morning," he said, his booming voice stabbing directly through my forehead. "Is Bert ready for me?"

Oh no.

Jeremy took the news that I'd forgotten to inform my father that he would be serving as Dad's in-home physical therapist in stride.

"It happens more than you think," he said, waving off my repeated apologies. (I was considering purchasing a shirt that simply read "I'm sorry" in flashing letters). After a hurried explanation and with his permission, I left Mom and Dad in Jeremy's capable hands. Relieved of parent-watch duty, I took myself off to work.

Chapter Seventeen

With Bud out making deliveries and Agnes sitting at the counter watching the empty showroom, I sequestered myself in Dad's office, ready to attack the remainder of his paperwork.

Pressure clogged my sinuses; I'd forgotten to take allergy medicine. I snuffled and reached blindly for the box of tissues. I shoved one up each nostril, afraid that blowing my nose would cause the top of my pounding head to explode. I rested my head on the desk, enjoying the smooth coolness of paper against my forehead. Work could wait while I took a quick nap, right? I closed my eyes. Bliss.

A soft rap at the doorframe was followed by a cheerful, "Hi, Daisy!"

I sat up, startled, an invoice stuck to my cheek.

Victor stood in the doorway.

"I brought you a client." The end of his sentence trailed upward into a question. He might have been addressing me or the tiny blond who appeared in the doorway behind him.

I had an out-of-body moment as I imagined myself through their eyes: Limp hair, heavy bags under my itchy red eyes, crumbs from a half-eaten sour cream doughnut trailing down my shirt like confetti at the world's worst party.

I spun my chair to the back wall and whipped the tissues from my nose. The invoice wafted through the air, landing delicately in the corner. "Hi!" I called, fumbling for my purse and makeup kit. "I... uh... gibe me one binute."

I pulled out my compact mirror and checked my tiny reflection. It was as bad as I feared. Clutching my bag, I stood and edged past Victor and his client. "Dosebleed," I said, improvising. "Bake yourselves at hobe." I gestured to the shop. "I'b just going to clean up. Audt Agdes?" I croaked. "Could you offer our custobers sobe water or coffee?"

The blond looked at Victor in confusion. "Bake ourselves?" she mouthed.

I hightailed it down the hall to the safety of the bathroom, where I blew my nose lustily and hoped it would provide enough relief that I could speak without sounding like a squirrel with a mouthful of acorns. I slapped tinted moisturizer onto my parched skin and raked my hair into a ponytail. After an exploratory sniff of my armpits, I pulled off my ancient Jayhawks sweatshirt and spritzed myself with Apple Cinnamon Febreze from the cleaning supply closet. I found an extra work shirt (a twin of the Dreaded Christmas Gift, I noticed) and buttoned it up, French-tucking the tails into the waistband of my black joggers.

It would have to do.

I rejoined the group, now gathered at the small white wrought-iron bistro table and pink-cushioned chairs that served as the shop's conference table.

Please, God, don't let me sneeze on anyone.

I pasted a smile on my face and held out my hand to the blond. "Hi," I said, projecting confidence and capability as if she hadn't just seen me looking like a feral wolverine. "I'm Daisy. It's nice to meet you."

She stood to shake my hand. She was so short that standing didn't change her height much. "Casey," she said, offering a firmer grip than I expected. "Victor said we had to come in to check out your bridal arrangements." She scanned the room. "I have to say, I was skeptical. But this looks much nicer than your expo booth."

I sent up a small prayer of thanks for Cecil's delivery this morning. Our cooler was stocked with loose stems, and I could pull out the lookbook for more specific examples. "We're pleased to…" I started, but Casey continued, stunning me with the most unexpected sentence:

"And, of course, I simply had to meet Agnes!" Casey beamed across the table to where Agnes sat, looking as content as a cat in a sunbeam.

"Of course you—wait, what?"

Casey whipped her phone off the table and turned the screen to me. Sure enough, there in her social media feed was a new video of Agnes holding a bouquet and doing a little two-step to "Wedding Bell Blues." I goggled at the staggering number of responses and likes.

"Casey is getting married in September," Victor explained as I regained my composure. "I wanted to show her some of Bloomin' Bert's famous wedding bouquets." He looked around, raising an eyebrow. "Do you have any examples?"

"Er… of course." I stood, motioning toward the workroom door. "Our head designer and our store manager are out this morning," I offered. "But I, uh, I mean, Agnes, can show you the arrangements they created for a style shoot later today." I'd learned my lesson: hand over the shoptalk to the pros. I belonged firmly in the background.

Agnes and Casey moved ahead of us, chatting like old friends. Victor and I hung back.

"Thank you," I said. "I appreciate this."

"You're welcome," he said. "You know, I looked this place up online after the expo. You do great work. And those posts of Agnes were fantastic." He cocked his head toward the back room. "Casey's a lifestyle influencer. Her specialty is highlighting small businesses and locally sourced products. I knew she would love it here."

I hesitated, wondering where to start. Should I attempt to explain my dinner invitation? Explain that he was the first person I'd connected with here who felt like an extension of my life in Kansas City? Would that sound creepy? No, what was creepy was just standing here, saying nothing. *Say something, Daisy!*

"Hey." Victor broke into my thoughts. "Would you like to get some lunch?"

Casey left half an hour later with a preliminary purchase order and a virtual appointment to discuss creative details with Chantal. I acted as Agnes's assistant, refilling coffees, getting order forms, checking the store schedule, taking notes, and nodding in agreement at the appropriate times. For the first time, I felt like I'd actually helped. Plus, I'd managed not to sneeze or throw up on anyone, so… winning.

Between discussing wedding details, Casey took several selfies with Agnes and promised to send more brides our way. She even took a video in the showroom with Victor as her videographer.

"I just love this cozy little shop!" she gushed, smiling for her audience. "It's a vibe. It's up to all of us to support local family businesses like Blooms by Bert." Victor turned slowly, hands steady, taking a final panoramic shot. Agnes struck a pose and made duck lips at the camera while I hid behind the counter.

Handing the phone back to Casey, Victor followed his client, calling over his shoulder that he'd see me in an hour.

The bell over the door was still jangling in their wake as Agnes eyed me.

"What?" I asked, avoiding the hard stare behind her giant black frames. I straightened up and smoothed the wrinkles from my work shirt.

"You like him."

"Victor?" I jotted a calculation in the margins of the purchase order, trying to look casual. "He's very nice. I hope Casey's video works," I said, switching topics. "Another wedding on the books would give us a couple more weeks' cushion."

Agnes would not be distracted. "Where did you and the wedding planner meet?"

"I met him Saturday. He helped me set up our booth." I blushed at the memory of myself falling, splay-legged, into a pile of stress balls, and how his appearance today was a sign of true professional compassion.

Agnes misinterpreted my discomfiture. "Honey, I wasn't born yesterday." She cackled. "You *like him* like him. It's a—what was the word Casey used—a vibrator?"

"A *vibe*," I corrected hastily. Slang in Agnes's hands was dangerous. "And no, I do not. At least, not in that way. He has a fiancée. He told me."

"Pish." Agnes waved my protest away like she was swatting a fly. "He might have said that, but trust me, his eyes told a different story." Humming tunelessly, she gathered the empty coffee cups and carried them, clinking in her shaky hand, from the room.

I arrived at the restaurant first and sat facing the door. I'd practiced my speech all the way over. First, I would thank him for the lunch invitation and for bringing Casey into the store. Then (and this was the tricky bit) I would explain that I hadn't been hitting on him when I'd invited him to dinner. I'd simply recognized a kindred soul and been trying, in my own prickly way, to make friends. There was a reason cacti thrived in deserts after all. They were not made for social interaction.

By the time Victor arrived, I had already downed two glasses of water out of nerves and my bladder was protesting.

"Sorry I'm late," he said, sliding into the booth across from me. "Bridal emergency." He still wore the pale-peach dress shirt and gray pants he'd had on earlier but had removed the tie and rolled up his sleeves in deference to the warm Colorado sunshine.

"No problem!" It came out much louder than I intended. He looked at me, bemused, as I rushed on. "I mean, hi. I was surprised to see you in the shop today. I mean, good surprised." Mercifully, our server interrupted my garbled attempts at small talk by asking Victor if he would like something to drink besides water.

"Iced tea, please." He looked over at me. "Do you know what you want to order?"

I hadn't even opened my menu; I'd been too busy staring at the door, waiting for him to walk through it. I scrambled to flip it over to the lunch specials. "You go first, and then I'll be ready."

After taking our order (mango salad without chicken for him; tortilla soup for me), the waiter whisked away the menus.

"Thank you for the invitation," I began just as his phone rang.

He grimaced as he glanced at the screen. I could relate. "Would you excuse me?" he asked. "I need to take this." He slid from the booth and strode to the door, holding the phone to his ear, murmuring. I took my chance and hightailed it to the bathroom.

When I returned, he was still on the phone, gesturing, features hardened into a scowl. Whoever he was speaking to was getting an earful. I sipped my refilled water and scrolled social media while I waited. Chantal's post had garnered even more likes. I found Casey's video next. "Met Agnes in person!" the caption read. "She and her store are just as adorable in person! Come see for yourself. #weddingflowers #imthebride." She'd tagged the store and our location.

I messaged Bud with the link and a note, "Casey is officially my new favorite customer." I smiled as I hit *Send*, happy to have some positive news to share for once.

"I apologize for taking that call." Victor slid back into his seat as the waiter returned with a basket of chips and salsa. "What's so funny?"

I took in Victor's flushed cheeks, his once-smiling face now pulled taut in a frown. "Oh, nothing. Just another funny Agnes post. Is everything okay?" I took a chip, biting down with an embarrassing crunch. I put it down.

He sighed. "Not really." He looked down at the bowl of salsa as if it were the cause of all his distress. "Are you sure you want to hear this? It's a lot for a lunch date."

I was so surprised to hear the word "date" come out of his mouth that I forgot my practiced speech. "Absolutely."

Still, he hesitated. "I feel bad. I hardly know you."

"Sometimes it's easier to talk to someone new. Less baggage. Less history." I bit my tongue from saying, "Less artillery with which to emotionally manipulate you and send you into a shame spiral that leaves you wanting to drink a bottle of vodka with your brother at four in the afternoon." This was his story, after all, not mine.

"True." He took a sip of iced tea and continued. "Okay. The short version is that Vicki—my fiancée—doesn't like me working for my mother." Victor took a chip from the basket, breaking off pieces as he spoke. "She says it's stunting my professional and emotional growth." Victor sighed, pushing the growing pile of chip crumbs to the side. "Can you believe her?"

"Hm." I hesitated, not wanting to confirm that yes, I could. Instead, I answered his question with a question. "And why do you think she feels that way?"

He considered this. "I think she's embarrassed. I think she thinks I'm taking the easy road, working for someone, rather than opening my own business." He looked up at me. "I mean, what's wrong with wanting to carry on a tradition? Why does following in my family's footsteps immediately disqualify me as a professional?"

My body stiffened. "Er..."

Victor caught my reaction and looked embarrassed. I wanted to reassure him that my reaction wasn't a judgment of his situation—his words were hitting closer to home than he knew. I had judged Bud, believing his choices were out of laziness, rather than respect. That he'd taken the easiest path, while I'd taken the difficult one. I wondered how often Bud had felt like Victor clearly did now.

"I'm sorry," I said, wishing I had better words. "That's unfair. And it sucks."

He laughed thinly. "You're right. It is. And it does."

Our waiter appeared with our food, breaking the tension. I'd never been so grateful to see soup.

"Anyway, enough about my drama." Victor recovered, picking up his fork and pointing it at me. "Tell me more about your designer—the one working with Casey."

It dawned on me then: I didn't need to give my speech. Against all odds, he saw me as a work colleague, a new vendor possibility. This lunch (aside from his momentary confidence, which I could tell he was now regretting) was about networking.

Phew.

Relieved from the duty of a formal apology, I told him about Chantal and Bud and their mission to rebrand and rejuvenate the business. Still trying to make up for my embarrassing show at the expo, I told him about Kansas City, my work with Event Artistry, and the plans for Ground Floor.

Victor relaxed as I talked, appearing happy to let me take the conversational lead as he finished eating. When the waiter came by to clear our plates, he ordered dessert for the table.

"So can you do it?" he asked over sopapillas. "Can you save the shop?" He lowered his voice, like a movie trailer announcer: "Big city girl, Daisy Greene, comes home to help her brother, Bud, restore the family business to its former glory..." He trailed off. "I have to ask, whose idea were the names? Daisy? Bud?"

"Says the guy who is half of a couple named Victor and Vicki," I retorted.

He held up his hands in mock surrender. "Fair enough."

Squaring my shoulders, I gave my canned response: "Mom and Dad were rebranding the business right around the time I was born and Mom thought Daisy Greene would be a cute tie-in. My brother is actually named Bertram after Dad, but since they'd fully invested in the flower theme by then, they nicknamed him Bud."

Victor licked powdered sugar from his fingers. "Well, she was right. Daisy Greene is cute. I mean, the name is cute," he corrected. "Just right for a florist."

"But I'm not a florist." I fought to steady my voice, rattled by his use of the word "cute." "I can't even stay in the store too long, or my allergies flare up." My face turned red, remembering how he'd walked in on me that morning. "I'm much better with events. All evidence to the contrary."

He laughed. "Anyone can have a bad event. I have some wedding stories that would curl your hair."

"You're just saying that to make me feel better."

"You're right. My events are always perfect."

I balled up my napkin and threw it at him, just as the waiter came by with the check.

"My treat," he said, brushing my hand away. "You can get it next time."

"Absolutely," I said, pleased. Denver wasn't home anymore, but for an hour, it had felt like it was in the neighborhood.

Victor waited at the curb with me until my ride arrived.

I paused before climbing in. "You know," I said, feeling my way through a thought that had been percolating during lunch. "Perhaps what Vicki is really trying to say is that she believes in you. Granted, she's not doing it in the most productive way, but maybe she's trying to encourage you to grow, expand, try new things. I bet if you asked her, she would say that traditions are great, but she also believes you have the talent and ability to do so much more. That you can do anything you want, if only you have the courage to try."

Victor considered this. "If that's what she really thinks, why wouldn't she say it?"

Why not, indeed. Had I ever said as much to my brother?

"Maybe she's jealous," I said, shrugging. "Maybe she's never been as sure about her place in the world as you are. Maybe she's misinterpreted your passion for passivity. But," I hastened to add, "I am sure she's very proud of you, and that at the center of her concern is also love. This may be one of those times where two people are too close to a thing to see it from each other's perspective. But if you each take a step back, you'll find that you can see the big picture."

"I never thought of it that way," Victor said as I climbed in. "Thank you, Daisy Greene." He mimed an explosion, as though I'd blown his mind with my insight. I didn't tell him that my speech had been just as much for me as for him. Let him think his new work friend was a genius at interpersonal relationships.

"You're welcome," I said, shutting the door. The car pulled away from the curb. I sat back, drained.

"That was quite a speech," my driver said. "You a therapist or something?"

"Nope," I said. "Just someone who needs to take her own advice."

"And your name is Daisy Greene?" he continued as he made a left onto Speer Boulevard.

I closed my eyes and leaned against the window. I knew what was coming. My headache returned in full force. *One... two... three...*

"With a name like that, you should be a florist."

Chapter Eighteen

I sat on the edge of Dad's bed. Bud and Chantal were still out on assignment. Mom had gone to pick up LilyRose from her afterschool program, waving away my offer to go instead.

"Carpool etiquette is too difficult to explain," she said while packing animal-shaped cookies and fruit-shaped gummy snacks into her upholstered purse as though she were leading an excursion to Everest rather than making a 10-minute drive to preschool. "Keep your father company."

I brought Dad a scoop of Moose Tracks ice cream (strictly verboten by Mom but okayed by Jeremy; I'd texted and asked). We ate silently; the television turned to a nature program featuring a lizard trying to make its way across the desert while unseen dangers closed in. I could relate.

"How are you feeling?" I asked as Dad ran his spoon hopefully around the bottom of his cup. I passed him my half-finished dessert and was rewarded with a happy smile, the first I'd seen since walking into his hospital room a week ago.

"Better," he mumbled, mouth full. "Although your friend tried to kill me this morning with his torture devices."

I laughed. "I think you mean exercise bands." I'd gotten the complete rundown from Mom when I'd returned. Jeremy would come once every other day for the next three weeks, then once a week, then once a month. He'd also refused to take payment, which had gone a long way toward Dad accepting his assistance. "Well," I said, moving the dishes to the top of the TV stand by the doorway, "I'm glad you're working with him. It makes me feel much better about going home." I watched Dad's reaction to this statement: a furrowing of the brow and fingers steepled under his chin. He had something to say. I waited.

"About that," he said after a prolonged silence. "I know you consider Kansas City your home."

"I do."

"And I know you feel strongly about your work there."

"I do."

"And despite what she says, your mother knows that too."

I snorted. "Right."

Dad shook his finger and *tsk-tsk*ed. "Now, now, Petal. Your mother loves you. She wants what's best for you. We both do." He held up his hand, stopping my reply. "I've been listening, you know, to you, and Bud, and Chantal. I've heard you say that you aren't *back*." He made air quotes. "I've heard Bud say that he and Chantal can manage on their own. I've thought long and hard about it." He broke off as a coughing fit overtook him. I rushed to get him some water, which he accepted.

After what felt like an eternity, he set the glass on the ottoman he was using as a bedside table and continued. "And I agree. Bud has come a long way. He's been working full-time at the store for more than a decade. He's learned every job. He works hard and asks for little in return. He's ready to take the next step up."

My mouth fell open, and my hands flew up, unbidden, into a victory stance. "Dad! That's great! That's magnificent! You won't be sorry, I know—"

"I wasn't done." My father's brusque tone cut my celebration off. For a moment, my arms remained extended overhead. I faked a stretch and lowered them, trying to seem nonchalant, and folded my hands in my lap, attentive.

"It's not Bud I'm worried about, Petal. It's you."

This was unexpected.

"Me?" I was shocked. "Why? I'm perfectly fine."

"Because when I look at you, I see me," he said simply, as though it were obvious. "All my life, I've worked hard. I've worked constantly. I worked to provide for this family. And I was happy to do it," he stressed. "But look where it's gotten me. Here, in bed, recovering from what the doctor calls 'a warning.'" He smiled briefly, the papery skin around his eyes accordioning. "And when I look at you and see how hard you're working, I worry that it will be the same for you."

"That's ridiculous," I said, shaking my head. "I'm perfectly healthy. Plus, I love my job. I don't want to let up." I thought of Tavia, her LED lights, the invitations. "I can't. And anyway, once John and I start our new company, we'll have to work hard to make a name for ourselves." I felt a surge of adrenaline just thinking about it: seeking out new clients, renovating office space, the long hours of unpaid start-up labor, not to mention the fact that until we had employees, we'd be doing all the work ourselves.

Just like Dad. Right before he collapsed, I reminded myself.

Quiet, brain. No one asked you.

Mom's voice rang out from the kitchen: "We're home!" Lily-Rose's footsteps pounded up the stairs, accompanying another song, this one about superhero pets.

Mom continued, "Bert? Bert? Are you relaxing yet? You know the doctor says you could die if you don't start relaxing right now!"

I gathered our ice cream bowls and hid them under the hem of my shirt. I stopped at the door and turned back to Dad. "I appreciate your concern, Dad. I really do. But I'll be fine. I'm ready to go home, where I'm supposed to be. And Bud will do great. I hope you'll talk to him soon. Make some plans."

I turned and went down the hall, feeling like a superhero myself. It was all coming together.

Bud, Chantal, and I sat at the kitchen table, my laptop and Chantal's side by side. Mom and LilyRose were watching *The Price Is Right at Night* with Dad and shouting wildly inaccurate guesses about the price of juicers and detergent pods.

"Okay," I said, turning my screen to face Bud. "Here's the breakdown of where we are with the store's finances." I tapped the screen with the eraser end of one of LilyRose's pencils, a sparkly silver number with a fuzzy pompom topper and googly eyes. The eyes clicked as I made my presentation. "And this—*click-click*—is the projected shortfall by the end of June."

"Four ninety-nine!" Mom bellowed from the other room.

"And here," I said, raising my voice to be heard, "is the difference we need to make up to implement your changes, including class materials and advertising. This—*click-click*—number includes a conservative estimate for what Casey's wedding will bring in." I looked over at Chantal questioningly. She and Casey had spent an hour discussing ideas and creating an inspiration board.

Chantal nodded at the numbers. "That looks about right. Plus, one of her bridesmaids is getting married in September, so assuming she likes the mockups, we'll get another referral soon." She looked to Bud. "And we should know about the other thing on Friday."

"What 'other thing?'" I asked, fingers pausing above the keyboard.

Bud waved his hand. "Don't worry about it." He pointed back at the screen. "So these numbers, these are based on everything in Pop's files?"

I glanced between Chantal and Bud. Something was going on. I opened my mouth to ask but let the subject drop instead. I didn't need to know. We were in the home stretch now. In a few days, I'd be gone, and they'd be here. "Everything except the bottom drawer of his cabinet. I couldn't find the key." I shrugged. "The only thing left is for you and Dad to approach Mom."

"On it," Bud said with confidence I hadn't seen before. "Dad and I are rehearsing while you're" he coughed before continuing —"out with Mom."

"Lord, grant me strength."

Bud clapped me on the shoulder. "You can do it, Sis. I know you can."

I put my hands on his shoulders, touching my forehead to his. "Team Greene?"

"Team Greene."

Chapter Nineteen

I checked the time. 11:45. Fifteen minutes before I had to go downstairs and collect Mom. I was taking her to her favorite Chinese restaurant and then a side trip to the silk flower store on Broadway. She and the owner were old friends, and I could be sure that their conversation would give Bud and Dad all the time they needed to hammer out a succession plan. The two of them could approach Mom together, and everyone would live happily ever after—them in their little codependent pod here and me, footloose and guilt-free, in Kansas City.

"Daisy, are you ready?" Mom's voice broke into my reverie just as I was returning triumphantly to Misery, er, Missouri, amid a ticker-tape parade and clouds of confetti.

"Coming," I called. I gave myself a once-over in the vanity mirror. I wore white jeans, a black sleeveless top tied with a bow at the neck, ballet flats, and my hair brushed and straightened, Mom's preferred hairstyle for me. I was as ready as I would ever be. I took my phone and my purse and walked down the stairs.

LilyRose sat in the kitchen, wearing a turquoise tutu and cartoon character T-shirt (I was surprised to realize I could now identify Doc McStuffins). Her yellow Crocs were on the wrong feet. Like me, she held her purse over her arm, although hers was in the shape of a fluffy Pomeranian with a zipper down its back. "I'm coming with you, Aunt Funny," she sing-songed. "Grandma invited me."

"Is that so?" I thought fast. This scenario was outside my skill set, but I knew from John and Zadie's stories that any time a child is involved, the time spent at a restaurant got considerably shorter. I'd planned on at least two hours for our excursion. Now, I wondered how fast Bud could talk.

Chantal appeared at the back door. "I'm sorry," she said. "My brother was supposed to take her, but his daughter has pinkeye."

Even I knew what pinkeye was. "No problem at all." I squatted down to smile at LilyRose, who held up her dog purse (purse dog?) for me to pet. "We'll have a girls' day, won't we?"

While Mom drove, I texted John, asking him for ideas on entertaining an almost four-year-old for an afternoon. "Ice cream," came his immediate reply, followed by "Build-A-Bear."

"What in the world is Build-A-Bear?" I texted back. He immediately sent back directions to a store that, to my uninitiated eyes, looked like something straight out of a nightmare.

"Trust me," read John's final text.

"Slight change of plans," I told Mom. I propped my phone on the dashboard and pointed to the map displayed. "We're going here."

Gradually, I became aware of the one-sided conversation LilyRose was holding with her purse dog.

"And then Daddy says we're going to move into our own house! It could be a castle with a moat and a drawbridge and"—she breathed, saving the best surprise for last—"our very own refrigerator!"

I glanced over at Mom. "Is that true, Mom? Are Bud and Chantal moving out?"

Mom kept her eyes on the road. She was a nervous driver, even after years of hauling flowers in the big, unwieldy delivery van. She stayed in the right-hand lane, only going up to one mile above the speed limit and often several miles under. For someone who was consistently deaf to her children's complaints, she was overly attuned to the honking of other cars, slowing down further when drivers communicated their frustrations.

"It's being discussed," she said evasively. A car behind us honked and pulled around. I felt our car decelerate in response.

In the backseat, LilyRose piped up. "Aunt Funny? Will you come to live with us in the castle? Mommy will be there, Daddy will be there, and I will be there."

I turned. LilyRose sat in her car seat, kicking her feet. She was missing a Croc, and the remaining one was hooked on her big toe. "I don't think so, honey," I said, feeling an unfamiliar squeezing sensation in my chest. "Your castle will probably be too far away from my job."

Her expectant smile turned downward, and she knitted her eyebrows together in such an eerie imitation of my mother that I instinctively drew back. "But you already have a job," she said, clearly impatient with having to explain the obvious. "You run the flower store with my Daddy."

Beside me, Mom chuckled.

An hour later, LilyRose was the proud new owner of a purple bear wearing a puffy-sleeved party dress and tiara. I carried the bear's cardboard carrier, its birth certificate (official name: Princess Sparkle Cupcake), the purse dog, and an entire season's worth of outfits because it turned out Grandma and Aunt Funny were suckers for stuffed animal couture.

We carted our purchases next door to the conveniently located ice cream shop. Mom and LilyRose snagged seats while I stood in line for two exorbitantly priced cups of mint chocolate chip for Mom and me and a small chocolate shake for my niece.

LilyRose sat between us, talking a blue streak thanks in part to Princess Sparkle Cupcake being an excellent listener and in part to her shake, which apparently had enough sugar in it to fuel a Wonka factory. Both bear and child sported chocolate smudges around their mouths. I reached over with a napkin, but Mom batted my hand away.

"It'll only spread it around and make it worse," she said, smiling fondly at her grandchild. "Wait 'til she conks out on the way home. That's when you pull out the Handi Wipes."

"Got it." I saluted with my plastic spoon.

"So…" Mom stirred her ice cream casually. Too casually. "What's this all about then?"

"Wh-what do you mean?" I asked, averting my eyes. "Can't a girl take her mother out for an afternoon of bear-related shopping?"

Mom stabbed her spoon into her ice cream. "Oh, come on. You've never invited me out for lunch in your life. I'm not dense, Daisy. What's going on?"

Of course, she would catch on. It had been absurd to think she wouldn't. "Game recognizes game," as John would say. And my mother was the reigning queen of mind games.

Taking a breath, I told her everything: Dad was ready to step down. Bud was ready to step up. I was ready to step out, and we all needed her to step back.

"Dad and Bud are at home right now, planning their strategy to talk to you about all of this." I pushed my cup away, glancing over at LilyRose, who was busy singing a song and rocking her bear. She caught my eye and put a finger to her lips. "She's sleeping," she whispered, planting a chocolatey kiss on Princess Sparkle Cupcake's tiara. I gave her a thumbs-up and turned back to Mom, who looked thunderous.

"If this is how you all feel, why didn't anyone tell me?" she demanded. "Why sneak around?"

"Are you kidding?" I exploded, earning another shush from LilyRose. "All we've done is try to talk to you. You don't listen. You're so focused on your plans that you tune out anything anyone else has to say."

"I do not," Mom said, piqued. "I'm very open-minded."

"Mom, you're as open as a bank vault. Why do you think I stopped coming to visit?"

The people at the next table stared with blatant curiosity. LilyRose had stopped rocking her bear and was listening intently, her head swiveling back and forth between us.

I continued, fighting to keep my voice down. "I don't visit because you refuse to accept that I'm different. I want to run my own business—not yours. I don't even like flowers. Meanwhile, all Bud does is try to please you, and you refuse to recognize any of his efforts." My hands rose off the table of their own volition. I clenched them in frustration. "You smother us with your expectations. You need to stop. You need to let both of us go."

Mom's face, so stern a moment ago, crumpled. Her lower lip trembled. Wordlessly, she snatched a napkin from the table dispenser and pressed it under her glasses to her eyes.

I stared in amazement and dismay. My mother was crying. I'd made her cry. This was worse than any blast-off moment.

Still clutching her bear, LilyRose slid off her seat and climbed into her grandma's lap. "It's okay," she said, her small hand patting Mom's shaking shoulder. "Shh... shh..." She shot me a look so arch, it would have made my mother proud.

Distract her, Bud said. *Keep her spirits up. Bring her home in a good mood.*

Fail, fail, and fail. Great job, Cactus Butt.

We drove home in silence. As predicted, LilyRose fell asleep almost immediately, dog purse and bear clutched to her chest.

At the house, I transferred LilyRose to her room while Mom carried in our purchases. Dad and Bud were still locked in the family room, their voices low, words unintelligible.

I took a moment in my room, smoothing my hair and gathering my courage. I had to fix this. For Bud. For my family.

For myself.

I found Mom sitting at the kitchen table. "Want some company?"

She shrugged. "Up to you. I wouldn't want to *smother* you."

I set out two mugs with English Breakfast and waited for the water to boil. Only after we were both sitting with our tea did I speak.

"I'm sorry I upset you." I reached over and took her hand. "Not sorry I said it, but how I said it."

This was uncharted territory. I usually planned out what I would say, thought it through, workshopped the introduction of difficult topics. In this conversation, at this moment, I was operating without a net, the most like my brother I'd ever been.

Mom took a sip of tea, avoiding eye contact. She didn't, however, release my hand. "All I want is for my family to stay together," she said, her voice shaking slightly. "I don't understand why that's so repugnant to you."

"It's not," I said, meaning it. "I've enjoyed being home this week. Well, mostly," I amended. "I didn't realize how much I missed you until I came back. But," I continued, gathering courage, "you have to allow that being a family doesn't necessarily mean wanting the same things. I'm different." I took a breath and dove (no net). "I'm always going to be the cactus in this garden of flowers."

"What?" she asked, startled.

"Don't you remember?" I pulled my hand away and toyed with the string on my tea bag. "You told a customer that I was the cactus in a bed of flowers."

"When did I—Oh, honey." She reached out and reclaimed my hand. "Is that what you think? That you don't belong in this family?"

Tears pricked my eyes. I pressed my tongue to the roof of my mouth to stop them. A napkin appeared (how *did* she do that?) and dabbed at my eyes.

Mom scooted in her chair until she was close enough to hug

me. "Oh, sweetie. I'm so sorry. Have you been holding onto that all these years?"

I nodded against the cabbage rose print of her blouse, sniffling.

We stayed that way, her rocking me, humming a meandering tune that bore a suspicious resemblance to the theme song to *Jeopardy!* Eventually, I drew back, hiccupping, and took a sip of tea.

Mom leaned forward, refusing to abandon proximity. "Do you know why I called you a cactus, Daisy?" she asked.

"Because I'm stubborn and prickly?"

She took my chin in her hand, forcing eye contact. "A cactus symbolizes endurance, resilience, and strength," she said, her eyes bright with tears. "You've always been my strong one. You know who you are, you believe in yourself, and you fight for everything you want." She took a deep breath. "I thought if I tried hard enough, I could convince you that what you wanted was to be here, with us." She paused. "I was wrong, and I'm sorry. Just because we're a family does not mean we have to be carbon copies of each other. Families should be allowed to bloom and grow. Even the cactus," she said, gently booping me on the nose.

"Ruth?" Dad's voice called, accompanied by the *screech* of the family room door. "Can Bud and I speak to you?"

I smiled, grateful for Dad's perfect timing. I had so much to consider, to mull over.

So much to un- and re-learn.

I found my voice. "You better go," I said. "They want to talk to you about the future."

"I guess I better go face the music." A small smile played across her lips. "But I might make them dance for it a little first."

"Go easy," I said. "Don't make them sweat too long."

"I promise nothing." Mom reached out and squeezed my hand. "And Daisy?" She patted my shoulder, then leaned down and pressed her cheek to mine. "I love you."

"I love you too," I said, reaching up to give her a one-armed hug.

I watched her go, smoothing down her shirt and touching her hair as she went. It was done. The store would go to Bud. Dad would recover. I was free. And I was, for the first time in my life, proud to be a cactus.

LilyRose woke from her nap and came downstairs, grumpy and hungry from her post-sugar crash. Chantal was in her studio, and Bud, Mom, and Dad were still sequestered away. I opened the pantry, searching for a snack for my niece. She pointed at a box of macaroni and cheese. "Princess Sparkle Cupcake likes blue box mac and cheese."

"Seeing as it's a royal request…" I smiled. "Come on, you can help me."

LilyRose kept up a steady stream of conversation through dinner. After years of eating alone, relaxing and listening to someone else's thoughts was a nice change.

Bud appeared as I finished clearing the dishes, his expression giving nothing away. "Sweetheart, why don't you go watch *Wheel* with GrandPop and Grandma? Aunt Daisy and I are going out for a while."

"Don't wait up," he called over his shoulder to our parents while pulling me toward the door.

Like spies on a covert operation, we ran down the steps to his car. He threw Arlene into reverse almost before my door was closed. I fell back against the seat as he roared down the alleyway, turning on the lights as we joined the main flow of traffic.

"Where are we going?" I asked, catching my breath.

"Out," he said simply. "We're celebrating."

"Does that mean what I think it means?"

Bud's grin grew wider. "You're looking at the new manager of Blooms by Bert."

"Yes!" I shrieked, hugging my brother with all my might. "You did it!"

"*We* did it," he said, hugging me back.

"No, Buddy." I released him and looked him straight in the eye. "*You* did it. You and Chantal. You saved the store." *And you saved us.* "Now," I said, grabbing his arm, "let's go celebrate."

We pulled into the parking lot of the Old Tavern Bar & Grill. Music blasted out from the upstairs patio, and he air-guitared along with it.

"Hey," I said as we crossed the parking lot, "before we start the celebration, I wanted to say again how sorry I am that I haven't been here when you needed me."

"But you're here now." He raised his voice to be heard over the music. "You came home when we needed you most. When I needed you. You helped make this happen. What came before doesn't matter. You're family. Family forgives and accepts. Family doesn't cut each other off."

My eyes watered. My sweet, goofy, big-hearted brother was more generous than I'd given him credit for. Chantal was right. Bud was 100% untapped potential.

I wiped my eyes and punched him in the shoulder to cover the moment. "Okay, but if you think I've forgotten that you used to ransom my My Little Ponies for Oreos…"

"Applejack knows what she did." He laughed, pushing the door open. "After you."

The bar was loud and packed. I claimed a sticky high-top table in the far corner of the room, feeling a moment of homesickness for Pavel's. Bud went to the bar and returned with six beers: two bottles under each arm and one in each fist. "Figured this would tide us over for a while." He handed one to me and raised his own in a toast.

I toasted back. "Here's to you, Buddy. And to Chantal and

LilyRose. To making something new, something special." Embarrassingly, my eyes threatened to water again.

We clinked glasses. "And to my big sis"—Bud cleared his throat as if presenting to a large crowd—"who likes to act tough, but underneath her ice-queen persona is secretly Aunt Funny." He clinked my glass. "I mean it. I know this isn't your favorite place to be."

"It's not that I don't like it," I said. "I always wanted different things. You, Dad, Mom, you all knew what you wanted. I always wanted…" I searched for the right word. "More. Not more, like more things or money, but I wanted to do more than Mom and Dad thought I could do." I paused. "I guess you know what I mean."

"Oh, you think so?" Bud raised a sarcastic eyebrow. "But you're right and wrong, Sis. I didn't want more, not for a long time. Until I met Chantal. And became a dad. That's when I realized I could be more. People were counting on me to be more." He spread his hands wide, making a joke. "I mean, who wouldn't want more of me?"

A voice piped up behind me. "As I live and breathe, it's the Greene siblings!" I twisted in my seat to find Jeremy at my side.

"Jer Bear!" Bud high-fived his friend. "Who let you out on a school night?"

Jeremy pointed across the room to the noisy group in the corner, all wearing matching cycling jerseys. "Instructor's night out. We're team building."

"Same," Bud said, recounting his good news while I sipped my drink, basking in the glow of my brother's happiness.

"Well, cheers to you both," Jeremy said, helping himself to one of Bud's beers. We clinked our bottles together. "To getting what you want out of life."

As if in agreement, the music changed to a rowdy up-tempo song. A cheer rose from the crowd.

"I love this song." Jeremy reached for my hand. "Let's dance."

"Oh no," I said laughing. "You're not getting me out there."

"C'mon! I've got some sweet, sweet moves to show off." Jeremy demonstrated a few dance steps. "See? Flawless. It'll be fun." Before I could object, he ushered me to the metal stairs leading to the rooftop dance floor.

Jeremy pushed his way through the crowd, navigating us to the epicenter, where lines of people stomped their feet in rhythm and executed a complicated set of moves.

"Watch!" Jeremy hollered, dropping my hand. I watched in amazement as he stomped, clapped, dipped, and spun and somehow ended up facing me as the movements repeated. Realizing it was either join in or get stepped on, I followed the crowd's stomping, clapping, and dipping. I looked over my shoulder at Jeremy, who nodded encouragingly.

"Great job!" he called.

I beamed. *This is what having fun feels like.* I wondered when I'd stopped having any. I remembered that long ago road trip and how I'd sung along with the radio. I never sang with anyone else. I'd never considered it before, but maybe only Jeremy brought out that side of me.

I didn't want the song to end, and when it did, I joined the other line dancers in calling for more. The next song was even faster. Jeremy seemed to know all the steps, and I was determined to keep up with him.

"I bet you don't do this back in your real life," he teased.

"Oh you think you know me so well," I retorted, breaking into a cross-rock-side-rock-quarter-turn sequence before rejoining the line. I laughed at his dumfounded expression. "I'll have you know that one of my clients always hosts a country music-themed holiday party for her employees. I wouldn't be a very good event planner if I didn't study up on the popular dances."

"You are full of surprises, Daisy Greene." Jeremy stopped dancing and stepped closer, his eyes intently fixed on me. A drop of sweat traveled along his cheek. I reached up and traced its path with my thumb.

"So are you." I didn't know exactly what I was going to say; I only knew I needed to say it. "Jeremy, I—"

"Get off the floor!" An irritated voice shouted as the line dancers spun past us. Surprised, I took a quick sidestep and crashed into someone. Beer splashed across my feet.

"I'm so sorry." I gasped, instinctively clutching the unfamiliar arm to steady myself.

Strike that. A familiar arm. I looked up, startled. "Victor?"

"Daisy?"

"Hey!" My shoes squelched as we moved away from the dancers. I turned to Jeremy who followed behind us. "Jeremy, this is Victor. We met at the wedding expo."

"Hey, man." Jeremy and Victor shook hands without warmth.

Jeremy faced me, and I realized that he had taken a direct hit from Victor's beer. He motioned to his sodden cycling jersey. "I'm going to go see if one of the other instructors has an extra shirt." He glanced at Victor, then back to me, lowering his voice. "You want to come with me?"

"No, no, I'll be fine. Just hurry back." I wanted to dance some more. I wanted to know what I'd been about to say.

With a reluctant glance, Jeremy turned and made his way to the stairs. I watched him go, then turned back to Victor, happy to see my friend.

"I am so sorry about your drink. Let me buy you another."

He regarded the little that remained of his beer. His eyes seemed to have difficulty focusing. "S'okay. I've probably had enough anyway."

"What are you doing here?"

Victor gestured loosely at the stage. "Checking out the music. I'm always on the lookout for the next great wedding band."

"Always working," I joked. "Speaking of work, my brother is

downstairs. I'd love for you to meet him." A thought struck me and I looked around. "Are you here alone? Is Vicki here?"

Victor's expression darkened. He finished the dregs of his drink in one long swallow and set the empty mug on a nearby table. "No, she couldn't make it tonight," he said just as the music ended.

The lead singer, a skinny redhead with long hair and a handlebar mustache, waved to the crowd, promising the band would return in fifteen minutes. He was replaced on stage by a surly-looking man in motorcycle chaps and a bandanna, who sat at the piano and ran his fingers over the keys in a confident glissando. His voice poured out like melted butter over the crowd as he crooned the opening lines of "The Captain of Her Heart."

"Let's dance." Victor took my hand and weaved his way onto the dance floor. He pulled me close, fingers resting heavily on the small of my back.

Something felt off. I took a tactful step backward, creating space between us. At close range, I saw Victor's red-rimmed eyes, the stern set of his jaw. He wobbled slightly as we turned, and I wondered how many drinks he'd had before the one I'd spilled.

"Hey," I said, trying to lighten the mood. "This guy is good. You should get his number—" I broke off as Victor crushed his mouth to mine.

I froze at the unexpected contact, my eyes wide. Over Victor's shoulder I saw Jeremy approaching, his expression at first shocked and then... what? Disappointed? Upset?

Jeremy turned and vanished into the crowd. I pushed Victor away.

"Daisy!" Victor called after me, swaying slightly, his focus shifting between me and the floor. "Daisy, I'm sorry!"

Leaving him, I elbowed through the dancers and raced down the stairs, past Bud, and out into the parking lot.

"Jeremy?" My eyes swept across the cars for a glimpse of Jeremy's white jersey against the darkening sky.

But he was gone.

Chapter Twenty

"Good morning, sunshine," my brother greeted me. Showered and dressed for work, he sipped his coffee as he pointedly inspected my pajamas and bedhead. LilyRose sat at the kitchen table, eating a bowl of yogurt and sliced fruit.

"Sh'up," I snapped, checking my phone for the hundredth time before flipping it over in frustration and hip-checking Bud out of the way of the coffee pot. I'd been up half the night, staring at my phone, willing Jeremy to answer my texts.

"Grandmaaaa," LilyRose called, "Aunt Funny said a bad word!"

"Watch your mouth around my grandchild!" Mom's voice floated in from the other room, accompanied by the sounds of the Weather Channel.

Bud moved to the table and helped his daughter wipe her mouth. "Good morning to you, Bud," he said, adopting a high-pitched nasal voice, his impression of me. "And LilyRose, my favorite niece! I'm sorry to be so grumpy on such a beautiful morning." When I didn't laugh, he dropped the falsetto. "What's the matter, Cactus Butt? Something wrong at Events Fartistry?"

"Grandmaaaaaaa," LilyRose sang as she climbed down from

the table and carried her bowl to the sink. "Daddy's saying potty words!"

Mom's admonitions were lost as Chantal swept in, dressed in a green maxi dress. She wore full makeup and gold chandelier earrings that brushed her shoulders. Her hands, customarily tinged with paint, chlorophyll and soil, were bare and scrubbed clean. She looked incredible.

LilyRose broke the silence as she ran to hug her mother around the waist. "Mommy, you look like a princess," she said, her face pressed into the folds of Chantal's dress.

"My queen." Bud moved to his girlfriend's side and carefully kissed her lipsticked mouth. Chantal smiled, cupping her hand to his cheek. He caught her hand and turned it over, kissing her palm. "Good luck today," he said, brushing his lips against her cheek. "Not that you need it. You're going to knock 'em dead."

"Thank you," she murmured, giving him a look so tender and intimate that I felt guilty for witnessing it. "And you." Chantal squatted down to hug her daughter. "You be good for Grandma and GrandPop. I love you."

She straightened and was out the door before I could add my compliment or ask what she didn't need luck for and who "they" were.

Bud hoisted LilyRose into his arms as they stood at the back door and waved.

"You really punched above your weight with her," I told him.

Other people might have been offended by such a remark. My brother looked pleased that I'd noticed. "Riiiiight? I mean, come on. She's amazing." He rubbed noses with LilyRose. "Isn't Mommy gorgeous? And smart?" His eyes went dreamy as he continued, "And artistic and brilliant and funny and caring."

"Then I suggest you make things official soon and propose." Mom entered the kitchen, Dad trailing behind with the help of his walker. She went to the fridge, opened it, and fished out a yogurt cup.

"Ease up, Ma." Bud groaned. "We're taking things at our own pace." LilyRose struggled to be released, sliding from his arms and running to her grandmother's side.

Mom held out the yogurt to Dad, who looked at her blankly before indicating the walker. She sighed and stuck the cup into his shirt pocket, along with a spoon from the silverware drawer. "If you ask me—"

"Which I didn't," Bud reminded her.

Mom continued as if she hadn't heard him. "Your pace is a bit…" She paused and put her hands over LilyRose's ears. "Out of order. You should marry that woman before she finds someone ready to commit." She took her hands away and smiled down at her granddaughter. "Come on, sweetheart. Let's go help GrandPop back into bed. I bet he'd like you to read to him while he has his snack."

"Good talk, Ma. Thanks!" Bud called at her retreating back. He rolled his eyes at me. "See what you'll be missing when you leave? How could you possibly want to miss all this fun, lighthearted banter?" He picked up his coffee cup and headed upstairs, calling, "Be ready in an hour. I've got a surprise for you."

I sat on my bed in my underwear, wet hair wrapped in a towel, staring at the long list of texts I'd sent to Jeremy.

From the dance floor: *Where did you go? Let's talk.*

In the car, as Bud drove us home: *Hi again. Can we talk?*

While brushing my teeth: *Please call me.*

Immediately after: *Sorry for all the messages.*

This morning: *Are you free for coffee today?*

"Come on, three dots," I whispered. "Where are you?" I imagined my messages stacking up like planes over Denver International Airport, the notifications buzzing like an insistent finger poking him in the arm.

I turned my phone face down, disgusted with myself and the situation.

Why had Victor kissed me? I didn't believe for a second that he was interested in me. It was more likely that I'd gotten caught between whatever was going on between him and Vicki at just the wrong moment. Which was too bad for all of us.

The real mystery was Jeremy. Why had he fled without giving me a chance to explain?

Was he angry? Annoyed? Or... my mind wandered to another possibility... jealous?

Heart pounding, I rechecked my texts. No response. But as I watched, three dots appeared. I held my breath. The dots pulsed, then vanished, then reappeared.

"Come on, come on," I whispered.

They vanished.

Sighing, I threw my phone down on the bed, where it bounced off and landed in Great-Aunt Marge's stupid wastebasket.

In just over twenty-four hours, I would be on a plane to Kansas City, back to my quiet condo and Event Fart—er—Artistry. Back to the world I knew and people who made sense to me. To Fiona and her backbreaking workplace. To John and our new partnership. To Eunice and Martin and even Tavia. I'd done what I'd come to do. I'd helped my brother, reconnected with my parents, met my niece and (if Mom got her wish) future sister-in-law. I didn't need another complication to upset the precarious balance I'd established in my family's new status quo.

I retrieved my phone and stuffed it into my purse. I didn't like leaving questions unanswered or loose ends dangling. It felt messy and out of character but so be it. I had only a little time left until I needed to be ready to go. I wouldn't waste it agonizing over something that was never going to happen.

. . .

Bud parked Arlene next to Chantal's Prius. "Hang on a sec." He jumped from the car. "I need to check something."

I watched as he unlocked the back door and poked his head inside. *Why is the store closed on a Friday?* I wondered. After a moment, he motioned for us to follow him.

I helped LilyRose out of the car, juggling all the items she'd deemed necessary for the five-minute trip: her purse dog, Princess Sparkle Cupcake, a plastic baggie of crackers, a travel cup emblazoned with turquoise and orange fish, and a battered copy of *Harry the Dirty Dog*.

"I'll be right back," Bud said in that same hushed voice as we entered, his footsteps receding down the hall.

The lights were on in the empty workroom. As I entered, I banged my hip against a table, startled to see that the room had been completely reconfigured. The long wooden table that normally bisected the space was pushed to one side, and several large, unframed canvases were propped up. Bold, jewel-toned abstracts swooped and zagged across the canvases, the paint thick and wet-looking in spots. I stepped closer, admiring the painting closest to me, jade green whorls with black slashes like branches, spots of red, blue, and yellow peeking out. It reminded me of my parrot chair. I found a signature in the bottom right corner: Chantal Rose Holt.

Of course. These were Chantal's paintings.

But what were they doing here?

Bud returned. "Okay," he said, voice back to normal. "We can go in. She's finished."

"Finished with what?" I asked, dropping LilyRose's things on the workbench and following Bud, who held his daughter's hand as they skipped into the showroom. "What's going on?"

I caught up with my brother and niece as Chantal and Agnes appeared.

"Ta-da!" Agnes called, throwing plant food packets in the air like confetti at a wedding.

"We wanted it to be a surprise." Chantal moved between Bud

and LilyRose, putting her arms around them. They were all smiling.

Bud kissed her head, beaming with pride. "Chantal is a finalist for a new reality show about flower arranging. Today was her video interview."

I gawped, speechless. Agnes came over and put her arm around me. She wore a very un-Agnes bright green dress with a high ruffled neck and long sheer sleeves. Her usually wild gray hair was smoothed and pinned back. She'd swapped out her regular Edna Mode-style glasses for a pair of stylish gold frames.

"Aunt Agnes, you were in on this?"

She laughed, a throaty guffaw. "Sure, honey. After my Tic Tacs went virile"—*Tik-Toks, viral*, I translated mentally—"Chantal thought including me would add a little extra pizzazz." She swept out one gauzy arm. "I was like a *The Price Is Right* model," she cackled. "Come see for yourself."

Dazed, I followed her around the store that had been magically transformed into a riot of color and flowers. Massive arrangements in a variety of colors and styles were placed around the room, each paired with one of Chantal's original artworks, which served as both backdrop and companion piece. Gone were the silk flowers, and the coffee bar and conference area had been relocated near the front door. It was the sights and smells of my childhood, but in a new and unexpected way that made me see it—really *see* it—for the first time. The reach-in cooler was full of fresh blooms and, when I opened the door, the smell created a heady time-travel effect. I was five, ten, thirteen years old, spending afternoons and weekends reaching my gloved hand into the cooler, delivering single stems or pre-wrapped bouquets to customers, and pulling out boutonnieres and corsages for prom. I was seventeen, arguing about Career Day and the right to live my life. I was twenty-eight and tired of defending myself, of explaining that owning a flower shop wasn't a gift I wanted. I was thirty-two, standing in the doorway with my brother, listening to his plans to save the business.

I was all the Daisys I'd ever been, all at once, and I felt a moment of gratitude to the flowers whose scents had reminded me.

"Wow." I spun slowly, taking it all in, coming to rest on the people who were my family. "You really did it. You saved the store." I threw my arms around my brother, squeezing him fiercely.

"*We* did it," Bud said into my hair. He pulled Chantal and LilyRose into the hug. Agnes didn't wait for an invitation, throwing her stringy arms around all of us.

"This is wonderful," I said when we finally broke apart. My eyes were watering, and my nose was running, both from allergies and from crying. I didn't care. I locked eyes with Chantal and smiled.

"You're going to bake that show," I told her, not minding that all my "m's" sounded like "b's" again. I turned to Bud. "And you're going to bake the store a huge success." To Agnes, I said, "And you're going to be an eb-ployee with an actual salary."

"You sound like Dorothy in the Emerald City," LilyRose told me. I smiled and knelt to hug her. "But with a cold."

"Don't start saying your goodbyes just yet," Bud joked, his eyes suspiciously shiny. He noogied me affectionately. "We've still got you for one more day."

My last night turned into a party. Bud and I dragged Chantal's worktable down from her studio, hosing it off and covering the paint splotches with an old chintz tablecloth inherited from some long-forgotten relative's linen cupboard. I pulled folding chairs from the storage area in the front hallway, and Chantal and LilyRose hung a strand of Christmas lights between two scrub oaks. Bud lugged Dad's armchair outside, accompanied by much sweating and swearing, and placed it at the head of the table.

I texted Jeremy, inviting him to the party, but the text remained unopened.

The evening air held only the slightest hint of mountain breeze; summer was coming. Mom helped Dad down the back stairs. It was his first outing since coming home from the hospital. LilyRose tucked her Frozen blanket around his legs once he was seated.

Bud started the toasts. "To Bloomin' Bert!" We raised our glasses of sparkling grape juice (since Bud's vodka suggestion had been shot down). "May you enjoy the many offerings of semi-retirement."

"Hear, hear," we chorused.

"To Bud and Chantal," I added. "And their future success."

We'd gotten word just before dinner that Chantal had been selected as a contestant and would begin filming the following week. Although details were under wraps, we decided to throw a party at the store after the show's debut.

"To Aunt Funny," LilyRose piped in.

"To my family." Dad smiled. "And remembering that the freedom to be themselves is the greatest gift a parent can give their children."

"Besides a foot spa," Bud called.

All heads turned to Mom, who remained strangely quiet, her glass in her hand but still resting on the table.

"Ruth, would you like to say anything?" Dad asked.

She raised her glass, her eyes sweeping across the table and coming to rest on Bud and me. "To new beginnings."

Despite my argument that I could arrange a ride, we arrived at Denver International Airport at noon on Saturday—Mom, Dad, Bud, LilyRose, and I crammed into the delivery van. Chantal and Agnes had stayed back to mind the store.

"No, no, no," I argued as Bud started to turn into the short-term parking lot. "You've got to deliver the arrangements for the Montroses' fiftieth-anniversary dinner. You don't have time to park."

Bud pulled into the passenger drop-off lane and parked next to a "No Parking" sign. He joined me in the struggle to free my suitcase, which had become inexplicably tangled in a mass of electrical cords, floral wire, and drop cloths. By the time he successfully liberated it, my suitcase was covered in pollen. I sneezed as he swung it out.

"One for the road," he joked, joining Mom and Dad at the curb.

LilyRose came first, offering her hand. "It was nice meeting you, Aunt Funny," she said gravely.

"You too, sweetheart. Take care of Mommy, Daddy, Grandpoop and Grandma for me."

Dad was next. "Don't work too hard," we said simultaneously.

I turned to Mom. "Be good."

"Let me know the minute you land," she said, enveloping me in a crushing hug.

I booped her on the nose. "I promise."

Mom, Dad, and LilyRose climbed back in the car while my brother and I stood awkwardly, each waiting for the other to start. Bud rocked back and forth on his heels, putting his hands in his pockets and then taking them out.

There was so much I wanted to say—thank you, good luck, I love you—but the words jammed in my throat like cars during rush hour.

Bud broke the silence. "Safe trip back to Misery, Sis." His hug lifted me off my feet, a twin to the one he'd welcomed me with ten days ago. "I hate goodbyes."

I hugged him back. "I'm going to miss you most of all, Scarecrow," I said, pressing my forehead to his. "You're going to be great. Team Greene forever."

"You know it."

The honking behind us alerted us to the car waiting for our spot. Making sure Mom wasn't looking, Bud hastened to the driver's side, making a rude gesture to the impatient driver on his way. I stepped onto the curb with my luggage, waving as the van pulled out into traffic. I watched until it disappeared, then turned and walked inside.

In the span of two weeks, I'd gotten everything I ever wanted, and now I was going home.

Why wasn't I happier?

Chapter Twenty-One

After nearly two weeks of constant commotion, the silence in my apartment was deafening. The absence of noise created an irritating, high-pitched whine in my ears.

"Alexa, play classical music," I called.

Soft piano music filled the space, taking my tinnitus with it.

Abandoning my luggage by the door, I kicked off my shoes and prowled the condo, seeing it with fresh eyes. Everything was as I'd left it: spotlessly clean, with nothing to trip over, step on, or run into. I luxuriated in knowing my bare feet wouldn't encounter one of LilyRose's rogue Duplo pieces. I ran my hand over the quartz countertop and shivered. Had it always been so cold in here? Even though it was sunny outside, the room seemed dark and chilly. I opened the thermostat app and nudged the temperature up. Moving to the living area, I slid the panel curtains to one side, allowing the mid-afternoon sun to stream in.

Between music and sunlight, the space felt slightly warmer. Friendlier. More alive.

My phone vibrated on the counter: *Smother calling*.

"Hi, Mom."

"Daisy, it's your mother. I thought you were going to call when you got home."

I dropped onto the sectional sofa, sending a puff of dust motes into the air. They glittered in the sunlight. "You didn't give me a chance. I just walked in the door."

She continued, either accepting or ignoring my response, "Well, it's a fine mess you've left us with. Do you know that Chantal is leaving next week to film that show? And Bud is talking about taking night classes at Metro. Who is going to watch the shop while they're off gallivanting about, I'd like to know?"

I rolled my eyes and checked the time on my phone. Three and a half hours since I'd left Denver.

"Mom, we talked about this. Chantal is only flying out to do some prep work for a few days. Most episodes will be filmed during summer break while LilyRose is at day camp with her cousins." I heard Mom's heavy sigh and imagined her sitting in the kitchen, drumming her fingers against a mug of tea. "Bud's classes are online, so he'll take them in the office while Aunt Agnes handles any walk-in traffic. And Jeremy"—I was proud at how casually I said his name—"is working with Dad. There's nothing for you to worry about."

That was the problem, I realized. There was nothing for Mom to worry about. I made the blast-off motion to the empty room.

"This would be so much easier if you were still here," she said, sounding sullen.

"My big event is coming up. I couldn't stay away and keep my job."

"You could have a perfectly good job here."

The woman was tenacious, I'd give her that.

LilyRose broke in from the extension. "Grandma! GrandPop needs you!"

Thank you, sweet girl. Aunt Funny owes you one.

"Oh dear." Mom's voice brightened. *Here she comes to save the day*, I thought to myself, smiling. "I have to go. I'll talk to you later. Thank you. Goodbye."

"Bye, Mom," I called as she hung up. In the sudden silence, I whispered, "I miss you."

I typed out a quick text to my brother confirming my arrival. I added a plane emoji signifying Mom's impending freakout.

His reply came quickly: *On it. Enjoy Misery.* He ended his missive with a string of cactus emojis.

"I'm home," I said into the silence, testing it to see if it felt real. I closed my eyes and tried to picture the space around me. Instead, my mind drifted 600 miles away, envisioning Mom and Dad in the family room, Bud at the store, and Chantal packing for her new adventure. I pictured LilyRose curled up on her bed, reading *Hansel & Gretel* to Princess Sparkle Cupcake, explaining the benefits of edible building materials.

From there, my thoughts slid sideways to Jeremy… how was he?

I'd texted him one last time before boarding the plane: *I'm sorry.*

He never responded.

I had to accept that it was too late. Whatever "it" might have had the potential to be, "it" was over. And anyway, it didn't matter. I was here and he was there. He had a son and responsibilities. I was alone, responsible for only myself once again. *It's probably better this way*. Event Artistry and Ground Floor needed my full attention again. I didn't have time for any distractions, potential or otherwise.

I pulled up the message, ready to delete the whole embarrassing thread, when a bubble and three dots appeared.

Jeremy was writing back.

I held my breath.

With a *blip* his message arrived: *I'm sorry for not writing back sooner. I took Ethan to the mountains for a couple of days. When are you coming back?*

It wasn't an overwhelming declaration of love, but it also

wasn't a dismissal. Whatever door I'd thought closed between us was still open a crack. Forgetting everything I'd told myself moments ago, I wrote back: *Maybe in the fall?*

As much as I wanted to, I couldn't tell him about the reality series. We'd all signed nondisclosure forms forbidding discussion until the network officially began promoting the show and its contestants. "Mum's the word," Dad had said, chuckling at his pun.

Let me know. I'd love to meet up, he responded.

Me too.

A big smiley face appeared. I sent back two smiles and waited.

Nothing.

What happened? Was a double smiley face too much? Had I scared him off? Argh, see, this is why I didn't need distractions.

My phone buzzed again, and I jabbed at the screen, hoping to see his reply.

It was John: *Welcome home. Lots to catch up on. Call me.*

Not now, I thought, dismissing his message. *I'm busy.*

He sent another text: *Don't pretend you're not looking at your phone.*

I tossed it away onto the couch like a criminal caught red-handed. Phone? What phone?

I wasn't ready to talk to John yet. My body might be here, but my heart and head were still distracted by Denver.

Yawning, I curled up on the couch and pulled the soft white throw blanket over my legs. "There's no place like home," I murmured, closing my eyes.

I awoke to the sound of my suitcase toppling over. I sat straight up, pushing the hair out of my eyes with my hand. "Who's there?"

I'd slept long enough for the sun to set. The room was dark

despite the open blinds. I could see a figure frozen in the doorway, backlit in a wedge of light from the hallway.

"Hello?" I called.

A small growling shape darted into the apartment, heading straight for me. Instinctively, I threw the blanket from my lap over it. It stopped moving but continued to bark at my feet, giving the appearance of a tiny, annoyed ghost.

The light at the front door switched on, and I saw Mrs. Rudnicki, the red and gold football helmet keychain dangling from her fist.

"Hello, dearie," she called as though we were best friends, and it was perfectly natural for her to break into my apartment for a quick chat. "Precious and I brought over your mail." She held up a slim packet. From under the blanket, Precious growled, twisting back and forth.

"Oh, um, thank you." I gave the chenille-covered menace a wide berth. Mrs. Rudnicki looked up at me as I took the letters from her, blinking rapidly.

"Thank you for collecting my mail." I prompted. No response. I tried again. "I'm home now. So I'll take my key back."

She held it out, clearly reluctant to give it up. "But what if there's an emergency?" At her feet, Precious had bested his foe and was contentedly chewing the offending fabric into submission. My favorite blanket would never be the same.

"That's very kind of you," I said, forcing my voice to remain light and unconcerned. I would not be terrorized by a nosy neighbor and her tiny minion. "As you can see, it's only me here. So there won't be any emergencies." I stepped back, easing the door shut as I talked. "Thank you again, Mrs. Rudnicki, and Precious, for keeping my mail." *And probably reading it.* "If you'll excuse me, I've had a long day of traveling, and I'm exhausted. I really appreciate it, goodnight." I said in a single breath as I shut the door and secured the deadbolt.

I was alone again in my quiet house. The piano music had

given way to violins on my playlist, and the ringing in my ears returned. "Alexa, stop." The music disappeared, and it occurred to me for the first time that I couldn't hear my clock ticking.

The cartoon cat's eyes regarded me slyly as I replaced its batteries. The comforting *ticktock* returned, accompanied by a low growl. I scanned the room, looking for the Return of Precious, before realizing it was my stomach. I was starving.

There was very little in the refrigerator—some expired milk and a sludgy bag of lettuce. Discovering an unopened bag of wheat crackers in the pantry, I snacked as I unpacked my suitcase and started a load of laundry. The comforting *shush, shush* joined the *ticktock*, making me feel less lonely.

I spent the next few hours going through work messages, slowly constructing a timeline of activities during my absence, noting, with some concern, the low numbers of RSVPs received for the exhibit opening. I paused occasionally (okay, frequently) to check my phone for new messages from Jeremy, but none came.

By 10 p.m., I was yawning, the crackers were gone, and my stomach felt uncomfortably heavy. I half-heartedly washed my face, brushed my teeth, crawled under the covers, and slept until the sun streamed across my face, and it was morning again.

Reacquainting myself with the shape of life in Kansas City proved more challenging than I anticipated.

I woke late the next morning discombobulated by the silence, expecting to hear voices shouting, laughing, talking over one another. I ate breakfast, a lone vanilla yogurt only a few days past its expiration date and watched an episode of Mom's favorite baking show.

In the afternoon, I walked to the corner market with my small metal cart and reusable bags and loaded up on food for one. In addition to my regular list, I added a ready-made vegetarian lasagna from the freezer section, a new box of green tea, and, after a moment's hesitation, a box of English Breakfast. Moose Tracks ice cream and Goldfish crackers rounded out the list as I headed to the checkout lane. I skipped the wine and liquor section.

Waiting for the elevator in the lobby of my building, I perused a poster announcing an upcoming pet adoption event. Great. More Preciouses to avoid. It was a good thing I was going to be busy.

I unpacked my groceries, heated up the lasagna, and spent the evening on the couch wrapped in my now clean—but irrevocably chewed—blanket, watching Game Show Network reruns. I knew I should work but couldn't find the motivation.

To allay my guilt, I called John and asked him to catch me up.

"We have a site visit at ten and a staff meeting in the afternoon. I'm sending the latest outline." I could hear him typing as he spoke. A moment later, a notification lit up my screen.

I settled back, listening as he continued the checklist. I'd missed this.

"And we need to talk about Ground Floor's plan B." He paused. "I've got a lead on a new space I think we should look at. But I need to know, are you still in this, or—hang on." He covered the phone, muffling his and Zadie's conversation. "Gotta go," he said. "Zadie needs me to run out for French fries and ice cream. Glad you're home. See you."

I called home next. After a dozen rings, Dad answered.

"Blooms by Bert, this is—er, I mean—Hello?"

"Hi Dad."

"Well, hello, Petal." He sounded pleased. "How are you?"

"I'm good. How are you? I can't believe Mom let you get up to answer the phone."

He laughed. "I was just sitting in bed doing the crossword. Everyone else is at the park. Jeremy stopped by with his son. They were going pedal boating and invited your brother and LilyRose. Your mother decided to tag along."

"Mom did?" I couldn't imagine my mother on a pedal boat.

No, wait, strike that. I absolutely could. She'd be the coxswain—"Faster! Faster!" Whoever got her as a partner was in for a leg workout.

"Of course your mother went. She likes outdoorsy things. Don't you remember the foraging hikes?"

Until he'd said it, I hadn't. But the memories flooded in at the mention. My mother led Bud and me through the neighborhood, each carrying a small bucket, while she carried gloves and her "snips," clipping blossoms from neighbors' bushes and flower beds, scavenging greenery and fallen branches from vacant lots and public spaces. She never took more than one or two of anything and would never take the last flower. I remembered how embarrassed I was, how I'd complained that we were stealing. Mom countered that people would be flattered to see their hard work appreciated. It all seemed invasive to me, and as soon as I was old enough to stay home alone, I quit going.

"Daisy?" Dad's voice brought me back to the present.

We chatted a few minutes longer before I ended the call with a promise to check in the next day.

That night, I dreamed I was a contestant on *The Price Is Right*, being quizzed on the prices of different flowers. The prize was a pedal boat.

Chapter Twenty-Two

In a last-minute decision, I chose to walk to work.

I slipped on sneakers and threw my dress shoes into my bag, along with my laptop, chargers, and journal. I slotted my earbuds in and cued up my favorite meditation channel. After a block, I stopped and switched to a classic rock playlist, matching my pace to the music, my arms swinging in jaunty rhythm to the beat.

"Watch it!" A red-faced man in a much-too-tight polo shirt pulled down his mirror shades and glared at me, motioning to the travel mug I'd almost knocked from his hand in my exuberance.

I waved cheerfully and kept walking.

I breezed through Event Artistry's doors, expecting a round of cheerful hellos, perhaps a colorful hand-lettered banner welcoming me back.

No one even looked up.

I waited, thinking that if one person saw me, it might set off a chain reaction. We were an events company, after all. We knew how to celebrate. Of course, I would be gracious, demurring all extravagant outcries of how much I'd been missed, how the place was falling apart without me, how clients had been calling every hour, demanding my return.

Crickets. Tumbleweeds. Nothing.

Eunice swept in, caftan in full sail, brandishing two drink trays of coffee.

"Oh!" I jumped out of the way as people swarmed. Unbelievable. After years of dedication, didn't I deserve a more enthusiastic welcome than a triple venti iced latte? The dopamine high of my morning walk crashed and burned.

I searched the room for John without luck. Adding to my annoyance, my regular place at the community table was spoken for. Sliding into an empty chair, I surveyed the offender's setup: iPad, portable speaker, and a thumb drive in the shape of a poo emoji.

Don't tell me…

"Hello, Daisy." Tavia appeared, coffee in hand, taking her (my) seat. "John said you were back." She wore an all-black jumpsuit similar to the one I was currently wearing, her hair slicked back in a low bun. Her eyebrows knitted together in mock consternation. "I thought you were meeting us at the museum."

Us? I stared at her, mentally cursing my stupidity. Of course, Tavia would be in today's meeting. What had I expected? That upon my return, she would vanish in a cloud of smoke? Melt away like a witch doused in water?

What a world, what a world.

"Oh, I wanted to come in early. Make a few calls, return a few emails." I wrestled my face into a neutral expression, waving my hand nonchalantly. "I'm not meeting John for an hour." I stressed the words "I'm" and "John," hoping she'd get the hint.

"Great," she said, batting her eyes, the picture of innocence. "We can ride together."

Something told me she'd not only received my hint but lobbed it back in my face.

"Super." I gritted my teeth behind a closed-lip smile. Point one, Tavia.

"Daisy Greene," Fiona thundered through the loudspeaker. "My office."

Tavia smiled serenely at me before turning back to her computer.

My right eye twitched. This morning was not shaping up as planned.

I made it halfway up the stairs before realizing I still needed to change my shoes. I turned, narrowly avoiding crashing into Martin. He carried a box from which wires and cords trailed out like tin cans on a just-married couple's car.

"Oops. Watch out," he said, dodging to the left to avoid me and running into Eunice, who was carrying an equally full box of streamers. Cords and decorations cascaded down the staircase, causing everyone in the room to stop and stare.

Well, I'd finally gotten their attention.

"Daisy!" Fiona barked.

"Sorry," I called to Eunice and Martin and fled, steeling myself for whatever fate awaited me.

"Have a seat." Fiona waved me in between puffs of her vape pen. Already delicate after two weeks of continuous assault, my sinuses seized at the strawberry-scented fumes while my eyes watered and the back of my throat tingled.

I sat in the indicated chair, leaning as far back as possible without toppling over.

Fiona plunked into the chair beside me. "How's your father?" She patted me with a sandpapery hand.

"He's find. Thangs for askink." I scanned the room, spying the box of tissues in a knitted cozy on Eunice's desk. "He's hobe. By brother is takink ober the store." I grabbed the tissues, dabbing at my eyes and nose, hoping my allergies would be construed as heartfelt emotion and garner some extra sympathy for my extended absence.

Fiona regarded me coolly. "I thought perhaps you were considering making your stay permanent."

No extra sympathy. Got it.

"Tavia proved an enthusiastic substitute during your sabbatical," Fiona continued. "I want you to continue working together on this event."

The color drained from my face. "What? Johd and I—"

"Is there a problem?"

I clasped my hands, nails gouging the skin of my palms. "Of course dot. If thad's what the cliedt wants, it's fide with me. Thang you." I waited, expecting further remonstrations, but Fiona flicked her hand, dismissing me. I started for the door.

"Daisy?"

I stopped and turned back. "Yes, Fioda?"

"Nice to have you back."

The atmosphere inside the car during the ride to the museum was so chilly that even our driver remarked on it. "A little cold for this time of year, isn't it?" he joked, earning matching glares from Tavia and me. We drove the rest of the way in silence.

John met us at the visitor's desk. "Well, if it isn't my two favorite p-art-ners in crime," he called, glancing between us. "Get it? Art?" Tavia laughed as though this was the funniest remark she'd ever heard. My right eye twitched as we headed to Reg's office.

John led the meeting as Tavia jumped in with the occasional clarification. I *mm-hmm*ed a lot, all the while growing more uncomfortable with the details being discussed. Glancing at John, I caught a glimpse of panic crossing his face when Tavia mentioned her latest idea: serving ceviche in tiny shells.

"For sipping," she explained.

"Well," Reg said, clapping his hands together, signaling the end of the meeting, "I trust that everything is well in hand. And Daisy—" He turned to me. Over his shoulder, Tavia's bright smile collapsed into a scowl. "I'm expecting those record attendance numbers you promised. I've assured our board that this opening event will be—how did you put it—the 'jewel in our museum's crown.'" His eyelids lowered just a fraction, delivering a subtle but unmistakable message: *This is on you.*

John, Tavia, and I settled into a booth at the museum's café for a meeting debrief. My mind reeled as we waited for our coffee. While I'd been assured nothing would change during my absence, the presentation I'd just seen no longer felt like a traditional art show reception geared toward faithful donors who preferred passed hors d'oeuvres and light jazz. Somehow, it had morphed into an edgy exhibition that seemed more closely related to an underwater nightclub.

"Daisy?" John's voice broke into my thoughts. I realized he'd asked me a question.

I shook my head. "I faded out for a moment. What did you say?"

John studied me. "I asked if you were happy with the direction of the event."

"It's certainly different," I hedged. On one hand, I hadn't exactly been helpful the past two weeks, essentially handing over the reins and disappearing. On the other hand, Reg's parting comments made it clear it was still my neck on the line. It struck me that this must be how Mom and Dad felt watching Bud take over their store—constantly conflicted about when to step in and when to step back. *Oh, irony, you crafty devil.*

Rather than answer the question, I turned to Tavia. "John mentioned some concerns over the invitations?"

She shifted in her seat, quickly glancing at John before answering. "Oh, well, yes. The invitations were a little… funkier than previously discussed. But all the best marketing involves an element of risk. Even the patrons who didn't like them remembered them."

"True," I said, inclining my head to acknowledge her point. "But we need them to also get people in the door. It's not just awareness we're raising. It's patronage." I thumbed through my phone to the photos I'd taken of Chantal's artwork and flower arrangements. "What if we pivot to something like this?" John and Tavia watched as I swiped through the images. "We pair local florists with a painting and have them create floral interpretations of Ms. Maxwell's work." It was an idea I'd had on the plane ride home. I spoke faster, excited. "We expand our invitation list to include both the art and floral worlds." I turned to Tavia. "We can still work within your elements theme. And your lighting solution is very good. We simply need to *soften* the edges." Another idea struck me, something Agnes said. "We could also set up selfie stations around town. We'll request permission to create banners of a few of her works. John, you call around to businesses for locations. Make up a marketing sponsorship level, put them on the program, event signage, that kind of thing."

John typed furiously on his phone. As always when we hit our stride, John anticipated where I was going before I finished vocalizing my thoughts. Tavia stayed quiet, making halfhearted notes on her banquet order while John and I scrolled our contact lists and flagged potential partners. I almost felt bad for her. Almost.

"Tavia," I said, feeling magnanimous now that I was back in my zone. "Why don't you lead the social media charge?" I pulled up the store's accounts. Next to Agnes' latest post was a video of Chantal peering over a bouquet of wildflowers, just the top of her head and eyes visible. "Something's coming," read the caption, followed by the hashtag #whereintheworldisBloomsbyBert. Only an hour old, the post already had hundreds of likes and comments. "We could set up a scavenger hunt: find all the backdrops, be entered to win tickets to the exhibition."

Tavia nodded, looking thoughtfully at my phone screen. "I could also film some short-form videos, teasers with behind-the-scenes looks at the exhibit. Maybe Reg could persuade Ms. Maxwell to share some insights into her process."

"That's a fantastic suggestion," I said, genuinely impressed. I waited to see if my right eye would twitch. It didn't.

John looked up. "Just got a response from the printers. If we get artist approval today, they can have banners ready by Friday."

"I'll go talk to Reg," Tavia volunteered.

"We'll *all* go." I stood, gathering the notebooks and spreadsheets before remembering that these were her documents, not mine. "Sorry," I said, pushing the pile across the table. "Habit."

She took them from me, wordlessly following as John and I retraced our steps to Reg's office.

Not that I was keeping score, but… game, set, match, Daisy.

We left Reg's office with his promise to contact Ms. Maxwell immediately. Even Tavia thawed after several compliments about our team's innovative marketing approach, and John's suggestion that she be the one to assist Reg with any media appearances.

Outside, John rubbed his hands together (whether in satisfaction or to wipe away the remnants of Reg's latest unpleasantly moist handshake, I wasn't sure). "That went swimmingly. What say we go to lunch?"

"Sounds good to me," I said, buzzing with adrenaline. *I missed this.*

"You go on ahead," Tavia said. "I, uh, forgot my purse." She turned abruptly, high heels echoing against the marble floors. "Don't wait for me," she called over her shoulder.

I watched her retrace the path toward Reg's office. "Do you think—"

John cut me off. "I try not to. That's why I'm so happy all the time." He extended his arm. "Shall we?"

• • •

John studied me over his soup and salad. "You're different."

I wiped a dribble of balsamic dressing from my chin. "Whaddya mean?" I asked around a mouthful of Caprese sandwich.

He took a bite of salad and chewed thoughtfully while I drained my water glass. I'd forgotten how dehydrating life at high elevation could be. I'd been drinking water nonstop since returning home. However, I assumed that wasn't the "difference" John was referring to.

He gestured to me with his fork. "I don't know, exactly. It's your... aura. It's different."

I rolled my eyes. "Don't you think you're too old to use that word?"

He feigned indignation. "I am a very youthful thirty-eight, thank you. I still get carded at bars."

"For what? Senior discounts?"

He slapped the table. "See? That's different. The old Daisy didn't throw shade."

"And the old John would know better than to say *throw shade*," I retorted. "I was only gone ten days. How different could I be?"

"I don't know, but you can't deny you've changed," he said, switching from his salad to his tomato soup. "You were a million miles away at the beginning of our meeting. I didn't even think you were listening until you created that whole promotional campaign." He blew on his soup, slurped, and continued. "Nice work, by the way. I was nervous about the numbers."

"Thanks," I said around another bite of sandwich. "And you're not wrong. I do feel different."

"Ha! See? How do *you* think you're different?" He threw my question back at me.

"I don't know. I guess it's because of my family." I paused, considering. "All along, I've been thinking of them as the people they were last time I saw them. Like insects caught in amber." I shrugged. "Silly, I know. But seeing them, really seeing them, for who they are now changed how I felt about them. And how I feel about myself when I'm with them. And now, even though I'm not with them, I'm still not the same as I was." I looked up. "Does that make sense?"

John nodded. "Sure. You updated your reference frame, so now your interpretations are more accurate. You finally caught up."

I caught up.

John had put into words the very thing I'd been struggling to define. Before, it was like I'd been wearing glasses with an outdated prescription. Now, I was seeing clearly. Mom, Dad, and Bud were no longer blurry outlines, cartoonish and two-dimensional. My time at home had brought them into focus, giving them depth. They were three-dimensional again.

And so was I.

John cleared his throat. "Not to interrupt this illuminating deep dive into the psyche of Ms. Daisy Greene, but while we're alone, I also have an update on the new space."

I remembered John mentioning an alternative after I'd cost us our prime location. "What's up?" I asked. "Is it still available?"

"Yes and no. The current tenants have a scheduling conflict and want to postpone their move-out date by at least two months. The landlord is okay with it if we are. Personally, I don't mind waiting. Another few paychecks won't hurt my bank balance. And we'll get a prorated lease when we do move in. But I know how anxious you were to put in your notice with Fiona and get started." John gave me a meaningful look. "At least, that's what you said before. Maybe that's not how you feel now."

I thought for a moment, letting the news sink in and examining how I felt. How I *really* felt.

Yes, I was still excited to start a new business with John. However, I didn't have the burning desire for escape I'd had two weeks ago—the need to break out, break away, and be seen as someone new.

"It's not a problem. I can wait."

"Great." John hesitated before adding, "Are you sure?"

"Of course. Why would you ask?"

He played with his spoon. "It goes back to what we were just talking about. How you seem different. First, you extend your trip to help people you've spent years avoiding. Then, you forget to sign the lease agreement. And now you're back, but you're only half here."

I was confused. I hated feeling confused. "But we've been planning this for months. It's the opportunity I always dreamed about."

"Dreams change. People change. Even Ice-Queen Daisy Greene."

"But what else would I do?"

"I don't know... Move home and run a flower shop with your brother?"

"No," I scoffed. "I might be different, but I'll never be *that* different."

"Great," John said, picking up his phone and starting to type. "I'll let Maggie know."

I popped the last bite of the sandwich into my mouth and gathered my belongings. Turning over my phone, I saw a new text notification.

Jeremy: *How's Day 1 back in real life?*

I snatched my phone away, but not before John saw the screen.

His eyebrows shot halfway up his forehead. "Who is Jeremy?"

"Nobody." I stuffed my phone into my purse. "Back to business. If your projections are correct—"

"My projections are always correct," John interrupted. "And that's not a 'nobody' face."

I gave up. There was no use protesting. John knew me too well. "Okay, he's somebody. But it's nothing." I hurried on. "I mean, he's there and I'm here and you know I'm better on my own. Alone…"

"But not lonely," John recited with me. "Yeah, I know. But since when does being yourself mean you have to be alone? I mean, you don't even have a fish or a houseplant to call your own."

"I based my whole career on being on my own. I'm not going to change my life because of one person."

"Of course you're not. The only person you should change your life for is you. But isn't it possible that other people could be *part* of the equation? It doesn't have to be all or nothing. There's room for all sorts of flowers in a garden."

I snorted. "I see what you did there."

"I wasn't trying to be subtle." He stood, grinning. "Think about it. Not for me, not for Jeremy. For you."

Chapter Twenty-Three

The rest of the day passed by in a flurry of details and the organized chaos of getting caught up after my absence. Midway through the afternoon, I received another text. Not from Jeremy, as I'd hoped, but from Victor: *I know you are traveling, but please call when you can. I owe you an apology.*

At 5 p.m., I slipped on my tennis shoes and packed my bag. I waved cheerfully to John, relishing the stunned look on his face at my leaving while the sun was still out.

On the way home, I called Victor. Business-mode Daisy knew it was always best to get the harder phone call over first.

He picked up on the third ring. "Daisy! Hi!" His words were jagged, breath coming in short gasps.

"Is this a good time?"

"Sure. I'm out for a run. Before you say anything, I apologize for the other night. I did some tequila shots before you showed up, and the buzz caught up with me at the wrong time."

"It's okay, I—"

"Vicki and I had been fighting earlier, and I was feeling, well… conflicted. After you left, I went straight home and we talked things out. But my behavior with you was inexcusable."

His breathing slowed; he was walking now. "I really am sorry. I hope you'll accept my apology, and we can stay friends."

I smiled as I answered. "I do, and I look forward to being work friends."

"Thank you." I heard the relief in his voice. "Speaking of work, I have another client I'd like to bring by the store. Do you think your brother can fit us into his schedule this week?"

I assured Victor it would be no problem, and we hung up. Happiness surged through me as I texted Bud: *Better late than never! More wedding clients coming your way as promised.*

He replied a minute later: *Never doubted you for a minute.*

As I approached my building, I texted Jeremy: *Just getting home from work now. All quiet so far.*

A wall of animal noises and delighted squeals hit me as I opened the door. Everywhere I looked, the lobby was full of crates and temporary enclosures. Parents, children, young adults, and older couples milled about clutching clipboards. I saw and smelled dogs, rabbits, cats, and hamsters.

The pet adoption event. So much for "quiet."

A bright green parakeet flew at my head. A voice hollered, "Close the door! Close the door!"

I yanked the door shut, thwarting the bird's bid for freedom.

"Thanks." A red-faced man in a bright yellow shirt raced by me. "Here, Betsy, good girl!"

I edged along the lobby's perimeter toward the stairs. Across the room, I saw Mrs. Rudnicki and Precious peering into travel crates. I quickened my pace, hoping to avoid conversation. As though reading my mind, she turned in my direction. I ducked behind a pillar and smacked into another volunteer in a yellow polo shirt, her hair tied back in a ponytail.

"Hi! I'm Katie. Can I help you?" she chirped, holding out a clipboard. "Are you looking for someone special?"

"God, no." I shook my head. "I'm just, uh, inspecting the structural integrity of this post." I gave the plaster column a rap with my knuckles. "I'm incredibly interested in the architecture of... lobbies."

Mrs. Rudnicki was now petting something that looked like a squash with fur. I seized the opportunity, fleeing up the stairs. I reached my apartment door and fit the key to the lock, slamming the door behind me as though I'd narrowly escaped a harrowing fate.

My heart rate had just slowed when my phone blipped, signaling a new text from Jeremy: *Quiet after family or quiet for real?*

Not so quiet after all, I responded. *Pet adoption event in the lobby. Mayhem.*

A moment later, his video call came through. I ran my hands through my hair before answering. I hoped I didn't have any leftover basil in my teeth.

"Hi!" Was my voice too loud? Was my smile too wide? Did I look overeager?

"Hi!" Two faces appeared onscreen, one big, one small. Jeremy and his son Ethan sat on a couch in what I assumed was his father's living room, a framed poster of Coors Field behind their heads. "E and I want to see some pets. Will you take us to meet the doggos?"

"I, uh..." I stammered, caught off guard. Just because I was "Aunt Funny" to LilyRose didn't make me an expert with other people's kids. "I mean, I guess I can..."

"Pleeeeease?" Father and son made matching puppy dog eyes.

"Okay, okay," I capitulated. "But I'm not petting anything that looks the least bit dangerous. Or hungry."

I headed back downstairs, listening as Ethan, prompted by Jeremy, began listing all of his favorite types of animals. I scanned the room for Mrs. Rudnicki, but she had disappeared. I breathed a sigh of relief and stepped toward an enclosure of rabbits.

"Hi again." It was Katie, the chipper volunteer. "Back to inspect more columns?"

I whipped the phone behind my back. "Uh, no. I'm just browsing."

Katie's smile widened. "That's what they all say," she said and handed me a clipboard. "Take this in case you change your mind. I'm here until 7." She wandered away, approaching a family peering into a cage where a giant white rat with red eyes sat nibbling on a carrot top.

"Um, Daisy? Why are we staring at your butt?"

Oh crap. I thrust the clipboard under one arm and brought the phone around. Jeremy was covering Ethan's eyes. Both father and son were giggling. "Sorry, sorry." I flipped the camera view toward the action. "Where do you want to start?"

For the next hour, Jeremy, Ethan, and I walked around, meeting all the adoptees. By the time we got to the last crate, I had been almost bitten twice—once by a budgie with an attitude and again by the furry squash, which I'd learned was a chinchilla. My hands and phone case were covered in animal hair and slobber. Ethan was wildly enthusiastic about every dog, from the energetic miniature pinscher whose owner had been allergic to the massive sheepdog rescued from an unethical breeder. His adoration was contagious, and I became more adventurous, squatting down to pet each animal at his request.

I was putting on sanitizer for the umpteenth time when Jeremy broke in. "Daisy? We have to go. My dad just got home."

"Oh, okay," I said, strangely disappointed. Once again, I'd found myself having fun. Something about Jeremy brought it out in me. I waved goodbye to father and son, then slid my phone into my jacket pocket and spritzed another coat of sanitizer on my hands for good measure.

Katie reappeared at my side. "Hi! Did you find a furrrever friend while you were browsing?"

I winced at the phrase "furrrever." "Honestly, I'm not an

animal person. I was just showing my friend around. His son likes animals."

Katie frowned and made a *tch-tch* noise. "I was watching you interact with the dogs. You have a real gift. They respond to you." She motioned me closer as if she had a secret. "There's someone I want you to meet. I don't have him out with the other adoptees because, well, he's a special guy. One of our volunteers found him on the side of the road and brought him in. No collar, no chip. We've been holding onto him in case his family came looking. But it's been a month, and no one's stepped up, so..."

She led me behind a long folding table where the other volunteers were processing adoption paperwork to a travel crate draped with a colorful patchwork quilt. I could hear snoring from inside, which ceased when Katie lifted the quilt and opened the door.

"Doggo," she whispered. "Doggo, there's someone here to meet you."

There was a snort, a *woof*, and the sound of nails scrabbling, and then Doggo came out. The first thing I saw was a big slobbery grin, drool hanging from each side of his mouth. The second thing I noticed was how he moved, a cross between a walk and a hop.

Katie noticed me noticing. "Doggo's what we call a tripawd," she explained. "He was born without his left back leg." She scratched behind his ears, and he hop-walked over to her before falling to the ground and offering up his belly for more. She laughed. "You can see it doesn't slow him down any. He's Mr. Personality." She rubbed his belly while he snorted and chuffed in pleasure. She looked up at me. "He's all alone and doesn't deserve to be. He needs a home, a friend."

My right eye twitched. I knew what she was building up to.

I thought of John and his comment that I didn't even have a pet fish or a houseplant to care for. I thought of Mrs. Rudnicki and Precious and how big and empty my apartment felt after two weeks of living with my family.

I looked down at Doggo, who was smiling at me.

"Will you take us to meet the doggos?" Jeremy had asked. Like it was some kind of sign.

I'm not.

I'm not, I'm absolutely not…

Oh no.

"Come on, Doggo."

I pushed the apartment door open with my foot, my hands full with Doggo's leash, foster papers, food dish, and the quilt from Katie. She'd insisted it was a gift and would make Doggo feel at home in his new surroundings since it already had his scent.

It was scented, all right. Did all dogs smell like wet cheese?

I dropped everything on the kitchen counter and stood in a daze, staring at a dog—*my* dog—and wondering what in the world had come over me.

"You're different," John had said.

Well, this was certainly different.

"Sit, Doggo." I pointed at the floor. He barked, drool cascading from his open, panting mouth.

"Lie down, Doggo." I motioned with both hands flat like Katie had shown me. "He knows all sorts of commands," she assured me. "He's very smart."

Doggo did his little walk-hop in a circle three times before sitting down and staring at me. His stubby black tail thumped against the floor.

"Stay." I backed away from him, holding my hands out like a traffic cop. Doggo jumped up and followed me, nipping playfully (I hoped) at the hem of my pants.

"Fine. Whatever," I said, throwing up my hands. As if spring-loaded, Doggo jumped up with surprising agility and gave me a big slobbery lick on the chin. Saliva splattered my face and chest.

"Ack!" My hands flew to my face as I wiped the moisture off furiously, shaking droplets off my hands.

Opening my eyes, I saw Doggo sitting and smiling up at me as if he were the best, most perfectly behaved canine on the planet.

"*Woof*," he said happily.

"Oh, *woof* yourself," I grumbled and went to collect a towel from the bathroom.

The rest of the evening was spent dog-proofing the apartment. My shoes moved to the closet, and I rolled up my rugs and stowed them under the bed, where Doggo's drool (*or teeth*, I thought, remembering Precious) couldn't get to them.

Katie said he was probably mostly American Bulldog with a streak of Pug somewhere in his little doggie family tree. "You can change his name if you want," she said as we completed the foster-to-adopt paperwork. "But don't wait too long. He's already responding to Doggo."

How could I explain that his name, Doggo, made this unlikely scenario happen in the first place?

I just shook my head. "Doggo's fine. He looks like a Doggo," I said, as though I'd grown up around dogs and was naturally attuned to their naming preferences.

Now, Doggo followed me to the bathroom, walk-hopping beside me. I stopped him. "Stay," I said, sliding the door shut.

I undressed, waiting for the water to heat and listening to Doggo's whines, the *scritch-scratch* of his nails on wood. I'd refinished the sliding barn door over two long weekends and couldn't bear to imagine the glossy black paint being ruined. Clutching a bath towel around me, I cracked the door open. My roommate bounded in, snapping enthusiastically at the steam clouds, his nails clicking against the tiles.

I stepped into the shower, self-conscious about having an audience. I closed my eyes and lathered shampoo into my hair. *Get over it*, I scolded myself. *It's a dog*. Nevertheless, I took the fastest shower of my life, opting for the leave-in conditioner and skipping shaving my legs.

"Enjoy the show?" I asked as I slipped my robe around me, tying it tightly. I hung up the bathmat and used the hand towel to mop steam from the mirror and dog drool from the floor. "Come on, creeper. Let's go find something to eat."

In the kitchen, I pulled out the small bag of kibble from the pile of necessities Katie had pressed on me. "This will get you through tonight and tomorrow morning," she promised. "But you'll need to go supply shopping soon. The best thing you can do for your tripawd is to ensure he eats healthily and stays active. Extra weight is hard on the joints."

"Here you go." I bent down and offered the food to Doggo, who sniffed suspiciously at the unfamiliar dish before digging in like it was his first meal in days rather than hours.

"Good boy." I patted him when he was finished. He rewarded me with a big, sloppy kiss followed by a blast of the worst breath I'd ever smelled. "If this is how you say thank you," I told him, fanning my face, "I'd prefer a handshake."

At the word "shake," he put his front right paw on my knee. "That's better," I told him and shook it.

He smiled, drooling.

I smiled back.

After dinner, I took out my laptop and notes and began working on the gala's new promotional plan.

Doggo slept at my feet for a while, then moved to sit by the door. Quiet at first, he gradually grew louder, pawing at the door and chuffing, insistent *woof-woofs*.

"Shhh! I'm trying to concentrate," I chided.

He continued whining and scratching, looking back at me.

The light dawned, and I jumped up. "Oh! You need to—"

Too late.

. . .

"We'll do better tomorrow, I promise," I told him as I threw the last rags into the washing machine, along with my robe, which had urine stains on the hem from where I'd knelt to clean up. For good measure, I threw in the clothes I'd worn to the pet adoption and the drool towels from the bathroom. "For someone who doesn't wear clothes, you generate a lot of laundry."

"*Woof,*" he agreed.

It was nearly midnight by the time I switched the laundry to the dryer. Packing my laptop and papers away, I turned and realized my bed was no longer unoccupied. Doggo was stretched across my pillows, snoring, tongue lolled to one side, while a wide drool stain darkened my special, wrinkle-reducing silk pillowcases.

I tried wrestling a pillow away but only managed to shift his sleep-laden tree-trunk body a few inches. "Fine," I grumbled, climbing into bed. "We can share. But just for tonight."

A low rumble erupted from Doggo's stomach. A moment later, a foul kibble-laced stench hit my nose. I rolled over, gasping.

As I drifted to sleep, I could swear I heard Doggo laughing. In my half-awake state, he sounded just like Bud.

Chapter Twenty-Four

I was nearly two hours late for work the next morning. By that point, both Eunice and John had phoned, warning that Fiona was threatening to send police to my building, claiming that the only reason I would dare to be so incredibly tardy was if I'd been murdered in my sleep.

Considering Doggo's nocturnal intestinal shenanigans, she wasn't that far off from the truth.

I'd woken early and taken Doggo for a walk, not wanting a repeat of last night's accident. On the way back, I'd stopped by the local market, purchasing the most upscale brand of dog food available, the one that claimed to help my pet maintain a healthy weight and a happy digestive system. I planned to call Katie later to ask if, by any chance, my "furrever friend" had some kind of terminal gut rot. I'd experienced smells over the last few hours that I hadn't known existed in this world.

And that was after a childhood with Bud. Which was saying something.

I'd adopted the canine version of my brother. *Let a therapist try to figure that out,* I thought, smiling to myself as I raced into Event Artistry.

This time, everyone looked up. But not in the happy anticipation or congratulations I'd expected the day before. This was the type of look that says, "Uh oh." I glanced down, making sure my shirt was correctly buttoned and my pants were zipped. They were. So what was—

"Daisy Greene," Fiona barked over the loudspeaker. I looked up and saw the top of her red hair in the office window. "Come see me right now." A screech of feedback punctuated the order as she switched the intercom off.

Everyone's heads swiveled back to their desks, feigning interest in laptops, phone screens, food, and banquet contracts. Anything to avoid eye contact with me. Even John and Tavia kept their heads down, looking at something on John's laptop.

Cowards.

I trudged up the stairs to Fiona's office, sidestepping Martin as he came barreling down the stairs with an armload of tablecloths.

"Yes, Fiona?" I decided to play dumb. I knew that she knew I was grievously late. But she didn't necessarily know that *I knew* she knew. I marched in and sat across from her in the same chair I'd sat in yesterday, grabbing a preemptive tissue on my way past Eunice's desk in case my allergies staged another comeback. I crossed my ankles, hands on the arms of the chair. I was the definition of open body language: nothing to hide, no defensive postures.

"Shut the door, Eunice," Fiona barked. Eunice scuttled from the room, looking apologetic as she closed the door.

Fiona sat back in her chair, feet on the desk, hands folded across her stomach, looking for all the world as if she was about to make me an offer I couldn't refuse.

"How long have you worked for me, Daisy?" she asked conversationally.

"Um, almost five years now." *Four years, eleven months, and a week, to be exact.*

"And have you enjoyed working here?"

"I've learned a lot," I noted with concern her use of the past tense *enjoyed*.

"Do you see yourself still working here in, oh, say, another four years?" she asked.

Caught off guard, I stammered out the best evasion I could think of. "Oh, well, yes, I could see that." Technically, I could.

She leaned forward, her legs knifing to the floor quickly for a woman her age, heck, for a woman my age. It made me wonder, if things went south, could I make it to the door ahead of her?

Fiona went on, unaware of, or possibly enjoying, my discomfort. "I like you, Daisy. You remind me of me ten years ago."

Ten years ago? I was getting my wrinkle-reducing pillowcase back from Doggo tonight.

I willed my voice to remain steady. "That's very kind. I'm happy you're pleased with my work." Where was this going?

Fiona stood and, moving with surprising speed again, came around the desk to stand over me. Her high heels made an impressive *snick* noise like they'd pierced the wooden flooring. "I'm going to let you in on a secret." She beckoned me closer. "I'm retiring. The events management industry is a young person's game. And I am not a young person anymore."

I sat back, genuinely stunned, all my fears of dismissal forgotten. Fiona, retiring? I'd imagined her simply keeling over at her desk one day, somewhere north of her hundredth birthday, vape pen in one hand, her beloved intercom mic in the other.

"Fiona, I don't know what to say." No need to parse words this time, I told the truth. "I can't imagine Event Artistry without you."

Her eyes sparkled, and she suddenly looked like a mischievous little gnome. "That's why I've decided to make you my successor," she said. "I want you to take over Event Artistry."

She wasn't a mischievous gnome. She was Willy Wonka offering the keys to the chocolate factory. And I was Charlie.

She mistook my silence for acceptance. "I'm sure you're

feeling overwhelmed, especially since you've just come back from seeing your family," she said, her voice softening to the point of almost being maternal. "We can make the announcement after Millie Maxwell's event." She waved a hand at the door, dismissing me. "Now, shoo. Get to work. Don't think I didn't notice what time you got here." She dropped an enormous wink, her dramatic black lash extensions fluttering. "When you're the boss, you're going to have to be more punctual."

Chastened, I hurried toward the door, but she called me back. "And Daisy?"

"Yes, Fiona?"

"Don't tell anyone yet. Not even John."

"Of course not. My lips are sealed."

"She WHAT?" John goggled at me.

We sat in our booth at Pavel's, drinks untouched.

"I KNOW." I slapped the table with each word for emphasis. "Can you believe this? She burned the gangplank before we could jump ship." I shook my head. "It's *such* a Fiona thing to do."

"What did you say? Did you give her your notice?"

"No way." I shuddered at the idea. "If she even *suspected* I—we—were leaving, she would fire us both and give the whole company to Tavia out of spite."

John looked thoughtful. "What if, just for the sake of argument, what if you—we—stayed? What if we put our funds into running Event Artistry instead of putting all our money into going up against them?" He held up his hand, anticipating my objections. "Think about it. No start-up costs, no new building lease, no having to install lighting or buy office furniture, no having to hire a marketing company to design a logo."

I thought of the nights I'd spent sketching out logos at home. "I concede your point," I told him. "But let's think about the other side. What we gain in finance, we lose in terms of creative control. You know that even if she steps back from the day-to-day, we'd never really be free from Fiona. She'd still consider it her company and find a way to appoint herself chair of the board of directors or something. We'd still be her lackeys, just on a different pay scale."

A dreamy look came into John's eyes at the mention of pay scales. "I'll be honest. There's a number in my head. If we could hit that, I would put up with a board full of Fionas." He picked up his drink and drained it in one long swallow. He slid from the table. "I promised Zadie I'd be home on time tonight. Text me later and let me know what you're thinking." He stopped at the bar to pay our tab before heading out into the dusky evening.

I nursed my drink, lost in thought. I felt like I'd dodged a bullet, but I wasn't sure for how long. Fiona said I could have until after the KCAM event. And the lease on the new space had been pushed back. I was being offered more than everything I'd ever wanted. So why did it all feel wrong?

It would be like the flower shop all over again, I realized. Fewer allergies but the same triggers. I'd be taking over someone else's dream instead of creating my own.

So that was a no.

Right?

Arriving home, I kicked off my shoes, too tired to put them away properly. I dropped my purse and bag on the kitchen chair and flopped onto the sofa face-first.

"Uhhhhhhhh…" I moaned into the cushion, my voice reverberating back in the silence.

Afraid I would fall asleep if I didn't move, I forced myself up and headed for the shower, peeling my dress off as I went. As the water warmed, I shook my hair free from its bun and discarded my undergarments.

The hot water hitting my skin was heaven. The knots in my

shoulders melted, and I rolled my neck, releasing the tension that had been building all day.

"Mmmm," I groaned again, the echo of my voice the only sound in the otherwise empty room.

Silence...

Empty...

"Doggo?!" I scream-gasped, spluttering as the spray hit my open mouth. I fumbled for the shower knob, in my haste turning it to scalding before wrenching it off.

"Yiiiii!" I screamed and leaped out of the shower. Grabbing my robe, I opened the bathroom door and called, "Doggo? Doggo! Where are you?"

No reassuring *woof* answered me.

Oh my God. I lost an entire dog.

I dropped to my knees and crawled across the floor, checking under the bed, the table, and the couch, knowing he wasn't there, couldn't be there, but hoping I was wrong.

I pulled open my closet door, shoving clothes and shoes aside. "Doggo?"

Panic rising in my chest, I sat back on my heels, wet hair dripping down my face. Where was he? Had I been robbed? Why would someone steal a dog? Especially that one?

I was just considering whether to call the police and risk being arrested as the worst pet parent ever when I heard the sound of a key turning in the lock.

I raced to the door and yanked it open.

Mrs. Rudnicki stood on my doormat, Precious in her arms. At her feet, drooling and smiling, was Doggo.

I dropped to my knees and hugged him, not letting go even when my robe fell open. "Oh, thank goodness, Doggo. I thought I'd lost you."

"*Hmph.*" My neighbor sniffed as she strode past me into the apartment, settling herself onto the couch as though she lived here and I was the visitor. "He woke Precious and me up from our afternoon nap," she said, narrowing her eyes at me in accusation. I straightened, pulling my robe closed. "You can't leave a dog alone all day. They get lonely." As if to prove her point, Doggo trotted over and, with surprising grace, joined her on the sofa, snuggling up to her leg like she was a cozy blanket and not a meddling, sort-of dognapper. Precious wriggled from under her other arm and lay across her lap, head resting on Doggo's broad back, right in the middle of his black spot. Within seconds, both dogs' eyes were closed, and they snored in unison. "Luckily, I still have a key."

I glanced at my key hook, where the Chiefs keychain dangled. My neighbor's eyes followed my gaze. "Oh, that," she said, waving her hand dismissively. "Precious likes to hide things. Don't you, sweetie?" She nuzzled her dog's head. Precious raised his head a fraction and growled in agreement, eyes still closed. "So I had a few extras made, just in case."

My first instinct was to ask how many "a few" were and if I could please have them, but at the same time, I was immensely grateful for her forethought. What might have happened to poor Doggo if she hadn't made the extra keys? No, I was the one at fault here. I'd thoughtlessly adopted a dog without any plans for his care while I was at work. I couldn't get upset over some light breaking and entering.

Mrs. Rudnicki regarded the sleeping dogs, and her expression softened. "Precious doesn't usually like anyone," she said with a grin. "Your blanket can vouch for that, but he sure likes... what'd you say his name was again?"

"Doggo," I said, surprised by the pride in my voice as I said it. "My dog's name is Doggo."

At the sound of his name, Doggo lifted his head. "*Woof*," he said. Drool threaded its way from the corner of his mouth onto his savior's yoga pants.

"Well, you certainly can't leave him by himself every day." She looked at me as if making up her mind. "Drop him off on your way to work. He can stay with Precious and me."

I was flustered by her unexpected generosity. "I couldn't possibly impose…"

She waved me off in a move that was so like Fiona I had to wonder if they were related. "Sure you can. Buy another bowl and an extra bag of whatever food he likes. He's good company for Precious, and he was very well-behaved at the park." She heaved herself to her feet, disrupting her charges. Instantly, Precious was awake and growling at my ankles. I stepped back, aware that I was still only in a robe. I escorted my neighbor (and her little dog, too) to the door. She turned. "Pay me whatever you think is fair."

"Thank you so much, Mrs. Rud—"

She wagged her finger at me. "Please, no more 'Mrs.' nonsense. My name is Agnes." She crossed the hall, whistling for Precious, who gave me one last parting growl before disappearing into her apartment.

"Ye gods, there's another one," I told Doggo in disbelief.

"*Woof*," he replied, thumping his tail.

After dinner, dressed in sweats, tennis shoes, and a ball cap, I walked my dog.

I searched online for dog parks in the area and found one less than a ten-minute walk away. I recognized the street name as the address of one of my favorite takeout spots. Somehow, I'd traversed this street for years without noticing anything beyond the sushi restaurant on the corner.

It seemed like the universe was enjoying showing me all the ways I'd been living a half-existence, looking straight ahead but never around.

I called home as I walked.

"Daisy?" Mom sounded concerned. "Is everything all right?"

"Hi to you too. I'm just calling to check in."

"Everything's fine," she said, still mystified. "Where are you? You're huffing and puffing. Are you smoking?"

I was, in fact, huffing and puffing. Doggo was faster than I anticipated. I made a mental note to buy new running shoes. "I'm not smoking. I'm walking... going for a walk." I didn't want to bring up Doggo yet. I'd already had one lecture on responsibility tonight. "How are you? How's Dad?"

"Your father is fine. Exercising with Jeremy, driving me crazy." Mom paused and I heard her take a sip of tea. "I don't know what I will do with him all day. He's already bored silly here, and I certainly can't keep him entertained."

"Mom," I said as I bent and unsnapped Doggo's leash so he could join the other dogs. "Dad doesn't need you micromanaging his activities. Get him an iPad and a *New York Times* crossword subscription and leave him alone." I didn't add that otherwise, she would likely send him straight back to the hospital. Her idea of entertainment for Dad usually involved home repair.

"*Psh.*" Mom dismissed this. In the background, I could hear the chimes of *Wheel of Fortune*. "Do you know what Bud and Chantal are doing this weekend?" She didn't give me a chance to guess. "Looking at houses."

I grimaced as, across the park, Doggo put his face into the backside of a prim-looking standard poodle. "Mom, you've been after Bud to grow up since we were kids. Now he's finally doing it and you're upset?"

"I meant things like keeping his room neat and not growing marijuana in the basement." (I choked. I hadn't known about that.) "I didn't mean he should move out." She gave a self-pitying sniff.

"He's got a family now. He probably wants to get out of your way."

"Why would he ever think he was in my way?"

"Probably because you complained about it every day," I muttered. Louder, I said, "Things are different now. Bud is stepping up. You and Dad have free time for the first time in your lives. Bud doesn't want to bring stress home to you. He wants you to relax and enjoy yourselves."

"But how am I supposed to enjoy myself when my children are gone?" she wailed.

Doggo romped through the park, the poodle bounding after him, barking happily.

"Mom, we're not gone. We've grown up."

"Same difference."

I gave up. "Can I talk to Dad?"

There was an exasperated sigh, assorted scuffling noises, and then my father's voice came on the line. "Hi, Petal."

"Hi, Dad. How are you feeling?"

"Oh, fine. Your mother is," he paused, "taking excellent care of me."

"She's standing right next to you, isn't she?"

"No, I'm not," Mom piped in from the upstairs extension.

"Mom!"

"Fine." She hung up.

"Are you getting enough rest? You have to rest to get better."

"I nap when I can. And I do those torture exercises your friend gives me."

I laughed. "That's good. He's supposed to torture you. Mom's the one who is supposed to be nice."

"I'm nice." Mom was back on the phone. "Tell her I'm nice."

"She's nice," Dad confirmed, chuckling. "When she wants to be."

"Bertram!"

"Mom! Hang up."

A sigh. A *click*.

"How are you, Petal?" Dad asked. "Not working too hard, are you?"

I told him about the event, including the new floral-inspired marketing campaign and the pressure on attendance and fundraising. I told him about Fiona's offer; what it could mean to take the job, what it could mean if I didn't.

He listened without interruption until I finished. "What do you want?"

"I don't know." I shook my head as though he could see me. "I want to have my own business. That's always been the goal. But I can't deny it's tempting to take over something already established."

"Just remember, Petal," Dad said, and I imagined him holding his index finger along his cheek, as he always did when dispensing advice. "It's important to work hard but also to find a balance. You don't want to end up like me, hospitalized, worried about mon—"

"Bert?" Mom broke in. "It's time for bed. Since you're so worried about his rest levels," she grumbled for my benefit.

"Ruth, it's not even eight—" The line went dead.

I pocketed my phone and called to Doggo. He came bounding back, hopping up to give my hands a slobbery welcome. Dismayed, I saw that he'd rolled in something dark and sticky. I hoped it was mud.

"Come on, you." I clipped his leash, thinking of the days when I only had myself to worry about. Now, I had an ever-growing cast of characters to fret over, and mud was considered a "best-case" scenario.

John's voice haunted me. *You've changed.*

If you could see me now, I thought, as Doggo and I started for home.

It wasn't mud.

I lay in bed, listening to Doggo snore on the pillow beside me. I cuddled up, throwing an arm around his doggie shoulder, and he licked my face automatically. I could smell chicken treats on his hot breath. It was comforting to have another living being in bed with me. Stinky but comforting.

At the idea of comforting, my mind shifted to Jeremy. I wondered what he was up to this evening. Was he with Ethan? Or his Dad? Or on a date? And what right did I have to care?

My phone buzzed on the nightstand and Jeremy's name appeared as though summoned. I ran a hand through my hair before sliding my finger across his picture.

"Hi," I said quietly, smiling at the face filling my screen.

He smiled back. "Hey you, I hope I'm not interrupting anything." He squinted. "Are you in bed?"

"I am." I lowered my voice, my tone teasing. What was happening? I was never this flirty. "And we'll have to keep our voices down because"—I paused for dramatic effect—"I'm not alone."

His eyes widened. "What? You're... Why on earth did you answer the phone?"

I giggled at his horrified expression and shifted my face next to Doggo's. "Don't worry, he's not the jealous type."

"No. Way," he said, making each word a full sentence. "Is that a DOG?"

His voice startled my bedmate. "*Woof,*" Doggo said, jumping up and attempting to lick the phone. I pulled it away, afraid he might swallow it whole.

"See what you made me do? You force me to one doggie meet-and-greet, and I end up with a roommate who hogs the bed."

"Wait until I tell E." Jeremy laughed, delighted. "We knew you'd find someone to keep you company. What's his name? What breed is he?"

"Doggo. He's a bulldog mix, we think," I said, showing off my new knowledge. "And he's a bit of a flirt." I recounted the shower incident from Doggo's first night and his new girlfriend-slash-dogsitter across the hall.

"I would have loved to have been there to see that," Jeremy said. There was an awkward pause. "Er, I mean... you know.

Anyway, I was just calling to say hi. I should go. I'm happy for you and Doggo. Talk to you soon."

He hung up, and I was left holding a silent phone and telling an empty screen "Goodbye." In the excitement of introductions, I had forgotten to ask about Ethan, or how Jeremy's day had been. I hadn't even told him I wished he were here, too.

"*Woof.*" Doggo licked the screen, leaving a silver trail of drool across my hand.

"Yeah, you like him, huh?" I said, scratching his ears. He rolled closer, nosing my hand in encouragement. I kept scratching as I snuggled under the covers and closed my eyes. "I'll tell you a secret. I like him too."

Chapter Twenty-Five

It is a truth universally acknowledged that when you have a deadline, time races to meet it.

The next three weeks passed in a blur. John and I were the first to arrive each morning and the last to leave at night. I found myself begrudgingly grateful for Tavia's unrelenting work ethic. Her marketing copy was impeccable, rarely needing more than a quick proofread. Her social media campaigns were creative and fun. She and John continued their good working rapport, leaving me free to focus on the installation of the artist backgrounds around town and the floral companion pieces.

Time grew short and tensions ran high. Still, attendance numbers began to rise, first to conservative estimates, then to our goals. Finally, the day before the event, we crossed the line into record-breaking. It was official: the Millie Maxwell show would be the single largest exhibit opening in KCAM's history.

The night before the opening found me riding the elevator up to my apartment, exhausted, at 9 p.m. It had been an incredibly long day after weeks of long days, culminating in a final two-hour all-staff logistics run-through. All I wanted was to eat, change into PJs, and snuggle with my dog.

As the doors slid open, I heard the now-familiar symphony of Doggo's booming barks and Precious's answering yips.

I smiled to myself. *Thank goodness for nosy neighbors.* In just a few weeks, Agnes Two (as I privately called her) had become as indispensable to me as Doggo had.

I knocked on her door before letting myself in, holding up a brown bag from our favorite dumpling house as a greeting and apology. Agnes Two and I had discovered a mutual love of take-out, and, as part of her payment for Doggo-sitting, I'd begun bringing us dinner.

"Come in, come in." Her face brightened at the sight of the restaurant logo. She bustled around the kitchen, pulling brightly colored plates from a shelf.

Where my apartment was black and white, Agnes's exploded with color. Having spent her younger years in Santa Fe, the southwestern influence remained apparent from her Fiestaware place settings to her adobe-colored wall paint, to the turquoise rings on her fingers and the Georgia O'Keeffe prints on the walls. We often ate together at the small mosaic table in her kitchen. Her apartment always felt warmer and sunnier than mine, even at night.

I shook my head. "Thank you, but I won't stay. I'm ready to crash." I opened the bag and removed one of the to-go boxes. Doggo hop-jumped at my feet, growling in the way I'd come to recognize as excitement to see me. Meanwhile, Precious snapped and growled in what I translated as, "Your ankles look tasty and I want to bite them."

I took my food and my dog and made a hasty exit. "Have a great night. I'll drop Doggo off tomorrow around three."

Already digging into the bag, Agnes Two didn't bother looking up. "Okay, dearie. See you then." Precious gave a parting snap at my foot as I closed the door.

Back in my apartment, I slid to the floor in a heap in front of the couch. Forgoing silverware, I ate dumplings straight from the container with my fingers, splitting them with the canine garbage disposal I'd adopted.

We made quick work of dinner. Doggo climbed into my lap, licking sauce off my face. "Stop, ugh, stop," I admonished, laughing. "Where did she take you today? You stink."

Still hungry (I'd skipped lunch), I pushed myself off the floor and went to regard the refrigerator. The long work hours had taken their toll, and the kitchen again looked forlorn and empty. I unearthed a package of frost-burned waffles from behind a bag of mixed vegetables and popped two into the toaster. As I waited, I changed into leggings and a T-shirt, washed my face, and checked work messages. John texted to ask if I'd confirmed the valet and bag check staff. *Yes, and yes,* I responded. Tavia sent a copy of the band's audio-visual requirements and set-up schedule. We'd gone with jazz, not death metal.

The waffles popped. I stuck one in my mouth, dry, and tossed the other to Doggo, who caught it neatly in mid-air.

"You are a dog of many talents," I told him.

Walking across the floor, waffle still in my mouth, I refreshed my messages.

A new text appeared: *Daisy, this is Reg Davis (my personal number). I propose we have a drink tomorrow night after what is sure to be a successful evening.*

I gaped, the waffle falling from my mouth. Doggo grabbed it and disappeared behind the couch.

Was Call-Me-Reg asking me out? I cursed myself for opening the message instead of reading the preview.

Three dots appeared, followed by: *I do hope you will say yes.*

I was stuck. Having a celebratory drink with a client after a big event wasn't unusual. It was good manners as well as good relationship-building. However, this was the first time a client had asked beforehand. I doubted John had received the same message.

As much as I wanted to, I couldn't ignore Reg's texts. After careful consideration, I typed: *I look forward to raising a glass in celebration with the whole team tomorrow. Cheers!*

Hopefully, he took the hint, and that would be the end of this awkward and unwelcome invitation.

When no further response appeared, I relaxed and popped a third waffle into the toaster. Doggo sat at my feet, clearly waiting for his next dinner.

"Oh no," I told him. "This is mine. My waffle."

As I ate, I FaceTimed Bud.

I'd kept my promise and stayed in touch, although with Bud as busy with work as I was, we'd mostly stuck to sending short texts and silly memes. I knew Chantal had started filming, meaning she was gone from Wednesday to Sunday each week. Meanwhile, traffic at the store had picked up, thanks partly to wedding season (thank you, Casey and Victor) and some of Bud's recent changes, including a highly successful centerpiece design class and a new booth space at a popular midweek farmer's market. Even Mom, at Dad's urging, was putting her powers of persuasion to good use by calling local businesses about the store's new bouquet subscription service.

All's well that ends well, I mused as I waited for my brother to pick up, which he did after six rings.

"Daze!" He was in his bedroom, and from what little I could see around him, he was either in the middle of a tornado or Chantal's organizational skills were sorely missed during filming.

I grinned. "Hey. Just checking in to see how you're getting on without your better half."

LilyRose popped into frame behind Bud's shoulder, sporting a fuzzy orange headband with cat ears and a blue juice-rimmed mouth. "Hi, Aunt Funny! I'm playing dress-up."

"You sure are." I brought the phone closer. "Are you a kitty cat?"

"I'm a lioness." She scowled, clearly disgusted with the stupidity of adults. "They're apex predators."

"Why don't you go visit GrandPop and Grandma?" Bud suggested to his daughter. "I'm sure they have some fresh gazelle snacks for you." She nodded before scampering off.

He paused, listening as the door scraped closed and his daughter's footsteps grew fainter. "Okay." He turned back to me, grim. I noticed how tired he looked. "Have you talked to Ma or Pop lately?"

In addition to texting my brother, I made it a priority to check in on Mom and Dad twice a week. Dad was up and moving, regaining his strength with continued physical therapy. He also took LilyRose to summer camp and had started volunteering in their community garden. "I spoke to Dad on Tuesday. Why? What's up?"

From the look on Bud's face, I could tell this was something new. Something bad. A faint alarm began to sound in my head.

"The first of Dad's hospital bills came through." Bud ran his hand through his hair. "Did you know they let their medical insurance lapse?"

I sank onto the couch, hand to my face. A series of moments flashed by: That first day in the hospital when Dad insisted on doing the medical paperwork himself, the interrupted comment on the phone a few weeks ago. The locked drawer in his office.

I knew he'd been hiding something, but I'd been too wrapped up in my own agenda to wonder what. Or why.

"They stopped paying the premiums when finances got tight," Bud continued. "I don't know how we'll pay."

"How bad is it?" As if sensing my distress, Doggo trotted over and lay on my feet. I reached down and scratched him, the simple act offering a moment of comfort.

"Pretty bad." Bud looked grim. "They have some savings, but..."

"But what?"

"But we may need to sell the store."

I gaped at him. "Seriously?"

He nodded. "Seriously. Chan and I have some money we

were saving for a down payment, but it's not enough. Dad's been hiding how close he's been cutting things, financially speaking, but he finally came clean. They've been dipping into their retirement funds for more than a year, hoping things would turn around." My ordinarily optimistic brother slapped his leg in frustration, making me jump. "If only they'd told me, trusted me. I could have done something. I would have helped… I spent the whole day on the phone with the bank. There's really nothing left to do but to sell."

My heart went out to my brother. He'd finally received the keys to the kingdom, and it turned out to be a sinking ship.

"I don't understand," I said, trying to make sense of it all. "Why not tell us? Why leave you hanging like this?"

Bud shook his head. "Embarrassed, I guess. And I think he was still hoping that something would come through. You would decide to come back and help run the store, and we could solve the finances between us. Or maybe that the bills wouldn't be so bad."

I shook my head, mirroring my brother. Pride. Our parents had always been proud of the store, of the legacy they would pass on to their children. They'd been too proud to see that I'd wanted something different, too proud to ask for help when they needed it. And now that pride could leave them with nothing.

My mind raced ahead. I had savings, probably enough to cover the first of the bills and buy my brother some time. I could save the shop. I could do it.

"Bud, I…" I started, intending to say I had the answer when the truth dawned.

It might take everything, including the money I'd saved for Ground Floor.

Bud waited. To my shame, I offered a useless platitude. "I think it will all work out. Don't worry."

For years, I'd thought my relationship with my family couldn't get worse. That the pressure to run the family business was the biggest challenge I'd ever faced.

But now... I was in a position to help them, but it would take all I had, including my future.

But without it, what would they do? What would I do? How could I ever look any of them in the eye again, knowing that I'd had it in my power to help and hadn't?

I needed time to think.

"Hey, Buddy," I said, making my voice soft, like when we were kids and he'd had a bad dream. "It's going to be all right. I promise. We're going to get through this. But right now, I have to focus on tomorrow's event. I'll call you Sunday, and we'll make a plan, okay?"

"Okay." Bud sniffed, and a fresh wave of guilt washed over me. "Okay," he repeated, sounding stronger. "We'll talk Sunday. Thanks, Sis, and good luck." He gave me a watery half-smile before ending the call.

I sank back against the couch. Doggo hopped up and nestled under my arm, his head in my lap.

What was I going to do?

In my shock, I hadn't thought to ask how much the bills were. I did a quick online search and goggled at the astronomical costs of a typical hospital stay. And that didn't include any testing or medication. I clicked on a link for suggested payment options, pulling a pen from my bag and scribbling notes on a takeout napkin. Bud and I could split the cost of the hospital bills, and Mom and Dad could apply for a loan or a low-interest credit card. Of course, Bud and Chantal wouldn't be able to move, and John and I would need to find a third partner to bring into the business. Not ideal, but it could be enough to save the store and leave each of us with some savings.

I could pay the bills outright, and Mom and Dad would be debt-free. This was a better situation for my family, but it meant giving up the business with John or, at the very least, stepping aside so that he could find a new partner, while I stayed where I was.

Or... I could take Fiona's offer. My savings would be gone,

but a managing director's salary would help me recoup the loss quicker. John said it himself: we could continue growing and expanding an already established business. By implementing the values we had planned for Ground Floor, Event Artistry would eventually feel less like Fiona's and more like ours. Was this the answer?

I needed an outsider's opinion, someone not directly involved in the outcome. I texted Jeremy: *Do you have time to talk?*

After the pet adoption, we'd begun texting more often. Not daily—he was busy with his business and Ethan, and I was fully immersed in the art opening—but regularly enough for me to feel comfortable asking his advice.

Ten minutes later, my phone rang with a FaceTime notification. I'd been pacing the length of the apartment, Doggo at my heels, talking to myself, trying to make sense of the disparate thoughts racing through my mind.

"Wait, wait, slow down," he said when I stopped to catch my breath after pouring out the whole story. "Let me get this straight. Your choices are as follows," he said, ticking off each choice with a raised finger. "Help your family a little. Help your family a lot. And in doing so, you either start your own company, like you've always dreamed of or take over an existing business, which you never wanted to do." He paused. "Wow," he said finally. "Those are massive choices."

"I know," I said, gnawing at a cuticle. "Is it awful that I don't know what to do?" What must he think of me? I wasn't even sure what I thought of myself. I resumed pacing.

He scrunched up his mouth as he considered this. "Not awful. It's a big decision and I understand your hesitation. Do you set aside your dreams for your family? But if you don't, are you asking them to give up theirs?"

I let that sink in. Either way, someone was going to lose. And it was up to me to decide who.

"Remember, supportive families are a rare gift." Jeremy

cleared his throat, looking uncomfortable. "If you gave them the money, would you move back and help run the store?"

I stopped in my tracks, surprised. Doggo ran face-first into my calves. "I don't know. I hadn't thought about it."

"It's something to consider," he said slowly as if carefully choosing his words. "What if, instead of looking at it like giving up a business, you look at this *as* your new business? You could work with Bud. Keep an eye on your father's health. You'd be investing in the store's future and your family." He offered a small smile and I noticed his ears were bright pink. "It wouldn't be all bad to come back, would it?"

I caught my breath, hoping I was correctly interpreting his suggestion. "No, it wouldn't be *all* bad."

His smile widened. "Well, then, think about it."

"Thank you," I said, wishing for better words to express how much I appreciated his advice and how much it helped to have him listen.

"Let me know when you decide."

"I promise."

"Good luck tomorrow night."

"Thanks. Bye."

"Bye."

I sank onto the bed. Doggo jumped up, tail thumping. I hugged him, grateful for his solid, stinky presence. "Oh, Doggo. What are we going to do?"

Chapter Twenty-Six

The night of the event arrived. I dropped off my bag and jacket at the coat check and reviewed the registration materials. Entering the main exhibit hall, I bumped into Reg. He looked more reptilian than ever in a slim-cut smoking jacket of shimmery jade green. Next to him stood a woman, so tall and thin in an iridescent white floor-length gown, she gave the impression of translucency. Her pale, nearly silver eyes stared at me from underneath a veil of white-blond hair, and I knew at once I was meeting Millie Maxwell.

"Ms. Maxwell, it's a pleasure." I extended my hand in greeting. Her hand felt like eggshells, as if the slightest pressure would break her. How could this diaphanous woman have created such large, vibrant abstracts? The paint on the canvases probably weighed more than her.

She whispered something in return that sounded like "Chicken monkey boo," which I translated to "Charmed to meet you."

I was saved from further conversation by John, who materialized at my elbow and guided me away after a quick apology to Reg and Ms. Maxwell.

"The lobster tails arrived, but, funny story, they're all still attached to very live lobsters."

And just like that, the event was off and running.

For the next three hours, I greeted, directed, and managed the inaugural traveling exhibit event. Eunice and I checked names off lists and took photos of guests in front of fabric backdrops. I passed John and Martin as we served trays of appetizers—the lobster tail appetizers located and the live lobsters rounded up and waiting in their tanks to be returned—cleared glasses and dishes, and tracked down owners of lost purses and cell phones. Tavia and I helped some of our more robust partygoers into Ubers and directed people to the nearest bathroom. We all played security and escorted wandering guests back to the party. I scarfed two puff pastries and half a glass of mineral water during my single break of the evening when Reg stood on stage and introduced Millie Maxwell, whose entire speech consisted of a single mumbled sentence that, to my ears, sounded like "Murgle squash higflarp."

Judging by the applause, the event was a success, regardless of her public speaking skills.

Fiona flitted through the crowd, escorted by her ever-patient husband, Jürgen. As slight and intimidating as Fiona was, Jürgen was tall, wide, and mostly silent. He followed Fiona, clutching her child-sized beaded purse in his bear-paw hands as she entertained large groups with one anecdote after the next, screaming with laughter at her own punchlines. I had seen her arrive (fashionably late) but hadn't spoken to her. Fiona would never do anything as common as check in at a party she felt she deserved to attend. Which, from what I could tell, was all of them.

"Well done, Daisy Greene," she said, approaching me. Jürgen followed in her wake, holding out the tiny coat check ticket. Eunice ducked into the coat closet to retrieve Fiona's enormously gauche (and, I hoped, fake) fur coat despite the warm June weather. "I'll see you Monday," she called as she tottered away, clutching her husband's arm. "Big day!"

I ignored Eunice's questioning look and excused myself. "I'm going to check in with John," I told her, picking up my radio. "Call if you need me."

I walked in the general direction of where I'd last seen John ushering out some drunken gatecrashers who had mistaken our event for a bar. Turning the corner, I ducked into a room labeled "Supplies" and slid to the floor between a mop bucket and a "Caution: Wet floor" sign.

I looked at my phone, smiling automatically at a picture of Doggo on my lock screen. Being a dog and having everyone take care of me would be nice. Doggo's biggest decision was whether to nap before lunch or after his walk. If only my choices were as simple.

If I gave my family the money, their troubles would be over. I wasn't quitting my dreams; I was simply delaying them. Maybe taking over Fiona's business was the right choice. John and I could cut our managerial teeth before moving on in a few years.

But—my mind veered, like a moth to a flame, back to my original plan—it also meant delaying the opportunity to create something new. I'd left home to avoid taking over someone else's work. Could I justify escaping my overbearing, overly involved family only to take over for another overbearing, overly involved boss? Was I willing to put my hard-won autonomy aside, even briefly?

And what about Jeremy? I couldn't deny that he was becoming a factor in this. I knew if he were in my position, he would do everything he could to help his family. *Supportive families are a rare gift,* he'd said. What would he think if I stuck to my original plan?

And what about John, Sabrina, Zadie, and their baby on its way? I couldn't forget that there were more livelihoods at stake than my own. What would it mean to John if I pulled out of our business arrangement? Would he be mad? Disappointed? I didn't want our friendship to become a casualty of the wrong decision.

How had everything become so complicated? This was what happened when I opened my life and let my family in. A month ago, I'd had my apartment, my job, and a plan. I was sitting on top of the world.

Now I had a dog, a niece, a nosy neighbor, a crush who lived 600 miles away, and I was sitting in a supply closet, arguing with myself.

But I couldn't deny it: my life was better—messier but better. It was more than it had been. Hadn't I always wanted the chance for more? And now, here it was. It wasn't the "more" I'd imagined, but the "more" I'd never known to dream of. Everyone and everything around me was more.

My whirling thoughts were interrupted by a blast of static from the walkie-talkie at my hip. "Daisy?" Eunice called. "The event is wrapping. Do you want me to start packing without you?" It was her nice way of telling me to come back.

"On my way." I stood, smoothing down my black jersey dress and running my hands over my hair. My decision would have to wait a little longer.

"To KCAM," John called.

"To KCAM!" We hollered back, clinking our glasses.

"To Millie Maxwell," he said, raising his glass again.

We were crowded around two high-top tables in the corner of the exhibit hall. John, Tavia, Eunice, Martin, and several others had stuck around to help close out the event. Reg, for the moment, had disappeared.

Millie Maxwell had gone as well. As she left, she pressed a single finger to my arm, looked me in the eyes, and said, "Beans greenins."

"Congratulations, Ms. Maxwell," I said, nodding as if we were in complete agreement. I watched as she floated away into the night in her ethereal gown, perhaps to be beamed back up to the mothership.

"To Reg," Tavia said, giggling.

"To all of you," I said. "Thanks for stepping in when I needed help."

"You owe us," John called, refilling his glass.

I took in the faces around the table, feeling a swell of love, fueled by the adrenaline of a successful event and the fizzy rush of champagne. These people were my family. I loved my job. I couldn't abandon this, could I?

But they aren't your actual family, my mother's voice interrupted. *We are. And we need you.*

Need versus want. Family versus self. That was what it all came down to, wasn't it?

Go away, Mom, I told her and finished my drink.

"Daisy Greene," said a voice in my ear. Not my mother's. This voice was oily and cold and real. All my warm fuzzies disappeared. I turned to see Reg standing beside me, still immaculate in his shimmery, snakey tux. "Could I have a moment of your time?"

Trapped.

"Of course," I said, gathering my purse from the floor. I caught John's eye. "I'll call you in a bit to review the final numbers," I said giving him a pointed look. I turned, registering the sour expression on Tavia's face as I left.

We stepped into the silent main hallway where, only an hour ago, people had been milling about, smiling and snapping photos, dancing and drinking.

Reg took my arm. My skin crawled. "I thought we'd have that drink in my office," he said, steering me to the back hallway.

I followed, intentionally lagging a step behind so that his hand lost contact with my elbow. I shifted my bag so that it hung between us, a barrier. "A quick drink," I stressed, hoping he'd get the hint. "I want to review catering numbers so I can prepare your bill on Monday."

Reg chuckled. "Tonight was wonderful. Our board members

couldn't be happier. I can't imagine any issues with your final invoice."

That would have been the best news a month ago, the signal that my new life was beginning. Now, however, it just gave me more supply closet vibes.

In his office, I sat in the same plastic chair as before while Reg bustled around the room, collecting two heavy glass tumblers and pouring a finger of amber-colored liquid into each. He handed me one and took the seat beside me.

"Cheers," he said, raising his glass.

I raised my glass in return and took a cautious sip, nearly searing my tastebuds off. My eyes watered, and I forced myself to swallow a trace amount of liquid.

Reg watched me as I blinked, clearly enjoying my discomfort. "Strong, isn't it? I had it imported especially for celebrations."

He set his glass on the desk and leaned forward. I folded my arms and crossed my legs, classic "back off" body language.

He registered the move; one eyebrow raised in amusement. "Why, Ms. Greene. I do believe you think I have nefarious intentions. Not so." He pointed at me. "I wanted to talk about your future. I'm extremely impressed with your management of this exhibition opening. In a very short time, you created an event that will put this museum on the map."

I relaxed slightly at his assurances that I wouldn't have to deal with any unwelcome romantic gestures. "I appreciate that. But the real kudos belong to the Event Artistry team, especially John and Tavia. They stepped up while I had a personal emergency to take care of."

"Ah, yes." He nodded. "But a good manager knows how to direct her team. I think it speaks volumes about you that your team successfully planned this event with minimal disruptions to your client. And your contributions were the icing on the cake."

"Thank you," I said, setting my drink on a coaster and standing. "I'll be sure to pass on your kind words. Now, if you'll excuse me, I really should—"

"How would you like to be this museum's Director of Events?" Reg asked. "I think you are exactly the person we need."

"Oh." Flustered, I said the first thing that popped into my head, "What about Tavia?"

"Tavia?" He looked surprised. "She's a nice girl and clearly ambitious." He studied me. I got the sense he had expected me to accept his offer immediately and was put off by having to offer further explanations. "But you have experience. And focus. That's what I'm looking for. Someone to make the museum their life, 24/7. I've asked around, Daisy. I know that your work is your life."

I couldn't help feeling a little insulted. I hedged again. "It's a very generous offer."

"Let's not play games," Reg said, all pretense of friendly conversation disappearing. "People like us aren't happy where we are. We're always looking for more. Another challenge. We're managers, not team players. We prefer to be alone. In charge. Not one of them." He motioned toward the door, indicating the rest of my coworkers. "You and I could make this organization a top performer in Kansas City. I'm offering you the opportunity to do something great."

Speechless, I gathered my things. He rose to escort me back to the main hallway.

"Think about it," he called, his words echoing in the emptiness. "I'll expect your answer on Monday. And remember, I only ask once."

Chapter Twenty-Seven

I awoke the following day with a splitting headache.

Sunday. Deadline day.

"*Woof,*" Doggo said, nosing my face. I pulled my arm out from the twisted covers and pressed the top of his head.

"Snooze, Doggo, snooze," I begged. "Five more minutes."

I'd slept fitfully, fighting the thoughts that clamored for top billing, exhaustion willing me to close my eyes, only for a fresh jolt of anxiety to shoot through my brain as I remembered the choices before me.

"*Woof,*" he answered and jumped down from the bed. I pulled the covers up and dropped back into near sleep.

Moments later, I heard a bark and a clatter, followed by a splash. My foggy brain went on high alert as it tried to connect which actions could make those noises in that order.

I leaped to my feet and ran into the bathroom, where I found Doggo panting happily next to the toilet. My phone blinked at me from the bottom of the bowl, a long stream of bubbles trickling up to the water's surface.

"No, no, no!" I plunged my hand into the basin and pulled my phone out, cradling it like an unresponsive patient needing CPR.

Rice. I had to get my phone into rice. I lurched into the kitchen and tore through the cupboards. The closest thing I had was a packet of instant oatmeal. That wouldn't do. I pushed my feet into my shoes and threw a sweatshirt around my shoulders. Doggo trotted to the door expectantly.

"Oh no," I told him, shoving my bank card into my back pocket. "We are not going for a walk. This is a rescue mission."

"*Woof*," he agreed, following me out the door. I sighed and grabbed his leash.

At the corner market, I bought a box of Minute Rice and dropped my phone into it.

"Dropped your phone in the water, didja?" the cashier, a tall kid who looked to be in his late teens, asked. "Jackson," his name tag read.

"Not me," I said sourly. "Him." I jerked my head at my companion, who didn't seem the least bit concerned about all the trouble he was causing.

"You know the rice thing doesn't work. It's an old wives' tale." Jackson took in my disheveled appearance as he handed over the receipt. "No offense. Try using a lint-free microfiber cloth. And airflow. Your phone should be dried out and good to go in about a week."

"A week?" I shrieked. Jackson shrank back. "I don't have a week. I don't even have a day." I sighed. "Thanks for the tip."

We left the store. I turned to head home, but Doggo strained against his leash, obviously itching to get to the park. I fought to pull him the other way as he planted his butt on the sidewalk and refused to move.

"Oh, for... fine." I gave up, and the three of us headed to the park: me, my passive-aggressive dog, and my phone in its cozy new home.

The park was hopping. I'd never seen so many people and dogs in one place. Everyone chatted happily, sipping coffee while the dogs raced, barked, and sniffed each other. I unclipped Doggo, and he ran off to join the fun.

I watched him go. Somewhere during the last three weeks, spring had turned to summer, and it felt good to be outside. I closed my eyes and tilted my head back. My shoulders relaxed as the sun warmed my face.

"You couldn't bring a latte like everyone else?"

I turned and saw John approaching, pushing Sabrina in her stroller.

"What are you doing here?" I asked, happy to see him. "You don't have a dog."

John gestured to his daughter. "She likes animals. This is big entertainment for us." He looked at me quizzically. "What are *you* doing here?" He gestured to the box in my hands. "With *that*?"

Doggo chose that moment to bound up, barking merrily.

"Doggie!" Sabrina held her hands out. Doggo obliged by putting his front paws on her lap and giving her a slobbery lick. She screeched in delight, and he race-hopped back into the fray. I chuckled, remembering how just a month ago the thought of being at a dog park with animals and children had seemed like a fate worse than death. My, how times had changed.

"That's Doggo. He dropped my phone in the toilet, so I rewarded him by doing exactly what he wanted." I shrugged. "We're working on it."

John waved his hands in a "stop everything" motion. "Wait, what? How long have you had a dog?"

"Three weeks." I couldn't believe it even as I said it. "But it seems like forever."

"Huh." He stared across the park, watching as Doggo hopped around, making friends. In her stroller, Sabrina sang a song that I vaguely recognized as a mashup of "Let It Go" and "Let It Snow."

After a minute of silence, John said, "So, how was your *drink* with Call-Me-Reg?"

I shuddered at the implication. "Not what you're thinking. He offered me a job."

"Really? You're quite the belle of the ball lately." He took a too-casual sip of his coffee. "What did you say?"

"What could I say? I told him I appreciated the offer and would consider it."

"Are you? Considering it?"

I leaned against the fence, crossed my arms, and hugged the rice box. "Events Director? It'd be an amazing job." I saw John's look and hurried on. "But no. I can't back out on you like that."

Another sip of coffee. Another careful question. "What about Fiona's offer? To take over Event Artistry?"

I shook my head. "I don't know. I guess… I mean, I could take it. I mean, *we* could take it." I looked at him. He was still staring at the dogs, but his body language was attentive. "There's no way I'd do it without you. We'd be partners, fifty-fifty, right down the line. Like you said, it would be less start-up money, easier in many ways than starting our own business."

"Yeah, but like *you* said, it would also be less ours."

"That too." I paused and looked at Sabrina, who was falling asleep in her stroller as John rolled it back and forth. "There's more." I told him about my conversation with Bud. The store. The lapsed insurance. Dad's medical bills. "The thing is, I have the money to give. But it could mean clearing out my account and starting over. I wouldn't have the seed money to start Ground Floor with you. I'd *have* to take either Fiona or Reg's job offer." I looked at John. "So, I have to ask. Are you okay with me giving the money to my family?"

John stared at me as though I'd sprouted horns. "What are you even talking about? This isn't my decision. It's yours. That's what you've been fighting for all this time, right? The opportunity to do what Daisy Greene wants to do?"

I stared back, stunned.

He was right. This *was* the moment I'd waited for. Fought for. I had opportunities in front of me, all with their own risks and rewards. All my life, I'd been waiting to make my own path. All my life, I'd felt wrong for wanting something different.

For the first time, no one was telling me what I should do. My life, on my terms, was up to me now. The choice was mine.

And I knew. In a flash of clarity, I knew what I wanted. It wasn't a choice of me versus them. I didn't want more for just myself; I wanted more for everyone. I was making a choice for *us*.

I whistled for Doggo, and he came hop-skipping across the park, panting and stinky. I knelt and hugged him. "Come on, you big pain in the butt. We have to go home."

"Thank you," I said, turning to face John. "Thank you for being my friend."

He put out his hand. I pushed it aside and enveloped him in a hug. Momentarily surprised, he nonetheless hugged me back. "Good luck, Daisy Greene. And don't you worry, I'll be just fine." He stepped back and ran a hand over his bald head, striking a pose. "When you're this good-looking and talented, things naturally work out."

Still laughing, we parted ways—him pushing his sleeping daughter in her stroller home to his pregnant wife, and me and my exasperating dog, back to our apartment to pack and hopefully borrow Agnes Two's phone.

I stepped out of Denver International Airport into the dry evening breeze, my hastily packed weekend bag over one shoulder. Doggo was staying with Agnes Two for a last-minute slumber party.

I flagged down a cab and gave my parents' address. The driver gave a low whistle. "Are you sure? That's an expensive drive."

"It's fine," I promised. I'd already spent quite a sum on same-day airline fare. What was one more astronomical charge to my card? "Please. I need to go home."

Without a working phone (Jackson had been right. My phone's Minute Rice bath was a bust.), I'd spent the hour and a half flight jotting notes furiously, making a to-do list of everything from bank transfer rules to finding a one-bedroom apartment for rent ("Must take dogs" was a requirement). Buying a phone and calling Jeremy topped the list.

My heart and stomach did a little flip. What would he say when I told him I was coming back? That the ten days I'd spent here had opened my eyes to the possibilities before me and he was a part of that? I didn't have much more than a suspicion that he felt the same way. Still, as Reg had said—of all people, I couldn't believe it was *Reg* I was taking advice from—I was "the type of person who liked moving forward."

Years ago I'd moved out, thinking that staking my independence was the only way forward. Now I knew that I'd been running away. I had a family who loved me and whom I loved back despite their quirks and maddening habits. I had friends in two cities who cared about and supported me. There were opportunities everywhere, and this was the one I wanted to take the chance on. Not only to be a part of something new, but also to carry on a tradition alongside the people I loved.

It wasn't about me any longer.

The "more" that I wanted was about "us."

I stared out the taxi window at the mountains in the distance under the cloudless sky, just starting to turn dusky blue with a few stars on the horizon.

"I'm home," I whispered as we moved forward.

Bud opened the back door and stared at me. For the first time ever, he was speechless.

"Hey, little brother," I said, throwing my arms around him. "Do you want to run a flower shop together?"

Chapter Twenty-Eight

Bud, Chantal, Mom, Dad, and I sat at the kitchen table, mugs of untouched tea in front of us. LilyRose pulled the ottoman into the kitchen and sat holding a book that she was pretending to read while listening to every word.

"So, that's the deal." I finished, taking a sip of now-cold tea. "I'd like to be a partner at the store." I saw Chantal's eyes dart toward Bud, who made a big show of examining his cuticles. "As manager of your new event planning department," I clarified. "You two are fully in charge of the flower shop. I mean, I'll help when I can. I'll buy stock in allergy medicine."

Chantal looked calm and collected, even after her long flight from the show's set earlier that day. "How long are you staying this time?" she asked, giving voice to the elephant I hadn't realized had wandered into the room. "Another ten days? A month?"

"For good, if you'll have me. I'll have to go back to Kansas City to give my notice and pack, but I've thought about it, and everything I want for my future is here." I looked around the table before coming back to Chantal. "I'm asking you to trust me."

"Trust takes time," she said after a long silence. "But I trust

Bud. And that's close enough for now." She paused. "Promise me one thing."

"Anything."

"No more exhibit booths," she said with a grin.

"I promise." I looked her straight in the eye, expecting to see a challenge but finding only acceptance.

"Well, I think it's wonderful, Petal." Dad beamed.

Mom's eyes were uncharacteristically bright as she stood and pretended to fuss with something in the sink. "I'm sure we are all glad to have you here to take over—er, help Bud."

"I'm not helping Bud, Mom," I emphasized. "He's the one helping me. And we're both helping you and Dad. Because that's what family does." On a whim, I stood and hugged her, feeling her surprise melt as her arms came around me.

"Thank you," she whispered, patting me on the back like a child.

"Group hug!" Bud's arms squashed me against Mom, followed by Dad.

I laughed through my tears, trying to protest but getting a mouthful of fabric. "Let me go! Let me go, or I'll take it all back! I'll be on the next plane to Misery by morning."

One by one, they released me. Bud was the last to let go, arms held wide in joyous victory. "You couldn't stay away if you tried."

"I most certainly could."

He shuddered. "You sound just like Ma."

I punched him lightly in the shoulder. "Don't say that." But I was smiling as I said it.

Chantal took a protesting LilyRose to bed. "I'm not tired," she muttered, half-asleep across her mother's shoulder. Behind her, Mom led Dad, who was also only partially awake, to the first-floor bedroom. "Good night, daughter, son," he called as he shuffled down the hall. "It's good to have you both home."

"So what's next?" I asked Bud, who was rummaging around in the freezer.

He held up a bottle of vodka, one eyebrow raised. "Celebratory toast?"

"Absolutely not. Pun intended."

"Juuuuuust kidding." He put the bottle back and pulled out the ice cream carton. I grabbed two spoons from the silverware drawer.

"Next steps?" I asked again as we dug in.

"Oh yeah." He licked his spoon thoughtfully. "Since paperwork is your thing, you can call Teddy in the morning." He winked. "I'm sure there's some legal and financial stuff to sort out. We'll probably need one of your special spreadsheets. Then there's the question of location." He paused, waiting for that to sink in.

"Location? Like, moving the shop?"

"When Chan and I started looking for a place to live, we found a great apartment over a storefront on Santa Fe, right in the arts district." He pulled out his phone and thumbed through his pictures. "See? Here's the storefront. The apartment is up the back stairs. It shares a courtyard with a gallery—Chan's friend owns it, that's how we got the tip—and a bar." He swiped through the pictures as he talked. "It's everything we talked about—better location, more foot traffic, chances for cross-promotion. With some creative planning, we can partition off a separate office space for you." He looked at me. "The price is steep but not completely out of the question, especially with a partner. Once we sell the location here and pay off Dad's bills, we can still put down a decent down payment on the building."

I took the phone from my brother and scanned the pictures. He was right. It was a good location, and the shared courtyard area was set up for foot traffic and browsing.

"When would this all happen?"

"We can move quickly. Chan's artist friend put us in touch with the property manager, Joe. Turns out he's an old buddy of mine from the summer I spent following Widespread Panic. He's giving us a heck of a deal." Bud grinned, pleased. "Don't tell me I don't know how to network."

I shook my head. Bud the business owner, the networker, the boss. It was going to take some getting used to. "I love it. Great job."

Mom appeared in the doorway. "Well, your father's asleep. Now we can discuss the next steps."

Bud shot a glance at me, and I saw his hand lift off the table slightly in a mini-blast off motion. "All taken care of, Ma. I was just showing Daisy the site for the new store."

Mom stiffened, and I braced for impact. To my surprise, she nodded as if deciding something. "It's your store now. You two do what you think is best. I'm going to bed." She turned and left.

Bud and I stared at each other in amazement. "Did that just happen?" I asked.

"Bet she almost bit through her tongue, but yeah."

"Okay, let's act fast. Before our Smother returns."

"I'll call Joe right after I say goodnight to LilyRose," he said, moving to the door.

I stopped him. "One more thing... can I borrow Arlene?"

Jeremy's dad opened the door, his tough-guy resting face splitting into a grin beneath a gray beard at the sight of me. "Daisy! What are you doing here? Jeremy said you went back to Kansas City."

"Hi, Mr. Michaels," I said, suddenly shy. I smoothed down my wrinkled skirt. "May I speak to Jeremy, please?"

He stepped aside, holding the door open. "Of course, of course! Come on in. We're just finishing dinner. I know he'll be glad to see you. Jer?" he called, looking like a mischievous gnome. "You have a visitor."

Jeremy stepped into the hall, a stack of plates in his hands.

"Who—" He stopped as he saw me. "Daisy? What are you doing here?" He blanched. "Is your dad okay?"

"Let me take those from you," Jeremy's dad said, winking at me. "You two talk." He lifted the plates from Jeremy's unresisting hands and retreated to the kitchen. "Ethan! Come on, we're going out for ice cream."

From the back of the house, I heard Ethan's *whoop* of joy, followed by the sound of dishes being deposited into the sink and, a moment later, the back door opening and shutting.

"To answer your questions in reverse order: Dad's fine. Everyone's fine. They're all at the house, safe and sound." I took a deep breath; it was now or never. "And so am I. I've decided to move back and help run the store."

"You have?" He stared at me as though I'd announced I was moving to Mars.

"Uh-huh," I nodded, stepping closer. "And I needed to tell you something."

"What's that?"

"I think I'd like to be on the same page. You know, with you. In real life."

His smile told me everything I wanted to know. And when he took me in his arms and kissed me, I knew that I'd come home.

We sat on the back porch, our untouched beers resting on the same rickety picnic table I remembered from that long-ago summer.

"So, what happened?" Jeremy asked. "What made you change your plans?"

"It wasn't so much a change of plans," I said. "It was more like a change of heart." I told him about my conversation with John, and the question he'd posed: *What does Daisy Greene want?*

"I realized that I could have everything I wanted anywhere," I said. "All these years I thought being alone and being independent were the same thing. Turns out, I can be independent and follow my dreams anywhere. I can be myself anywhere. And where I'd like to do that is here. With my family." I looked up, grateful Jeremy couldn't see my cheeks flush in the dimming evening light. "And with you."

He reached out, his warm hand covering mine. "I'd like that." He leaned in and the second kiss was even better than the first. "I'd like that a lot."

This time, time was on our side.

Chapter Twenty-Nine

Six months later

"Daddy! Aunt Funny! Everyone's ready!"

It was the premiere of Chantal's reality show. She'd been extremely close-lipped about the results and about the eight contestants vying for top marks in flower arranging, but the early buzz around the show had been terrific. We'd already had several bloggers write features on her and the store. Of course, we'd invited them all to our grand reopening event.

I took a final look at myself in the full-length mirror. I was wearing a new black shift dress and my favorite ballet flats. Tonight was going to be busy, and I would be on my feet a lot. I smoothed back my hair, loosening my ponytail slightly so I didn't look quite so much like I was giving myself a facelift.

At the bottom of the stairs, the crowd assembled in the family room. Dad sat in his recliner, Doggo tucked under one arm. Bud and Chantal sat beside LilyRose on barstools purloined from the old shop's workroom, while Mom, Aunt Agnes, and Cecil sat squeezed together on the couch. Clementine happily chewed a piece of rawhide under the coffee table (I'd taken the precaution of removing all the potted plants), while Ethan lay next to her, eating Goldfish crackers and stroking her wiry fur.

As for me...

"I saved you a spot." Jeremy patted the empty inch of cushion on the parrot chair, which Bud had lugged down from my apartment above the garage. I snuggled in beside him. Ethan abandoned his crackers (much to Clementine's delight) and climbed into his father's lap, settling back and letting his head rest lightly on my shoulder. I reached up and smoothed his tousled hair, smiling. We were all taking things slowly.

The show began, and everyone cheered as the florists were introduced, starting with Chantal.

"That's you!" LilyRose shrieked and pointed. Chantal smiled and leaned over to kiss her daughter's head. She whispered something in LilyRose's ear, and the little girl's eyes widened.

"Mommy's going to win this challenge! It's a secret!"

Chantal clapped her hand to her forehead. "Baby girl, we are going to discuss the meaning of the word secret," she said as we burst into another round of applause. She picked up the remote from the coffee table and paused the show, freezing the genial-looking host mid-sentence. "Well, now that you know that, we might as well tell you our other secret." She looked over at Bud, who nodded, color flushing his cheeks as he rose and took Chantal's hand.

"We got married this morning," he said as they held up their hands to display matching gold bands. "Victor's going to help us plan a big reception later, but we wanted to make it official before the store reopened." He kissed Chantal on the cheek. "I have a feeling we're going to be very busy after tonight."

"This deserves a celebration," announced Cecil, pushing his way to his feet. "A toast, perhaps?"

"We don't have any champagne," I called. "But there's vodka in the freezer."

"No!" shouted Mom and Dad in unison.

Cecil waved us off. "Not to worry. I have a couple of bottles of champers on ice in the other room." He winked at Agnes, who ducked her head. "A little birdie told me we'd be celebrating more than the store opening today."

The next hour was filled with laughter, toasts, and cheers as we watched Chantal win the first challenge. I nursed my one drink, making it last, aware that the evening was far from over. I noticed Chantal and Bud doing the same. Mom, Dad, Agnes, and Cecil, however, looked as though they were ready to party all night. Dad had officially retired and was enjoying his third act spearheading a community garden project at LilyRose's preschool, where a new generation was learning to love flowers with "Bloomin' Bert." Mom was putting her considerable skills to use and helping me build a client database. She was rarely off her mobile phone, constantly calling and harassing, er, *networking* with all the local hotels, event venues, and restaurants. Agnes was finally a paid employee and our head of social media, in charge of the store's online platform under the name "TheInstantGramma." She was currently working on a series with Casey, chronicling our store's rebranding.

Bud, Chantal, and I had chosen the new store moniker. We'd brainstormed, debated, and finally come up with what we felt was the perfect name for the new direction: Blooms. And in smaller letters underneath, "Flowers & Events."

"Because it's not about us versus them," I'd said, repeating what had become my mantra. "It's about all of us honoring the past and creating new traditions together."

"It's about family," Bud agreed. "And doing your best wherever you are."

"It's about growth and beauty and fulfilling your potential," Chantal added.

Jeremy helped me clear the glasses as the revelry ended. It was time to head to the store for tonight's soft launch, followed by tomorrow's official grand reopening.

Bud, Chantal, and I piled into his car. Everyone else would follow behind. I ran over my prep list in my head. *Check decorations, turn on music, put out hors d'oeuvres...*

I bounced in the backseat, nervously smoothing my skirt.

Chantal reached back and patted my hand. "Relax," she said. "It'll be great. Have faith."

My phone began to buzz. I slid my finger on the screen to see John smiling and holding a champagne flute.

"Congratulations!" he cheered, then held his phone up so I could see the whole office staff—*John's office, John's employees*, I reminded myself—behind him. "We just watched the first episode!"

I handed the phone to Chantal to accept her well wishes.

"Thanks," I said as she handed the phone back. I was trying to will the tears that sprang to my eyes not to fall and ruin my mascara. I'd worn waterproof, but even so… "How are things at Event Artistry?"

"You mean Ground Floor," he corrected and tilted his phone again so I could see the banner hanging across the window of what had been Fiona's office. "Eunice sent all the paperwork through last week. And Martin's in the middle of creating our new company logo." Behind him, I saw Martin and Eunice wave. I waved back.

John continued, "And the employee doggie daycare is already a huge success." He swung the phone around to show me the back half of the office, which featured a gated play area and a wall of windows looking out onto a fenced grassy area. I could just make out Agnes Two engaged in tossing tennis balls to a joyous group of dogs. I imagined I could hear Precious's distinctive *yip* above the din.

So many familiar faces. Besides hiring Agnes Two at my suggestion, John had kept the entire staff when he'd taken over the business from Fiona. Except for Tavia. She had accepted a job as Director of Events for the Kansas City Art Museum. I wondered if Reg had told her she hadn't been his first choice. *Good luck to her*, I thought. I just hoped she didn't make her job her life. There was so much more out there. Speaking of more…

"How's the baby?"

John's smile grew wider. "Hugo's good. Chubby, smiling, and chill. Sabrina still isn't convinced about being a big sister, though. She keeps asking if we can trade him in for a dog." He chuckled. "Got any sisterly advice?"

"Tell her to hang in there," I said, glancing at Bud, who grinned at me in the rearview mirror while tapping his fingers on the steering wheel in time to the radio. "Tell her little brothers are worth it in the end."

I looked through the glass as I unlocked the front door, overwhelmed by the number of people waiting outside. Interspersed among the crowd, Aunt Agnes and Cecil stood near the front, and just behind them were Victor and Vicki, holding hands and leading what looked like an army of future brides. Mom, Dad, and LilyRose held places of honor at the front of the line, Dad leaning on a cane and looking dashing in his lime-green cowboy hat. Beside them stood Jeremy and Ethan, each holding a daisy and wearing proud smiles.

Bud touched my shoulder. "Ready, Sis?"

I nodded and opened the door wide. "Hello everyone," I called. "Welcome to Blooms."

The End

Daisy and Bud will return in Wedding Bell Blooms.

About the Author

Joanna Monahan lives in North Carolina with her husband, their two children, and two distracting cats. Her love of movies inspires her to write Women's Fiction for the young at heart—cozy, feel-good stories featuring quirky, memorable characters. Her first novel, *Something Better,* was named a 2024 Next Generation Indie Book Award winner in both the General Fiction and Chick Lit categories. She is a member of The Authors Guild, North Carolina Writers' Network and the Women's Fiction Writers Association.

When she isn't writing, Joanna enjoys theatre, baseball, and bookmarking recipes she will never make. A child of the 80s, she regrets that she no longer receives pizza coupons in exchange for reading books.

Find her at: www.joannamonahan.com or on Instagram, Facebook and Pinterest as @joannamonahanauthor.

Acknowledgments

Bushels of blossoms to the incredible writing community of North Carolina: the fabulous Raleigh chapter of the Women's Fiction Writers Association, the North Carolina Writers' Network, Page 158 Books, Persnickety Books, Broken Anchor Books, hOMe Yoga Studio and Winebrary, Bright Side Books and Wine, and the Wake County Library system. What a privilege it is to live in the "Writingest State."

And where would writers be without readers? Thank *you* for reading this book, and if we have met over the past few years at a book club, book fair, library event or other outreach program, or chatted over social media or email, please know that it is your encouragement and enthusiasm that carried me across some incredibly long miles to the finish line. A tussie-mussie to each and every one of you.

A parade of roses to Blue Ink Press, who welcomed me aboard in 2022 and made a home for me among their authors ever since. Stephanie, Sherry, Amanda, Christa, Liz, Tabitha, Scott, Jan, Kathryn, Robert, Alexandria, Joshua, Andy, and Joy—it is an honor to be part of this family with you.

Daisy chains to D.Allyson Howlett, TL Brown and Saffron Amatti! Your writing challenges helped me create these characters and their world. I thank you in playlists and Turvies and holiday fun. You are the stars in my sky.

Mary Furby of Thistle & Moon and Reagan Mountain of Faraway Gardens allowed me to interview them about all things floral and family businesses. They are as gracious as they are knowledgeable and talented. They are the stardust that made this story magical. Any mistakes are mine alone.

Garlands of greenery to my early readers: Tracey Atkinson, Donna Norman Carbone, Monica Cox, Charlotte Rains Dixon, Monica Frederickson, Hope Gibbs, Anna Gresham, Sabrina Hofkin, Cassandra Howland-Hunt, Elisa Lorello, Shail Rajan, Sue Reynolds, Cammy Sollie, Ava Teedro, Selena Templeton. Each of you made this story better through your caring feedback. And extra-special thanks to Jennifer Brasington-Crowley, author and alpha reader extraordinaire, and Tom Youngdahl, my creative sounding board. Thank you for guiding me through every existential and creative crisis. You are the flowers upon this cactus's soul.

A plethora of petals to the MH Literary Society. Bookish friends are the best.

To all my family members, near and far. I am so proud to have been planted in the same garden as you.

To my husband, who packs the car, carries the books, fixes the computer, attends the events and is my number one fan. You are my lobster, always. Thank you for turning on the fireplace months before you think it's necessary because you know I'm always cold.

Daisy and Bud began as minor characters in a collection of stories I wrote in 2020. Since then, they have become a love letter to my children. Millie and John, promise that you will always stay in touch with one another, if only to complain about me. I love you so very much.

www.ingramcontent.com/pod-product-compliance
Lightning Source LLC
LaVergne TN
LVHW040043080526
838202LV00045B/3462